CHRISTMAS IN FORTUNE'S COVE

CHRISTMAS IN FORTUNE'S COVE

A Novel

VICTORIA JAMES

alcove
press

Published in the United States by Alcove Press, an imprint of The Quick Brown Fox & Company LLC.

Alcove Press and its logo are trademarks of The Quick Brown Fox & Company LLC.

Library of Congress Catalog-in-Publication data available upon request.

ISBN (paperback): 978-1-63910-503-8
ISBN (ebook): 978-1-63910-504-5

Cover design by Lynn Andreozzi

Printed in the United States.

www.alcovepress.com

Alcove Press
34 West 27th St., 10th Floor
New York, NY 10001

First Edition: October 2023

10 9 8 7 6 5 4 3 2 1

To Megan: Thank you for your friendship and support and laughter. Here's to boundaries and lines and knowing when it's time to set them . . . xo.

CHAPTER ONE

Six weeks until Christmas

"You are making the biggest mistake of your life. It might take five months or five years, but your kids will hate you for this."

Annie Hamilton gritted her teeth at her sister Valerie's remark and pressed the button to close the trunk of her SUV, mentally cursing the slow-moving automatic close and nonthrilling click as the door shut. It deprived her of the release. She had wanted the satisfaction of slamming it.

You'll be gone in five minutes, just keep it civil, the kids are watching. She knew why her sister was saying this. It had nothing to do with Annie's kids. It had to do with Valerie. Because it was always about Valerie. "Thanks so much for your support, Val."

"I'm just saying. No need to get defensive."

The bitter, early morning November wind danced around them as they stood in the driveway of the house that Annie had considered their forever home just a few months ago. But forever could be as fleeting as a season, gone as quick as the biting winder wind. Annie took a deep breath and stuffed her cold hands in her pockets and told herself that she just needed to remain calm, that this would be their last in-person conversation for a very long time.

"I'm not defensive, but you literally just said that my kids will hate me in five years. That's not exactly supportive."

Valerie's mouth dropped open. "Wow, I never could talk to you. You have changed so much. You're not happy, Annie. I think this started when you put on five pounds last year. You need to be a better role model for your kids."

Blood rushed to Annie's ears and her childhood flashed before her eyes, unspoken words caught in her throat, never allowed to be voiced, threatened to bubble to the surface. But she couldn't. She just needed to leave. She could not lose her temper; it would be used against her by Valerie. "Thanks for the parenting tip. Really wish we could stick around longer, but we've got a long drive ahead of us."

Valerie pursed her lips. "You know it's not going to be like the movie, right? Like, no one actually moves to PEI from Toronto, right? You're not Anne of Green Gables."

Annie stood a little taller, welcoming the icy wind against her flushed cheeks, lifting her chin at the patronizing comments. She was trying not to get baited, but it was *so* hard. Her sister spoke with an air of authority and wisdom that was unjustified. But this was her usual tone, and Annie had learned to live with it. She wasn't going to let Valerie bring her down today. She needed all her mental energy focused on making her kids feel secure and supported. They were her priority, not her adult sister, who had never helped her, or her children, even when tragedy had struck their family. "Obviously I don't think I'm Anne of Green Gables.

And I'm an adult. A mother. A widow. Not an orphan. We've been there before and Matt and his family are there, and when the veterinarian position opened, I couldn't resist it. Matt is the kids' godfather and like an uncle to them. His family is amazing and will welcome all of us in. His sister has the perfect home waiting for us. We need this change."

It was only five in the morning, way too early to deal with this kind of discussion. She needed more coffee and less arguing—there would be enough of that on the car ride. At least the ocean was in their future. The ocean. She'd lived in a land of lakes her entire life. But the *ocean*. Prince Edward Island. Maybe she had rewatched the original *Anne of Green Gables* series a handful of times with her daughter, Maddy, but of course she knew it wouldn't be like that in real life.

Annie was trying really hard to end this conversation civilly—and the only way to do that was to keep her mouth shut. She had done it for years, after all. Annie was an expert at toeing the line and letting Valerie's comments go in one ear, jab her in the heart, and go out the other. Annie was the peacemaker. Or the pushover.

While their parents had been alive, Annie had promised her mother she would tolerate Valerie. But their parents were gone, and had it not been for the fact that Annie's two children had already lost so much in the last few years, she would have told her sister she was done with their one-sided relationship.

Annie ignored the stab in her chest as she looked at the two-story, red-brick, suburban home. They'd had good years here. Great years. Last night she and the kids had said goodbye to their best friends, and it had made Annie question this move. But her friends understood. They encouraged her. Since Cam died four years ago her life had spiraled, but her friends had been her rock . . . while her sister had just continued to take and demand and criticize. Annie wasn't surprised by this last-minute attempt to get her to change her mind.

There was no way to fully articulate what she was feeling, the restlessness in her, the nagging feeling that staying here wasn't working, that there was more out there for them. Better things. Real things. Lovely things. That there could be a new life if they really tried living again.

Or maybe not. Maybe she was completely wrong and they'd be back here in a year when their lease was up. But at least she would know that she'd tried. Tried to put her family back together and rebuild her relationship with her son. She owed it to Cam. He'd been a good father and a good husband and he'd never stopped until the very end.

And Matt had been a best friend to both of them since their university days. The three of them had been inseparable. When he'd made the suggestion in the summer, she'd dismissed the idea at first. But things had continued to decline with Adam, and Annie started reminiscing about their family vacation with the kids when they'd visited Matt five years go. It had been idyllic.

"Well, I'm their *real* aunt. Not a friend aunt."

Annie crossed her arms and forced herself to look at Valerie. Annie wanted to tell her that Matt was more like family than Valerie had ever been, but there was no point. Annie also wanted to tell her that real aunts actually spent time with their nephews and nieces. She didn't, though. But she was trying to assert herself, even if it wasn't natural for her. "Thanks for your opinion, but they're my kids. I'm trying my best here. I'm putting them first. I always do. I always have. I'm a single parent, just trying to keep it together." Annie stopped speaking abruptly because she was going to spiral. There was no point anyway. Valerie would never truly listen. And Annie didn't have to convince her of anything. She needed to stop responding like she was always on trial. But that's how it had always felt with her sister.

Valerie's mouth thinned to a perfect line. No one disagreed with Valerie. But Annie had started to. Here and there over the last month, Annie had stopped playing the lifelong game of pretending everything was fine—not consciously, but bit by bit, because she couldn't handle Val's needs anymore. Not when her sister was needier than Annie's kids.

Valerie called her five times a day and never asked how Annie or the kids were. She called her when Annie was working, she called her when Annie was at home, at the kids' sporting events or recitals. If Valerie did spend an hour with her kids, all she would do was badmouth Annie. She had never babysat her kids, never brought a meal over, never done anything to help Annie.

When Cam had been in a car accident and then been in the hospital for weeks until succumbing to his injuries, Valerie had made the entire thing about her. She had even burst into the ICU one morning saying she had been in an accident in the parking lot, and when no one reacted, spiraled and accused them of not caring about her. Matt had been there and ushered Valerie down the hall. Maybe that's why Valerie didn't like him—he hadn't put up with her pretend drama.

But this had all gone on long enough. She couldn't continue to put her grown sister over her own kids. This year, Annie had reached a breaking point. But she couldn't afford to be broken because she was the only parent her kids had. "And was that a Le Creuset pot in there? Since when do you cook? Or use designer pots?"

If that pot hadn't been such an indulgence, Annie would have liked to test their durability by chucking one in her sister's direction. Or letting it fall on her foot. But that was mean and she had to set an example for her kids. "Yes, it is. I bought it for myself as a treat. And I'm planning on doing more cooking because I'm only going to be working three days a week."

Why was she even on the defensive? She was thirty-four years old, and if she wanted to buy an expensive pot, she could. She didn't owe her sister any explanations. And cooking more, being more present, was one of her goals. After Cam had died, she'd taken a month off from her job as a veterinarian at a nearby clinic. But that month had been all about making sure the three of them simply stayed afloat. And then after that, she'd gone headfirst back into full-time work, with a nanny stepping in to help at the house. But she'd been fooling herself, she'd been running. It had only made things worse. To the point where Annie didn't want to come home at night because Maddy was so needy and Adam either didn't speak or picked a fight at every turn. She realized that if she waited any longer to deal with the muck, the hard stuff, with her kids, it might be too late to salvage what they once had. Because they had been close. The good life had been theirs, and had she known it wasn't theirs for keeps, she would have cherished it more.

"You can't just throw your career away."

Annie straightened her shoulders. "I'm not. Plenty of people work three days a week. It might be a good way to get some balance."

"You haven't even seen this veterinary office. It could be a hole in the wall. It probably is. Small towns are filled with weirdo rednecks. Especially small towns on small islands. There has to be a reason their population is so low. I think you're just rebelling like you did as a teenager and went away to university."

Annie blinked, not even knowing what she could possibly say to these remarks. They weren't even true. Annie had been the most boring teenager ever. And she had only gone two hours away from home to university. But she couldn't start with Valerie. Even the slightest rebuttal could send her sister into a tailspin. The best thing to do was leave when the conversation inevitably became this ridiculous. "I saw it when we visited last time. It's a great clinic."

Valerie's eyes brightened. "Actually, I was thinking, if you do insist on working there, maybe you could get Matt to make Penelope like the mascot. She is a perfect example of a Maltipoo."

Annie stood perfectly still. She couldn't even blink. She was tempted to look around to see if anyone else was witnessing this. Like, this kind of stuff was hard to even make up. Who would believe some of these conversations she had to listen to? How was it possible that she could go from absolute anger at her sister trying to control her life, to utter shock at this . . . suggestion. Annie cleared her throat. "What exactly do you mean by mascot?"

Valerie gave her a slightly grinch-like smile. "I mean, Penelope is adorable. People fall over her when we walk into a coffee shop or store. You should see. I could start an Instagram account and she'd be famous in a week. She would definitely have more followers than you. So Matt could have her painting on the wall, like a mural or something."

Annie's stomach was in a ball of knots tighter than an abandoned set of Christmas lights. She wasn't even sure she could be mad at this, it was so absurd. But she also knew it for what it was—Valerie trying to make Annie's new job, her new life, all about herself. "Well, I don't think I'm in any position to be walking in and demanding that murals of my sister's dog be painted on the wall."

Valerie's smile fell. "Why not?"

Oh, this was getting very serious. She cleared her throat. "It's not my clinic."

Valerie's lips thinned to a straight line. "Everyone loves Penelope. Ask him, Annie."

Annie took a step back. Every now and then she had flashes to when she was a child, Valerie ten years her senior. She did not like being reminded of the intimidation, the abuse, but the way Valerie's tone changed now brought the memories flooding back in. Of hiding in the bathroom from her rage, or her nails digging into Annie's skin. "I'm not going to do that. I'm sure other staff have animals and their portraits aren't painted on the walls."

"So, what, you're not even going to ask?"

She lifted her chin. "I'm not asking."

Valerie scoffed. "Wow. If he's such a great guy, you should be able to ask him. This whole thing is such a bad plan. You don't even know anyone there besides Matt. The kids don't know anyone. How can you say that taking them away from their home, from their aunt, is the best thing for them? If you're struggling with the house, why don't you move into my condo building? I think that would be good for you. Get a dog, like Penelope."

Annie tore her gaze from Valerie to her kids, each seated on opposite ends of the front porch bench, bundled up in their winter gear. They had to be freezing. Adam was sitting with his typical hunched posture and bent head, phone in hand. Maddy's hat was on so low, her posture so stiff, that she resembled a snowman. Time to go. She turned back to Valerie and stared over her shoulder, not quite able to make eye contact anymore. "Just because a condo is right for *you*, and a dog is right for *you*, doesn't mean it's right for me and the kids. Matt is very close to them. He calls weekly. He's visited. We have lots of friends who will come and visit. Both Adam and Maddy make friends easily. Small towns are like that, and I'm sure by the end of the month we'll know half the town. And Matt's family is amazing. They're all excited we're coming."

Valerie held up her hands. "Whoa. Relax. You always had such a temper. No need to get so angry."

Annie ran her hands down her face, trying to keep her real anger in check. "We really need to get going."

"Friends aren't family."

Annie clenched her teeth. Valerie used that line constantly, and it was like it was her free pass to treat their parents and Annie, Cam, and the kids like crap. But Valerie only had them. She had never had any long-lasting friendships or long-term relationships in over forty years. So she relied on her family as her only social circle. They were the only people who would put up with her. Annie cleared her throat. This would be their last in-person conversation in a very long time, she could handle it. "We tried staying here. It's been four years since Cam died. This . . . isn't working. I told you this. I've told you everything. It's not up for debate anymore. I'm their mom, and I'm making this call. I would think that if you truly wanted what was best for me, you'd support this."

Valerie pinched her lips. "Mom and Dad wouldn't approve."

Annie stared into Valerie's eyes, a thousand retorts springing to her mind, louder than a fire alarm. Her face heated, burned with pent-up anger, a kettle so close to boiling over. She had so much to say. So much she'd been holding onto. But Valerie really had no idea what their parents thought of her, how much pain she had inflicted on everyone due to her own selfishness. But there was no way Annie was going to make today about Valerie. She'd already stolen so many days from Annie and her kids.

"They aren't here."

"Do you even know where you're going? How dangerous this is?"

"I'm driving up the East Coast. In Canada. What's going to happen to us? A moose blocking traffic on a rural highway? It's a gorgeous drive, and the kids are going to love it. Speaking of which, I really want to beat rush-hour traffic."

"Mom? Are we going yet?" Maddy called out, the sweetness in it, the trust in it, sprinkling over her, scattering the retorts she had gathered into the wind, reminding her who came first.

"Yup! Let's go! Road trip!" She forced a bright smile even though the only one who actually returned it was her daughter.

Valerie's mouth dropped open and Adam glared at her, shoving his phone in his back pocket as he walked toward them.

"I'm not changing my mind. I know in my gut that I'm doing the right thing for my family. It would be nice leaving here knowing my sister had my back and could be encouraging for the kids' sakes," she whispered, at the very least wanting the last word.

Valerie raised a brow. "Do the right thing, Annie. Be kind. Be a team player."

Heat that started in her chest burned its way through until she was pretty sure hot lava would start pouring from her ears any second. Valerie had never gotten over the fact that Annie had grown up and had her own family. Adam and Maddy came to stand with them just as Valerie finished speaking.

Maddy frowned at Valerie, clutching her PEI tourism brochures to her chest. Adam just looked away. Sometimes there were glimmers of the kids they used to be. They had all had each other's backs when Cam was alive, and both kids had figured out the hard way that Aunt Valerie wasn't to be trusted. She made promises and broke them without ever acknowledging that she'd made promises in the first place. And no one was ever allowed to ask her why she'd broken a promise.

"Say goodbye to Aunt Val," Annie forced herself to say in as casual a tone as she could muster.

The kids mumbled goodbye and then clambered into the SUV. Annie wondered if it was petty that she was happy her kids didn't buy into Valerie's attempts at undermining her—even Adam, who was so mad at her. "So . . . see you later." She raised a hand, her keys dangling, not quite making eye contact, hoping she wouldn't have to give her a hug.

Valerie just shook her head, her mouth in that thin line again, and backed up a step.

Annie hopped into the driver's side of the SUV, relieved that she was able to drive away from at least one of her problems. The rest wouldn't be that easy to solve, namely the problem sitting beside her in the form of a very sullen fourteen-year-old who was hell-bent on hating her for everything.

She started the ignition and glanced in her rearview as she pulled out of the driveway. She chose not to focus on the sub-urban red-brick house they'd lived in as a family for a decade, because she couldn't deal with that right now; rather, she stared at the woman who was her only remaining blood relative, other than the kids. She searched for a pang of . . . something, but came up blank. Valerie had caused so much pain, had been such a huge burden in her life, that the farther down the road she drove, the easier it became to breathe. Valerie wouldn't be able to manipulate her when she was a thousand miles away. And if she were being completely honest, a part of her wanted to do a happy dance that she was leaving her behind.

She took a deep breath, forcing herself to turn the page and start this trip off right. "Okay, guys, this is it! I'm thinking we'll make about three stops today to stretch our legs, use the washrooms, and get food. And since we're on a road trip, how about we get McDonald's?" She was hoping for a resounding cheer because she was a relentless stickler for nutrition and rarely allowed fast food.

Maddy nodded, smiling at her in the rearview. "Sounds great!"

Annie glanced at Adam. Eyes glued to his phone. Not a word. "Well, Adam?"

He stared at his phone as though it held all the answers in the universe. "So, what, you buy me a Happy Meal and I'm going to smile and say that I'm happy to be moving to an island with a population of like, five, in a town with a population of like, two, during my first year of high school and you're basically ruining my life?"

Annie gripped the steering wheel tightly and forced her smile to remain intact. They had been over this. But she was going to be so patient because it *was* a big deal. She did regret the timing of all this. But he was partly responsible for the timing of all this, and she didn't want to get into all of that again in front of Maddy. "Of course not, but we still have to get breakfast. It's a long car ride. I just thought it would be a nice treat."

"How long again, Mom?"

Annie made eye contact with Maddy in the rearview mirror as they drove through their middle-class suburban neighborhood. It felt like only yesterday that she and Cam had won the bidding war on that four-bedroom brick house built in the eighties. They thought they'd have decades and decades of life ahead of them. "Eight hours today, but I'd like to push for ten if we can. Then tomorrow it's another eight. But the drive will get really pretty after we get out of the city."

"*Great.* We're going to get to the middle of nowhere even faster," Adam said, somehow managing to hunker down even further without being in a fully reclined position.

She rolled her shoulders, forcing herself to just let the comments roll off, and turned up the music as her kids retreated into their devices, and she kept her eyes on the road as she merged onto the quiet highway. They would beat Friday morning Toronto traffic, which was always a win. She had already programmed their destination last night when she'd packed the car and second-guessed this entire notion. It was the most adventurous thing she'd ever done. She was the only adult here. There was no one to fall back on. But as they drove in silence, Adam not engaging with either of them, she knew she was making the right decision.

I trust you with them, Annie. You're going to be okay. You're so strong. Whatever you need to do to get through it, do it. Thank you. For falling in love with me and marrying me and being my rock. You gave me a life I never thought was possible.

Annie blinked back tears as that memory of her and Cam's last conversation flitted across her mind. He'd been her first everything. He'd been her hero. He'd stolen her heart back in college and they hadn't even waited to finish school before getting married. They'd been passionate and idealistic and so young.

I won't be mad if you get married again. I want you to. Just make sure he's good to you. That he's good to the kids. Make sure he's strong, Annie. Watch out for Val . . . I don't trust her. Take care of you. I asked Matt to look out for you. He will. If you need anything, he'll be there.

She had already broken down at that point, holding onto him, hating the finality in everything he was saying. It had been impossible to imagine a world without him. Adam had been a surprise, but Cam had made sure Annie was able to pursue her dream to become a veterinarian, and they'd made it work. True partners. She hadn't argued with him then. But she would never get married again. And she would protect the kids.

Matt had been there for her. But they all had their own lives to live, and she wasn't the type to lean on anyone. Even now, she'd made it clear to Matt that they wouldn't be a burden. Matt was a good guy and she knew he felt like he owed it to Cam to keep an eye out for them.

And make sure whoever you marry isn't a cheap-ass like me. I should have bought you jewelry and all that stuff. Use the insurance money, Annie, and spoil yourself.

At that point, she'd been laughing through her tears. Cam *had* been cheap. But not stingy. Cam had grown up without money and had always struggled with feelings of poverty. He knew how to treat her well and he knew how to be a real husband and father, and he'd tried his best at everything. She would always love that about him. And she'd bought a luxury SUV with the car insurance money from his wrecked one. And then she'd been ridiculed by Val. Of course.

Build a new life for yourself. If it means leaving here, then go. Do all those things we said we'd do. And, Annie, I know you love your family, but duty won't make you happy in the end. How many years did we waste trying to keep them all happy? I regret every hour spent on the people who tried to take our happiness away from us. Don't waste another minute, Annie.

CHAPTER TWO

"Did you know that the Confederation Bridge is the longest bridge over frozen waters in the whole world? It connects mainland New Brunswick to Prince Edward Island."

"Who cares? What a waste of taxpayer dollars."

Annie shot Adam a glance. "I didn't realize you were so interested in government spending, Adam. But anyway, don't be rude. And yes, honey, I remember that fact. It's still a good one, though. Hard to believe it's such a quick drive from New Brunswick to PEI with the bridge," she said, dreading the upcoming bridge. She hated bridges. Especially ones that spanned an ocean.

Thankfully, crossing Confederation Bridge meant that this trip was almost over. Annie had heard Cam's voice over and over again in the car these last two days. Laughing. Or sternly telling Adam to watch his tone. She also saw Cam rolling his eyes at some of Adam's remarks. Then she'd see him ruffling Maddy's hair. And defusing the tension in the car with a ridiculous "dad joke" and then she'd see Adam laughing.

Last night, they'd stopped at a hotel just outside of Quebec. She'd made excellent time, mostly because she felt like she was trying to outrun teen angst and trying to get farther and farther from home. Like, the sooner they arrived at their new home, the sooner they could start living their new lives.

They'd driven through Kingston, where she, Cam, and Matt had attended university together and had all met for the first time. On their last trip to PEI, they'd stopped there with the kids to show them around. This time, it felt like she'd held her breath until all the Kingston highway exits were behind them. She had done the same as they passed through Ottawa, remembering how anxious they'd been to show the kids around Canada's capital on that vacation. But Annie tried to zoom past those memories so that none of them would get caught up in them. Memories of good times were dangerous when there were no guarantees of the future. This trip wasn't the time for memory lane.

"I need to go to the bathroom."

Annie glanced over at Adam, so many sarcastic comments on the tip of her tongue, but instead she forced a strained smile. "Well, we are in a really rural area. It's either here or it's probably another hour and a half until we get to our new house. Can you wait?"

"Can't I go in a bush?"

"Ew, that's so gross," Maddy moaned from the back seat.

"You're gross," Adam snapped.

Annie held up a hand. "Okay, no one is gross. People need to pee and since Adam drank the largest Coke possible two hours ago, I'm not surprised he needs to go."

Maddy erupted into laughter and Adam mumbled something under his breath.

She was mesmerized by the blue of the water on their left. Powering down her window, despite the light drizzle, she inhaled deeply. "Do you guys smell that?"

"Adam farted."

"I did not. That's how you always smell."

She was not going to let them ruin this for her. "The *ocean*. It's the ocean, you guys."

"I still smell farts."

"You're a loser," Adam snapped.

Annie decided to keep her window lowered in case it did smell like farts, and pressed the gas because she needed this car ride done ten hours ago. "Let's be nice to each other. And no one here is a loser. Adam, I'm not going to tell you again to watch your tone."

He crossed his arms. "Okay. It's always me, isn't it? I didn't even start this."

Annie's phone vibrated in the arm rest holder beside her, but she didn't bother glancing at it because she already knew who it was. "Keep your eyes out for a Tim Hortons or Starbucks because I need coffee."

"Better get it now because I don't think they have Tim Hortons or Starbucks on the island," Maddy said.

"We're still in Canada. Of course they have Tim Hortons. And Mom, Aunt Valerie's calling again," Adam said.

Annie ran a hand through her hair, listening to the GPS directions, and took a turn that led them down a country road with a view of the ocean that made it difficult not to turn and stare at it. Valerie who? This was freedom. She had already spoken to her sister three times and texted her back five times in the last two days. Considering Valerie had nothing nice to say, she was pretty sure she'd done her duty and then some. Besides, Valerie had now decided to spam her pictures of Penelope, demanding Annie show them to Matt. Now that she was almost on island soil, she could start her new life, the one where she wasn't a pushover anymore.

They drove in silence for the next ten minutes, Annie desperate to get to their new home before dark. And she wanted to see Matt. She'd missed him. She hated relying on people, always feeling like, if she did, they'd keep score and throw it back in her face one day. But she knew he wasn't like that. It was still difficult to ask for help. But maybe technically she hadn't. This plan to come here had been hatched late at night, after a brutal summer of parenting, when Matt had been her rock. They could talk for hours and he always wanted to know what was going on with the kids.

The silence in the SUV was different now as they stared out the window. There was something very real about the ocean beside them, a visual reminder that though this was the same country, though they'd been here before, this was very different than living in a Toronto suburb. The landscape was alive with blue and green and the white dusting of snow. Even though dusk was descending around them, there was still life in the air. Dusk was different here too.

"Mom, I gotta go now," Adam said.

Annie nodded. It could be worse. "Okay, this looks like a good spot to stop. Probably a ten-minute drive to the bridge from here, and there are no houses."

Five minutes later, Annie and Maddy were still waiting in the car for Adam to come back. "I think I should go look for him."

"Knowing him, he fell in the ocean."

That's exactly what Annie had been thinking, but there wasn't a steep drop to the ocean, just a sandy shore and some benches "I'm sure he's fine. Stay here, I'll be right back. I'm locking the doors."

"Mom, there's like no one here."

"Still. Stay inside," she said, before hopping out and closing the door.

"Adam! Are you done?" she called out, walking in the direction he'd headed. She shivered in the damp winter air and squinted against the drizzle that had started. She could see Adam in the distance, his head down, his back to her. "Adam," she yelled again when he didn't answer.

He turned around, his eyes shifting away from her, putting his phone in his pocket. "I'm not going."

"Excuse me?"

"I'll take the first bus off the island and go back home."

The waves of the Atlantic seemed harsh and mocking, reminding her how small she was, how unprepared she was to be a single parent, to move to an island when all they'd ever known was living in a city.

Annie blinked, desperate to hold onto her composure, to her authority as a parent. But as she stared at her son's red face, taut with anger, his large, strong body towering over her, the memory of him in her arms as a baby, grinning wildly, consumed her until she couldn't breathe. And where they were right now was the last place she wanted to be.

She wanted to be twenty again; she wanted him to be that baby boy in rocket ship onesies, looking at her like she was his entire world. She wanted to go back to when a cupcake could solve all his problems. She wanted to relive each and every moment, this time with the understanding that those days were fleeting and that they were the best days of her life, but she'd been too exhausted to realize it at the time.

She would never have days as good as those—when Cam was alive, when the four of them, a family, had it all. She wanted Adam to snuggle on her lap while she read to him. She wanted to pour apple juice into his *Thomas the Tank Engine* sippy cup and twist the lid shut and hand it to him as though she were handing him gold.

She wanted him to reach for her hand like it was life, like it was all he needed. She wanted him to play with his little sister and make her laugh. And she wanted Maddy to look up at him and know that he would always have her back, that he was her hero forever. She wanted Cam back . . . because that would have made this all easier. They would have drunk wine together and laughed about how impossible teenagers were. They could have taken turns, they could have whispered in the dark, in bed, about the best ways to deal with a teen. They would have had each other's backs.

This world she was in right now was hell. It was filled with beautiful memories of a life she treasured, a life that had passed by too quickly. And yet she relived it, far too often to ever be able to move forward. But this current reality, this was an unknown space that she wanted out of. She didn't know who she was anymore or if she could ever get herself back.

It was like her old life was a snow globe and she was holding onto it, staring at it from the outside, wishing for it to be real again, wishing to be let back in.

Adam was over six feet tall, a teenager, independent in so many ways, and she was on her own. But he wasn't sixteen. He couldn't leave. And if she had to remind him of that, if it came to that, she would.

She crossed her arms, her heart slamming against her chest. She was too exhausted to argue with him again. "We are a family and we stay together."

"Like Aunt Val? Isn't she family?"

Everything inside her stilled. Adam never defended Valerie. As much as Annie and Cam had tried to shield their kids from the shortcomings of some of their family members, they'd also been very clear so that the kids would know who could be trusted and who couldn't. Plus, the kids witnessed so much bad behavior that they knew Valerie was devious. But if she was manipulating his weaknesses and insecurities right now . . . well, he'd be easy prey. Annie clasped her hands together, trying to channel some of her tension so she didn't lose her composure. "Where is this coming from?"

He shrugged, attempting to pass her. Anger rushed over her. And she felt herself snap like the twigs she'd just jogged across when she thought something had happened to him. Like he was hurt or in trouble. She was worried and he was indifferent. No more. "Were you talking to her just now?"

She grabbed his wrist. "Open your hand. Now."

His eyes flashed. "She called me. She said that if I wanted to go back to Toronto, I could."

Blood rushed to her ears and she wanted to lose it. Right there. She wanted to scream and cry and then just check out. She was bone tired. Her eyes hurt. Her head throbbed. She had just driven nineteen hours. And now this. This was supposed to be the home stretch. "Adam, you have never even spent the night at Aunt Valerie's. You could go back there and she could change her mind—she's done it before. How many times have we gone over for a visit and she wasn't there, or basically telling us half an hour later that it was time for us to go home? How many times did she promise to take you guys somewhere only to never turn up? How many holidays did she not show up to? Or birthdays? Without even an explanation? I wouldn't trust a hamster with her, let alone my child.

"And then on top of all of that, do you really think that's an appropriate thing for an adult, who is also your aunt, to be saying to you? Don't you think someone who had your best interests at heart would be encouraging you and telling you to give this move a shot? Do you really think that my own sister should be saying this to my child?"

For a moment the façade cracked, like a gray-black sky opening up with rain. His chin wobbled, but he didn't say anything. She hated that Valerie had used him, had manipulated him, and now was making it even harder for him. "Adam, I love you and your sister more than this entire world. I would dive into that ocean to save you if you needed saving. That's what I'm doing now. You have to trust me. You have to trust that I know what's best. You have to trust that I'm doing what's best for our family. Yes, we're only a family of three, but we are a family. We stay together."

He kicked his foot into the sand. "I never wanted this."

Neither did she. She wished she could admit defeat and take them back to the only home they'd known, because this seemed like the worst plan ever right now. It was too hard. She wasn't cut out for this. She was a city girl. Her kids were city kids. Maybe she'd overreacted when Adam had been caught vaping and drinking with friends at school.

It had been the last day of grade eight, his last day in elementary school. But as she'd sat in the principal's office with the three other sets of parents, she'd known in her gut that this wasn't right. This wasn't her son. And the vaping and drinking weren't the only signs something wasn't right—he'd been struggling with his classes, he was always in a bad mood, barely making eye contact. He wasn't the boy she'd raised.

That day in the principal's office was her wake-up call. It was time for her to step in and be the parent no one wanted to be.

The other parents had taken it in stride. *"Boys will be boys,"* they'd said as they'd all left the principal's office. They had all laughed and joked and she'd walked down the hallway, her head to the ground, as though she were the one who'd just been scolded. It wasn't okay. It was a sign that her son, her family, was spiraling out of control.

That had been the final straw for her. She'd called Matt and they had hatched out this plan. His sister had a house already under construction, and there had still been time for Annie to have input on the décor. His sister had made sure the house would be ready for them. Then Annie had called a friend who was also a realtor, and as soon as they were able to get the house leased, it was time to go. Not ideal timing, but in a way it had worked out, because Adam was still hanging out with the wrong crowd and his grades hadn't improved in high school. It was the right moment in many ways.

"Neither did I, Adam. But sometimes we have to go through really hard things in order to get to the good stuff. You have to fight for happiness sometimes. But it's there. If you try. If you don't lose faith. Trust me."

He raised his head, his eyes filled with so much pain that if he begged her to go back, she might have actually considered it. She held his gaze, held her breath, held all the love for him in her heart, and prayed fervently that he trusted her, that he wouldn't go to Valerie. Never in a million years did she expect that not only would she be trying to start over but that she would also be fighting to keep her son with her.

The wind battered them, the sleet making all of this harder, and suddenly his stony expression gave way to a hint of her little boy. His chin quivered and his brow furrowed. "I miss Dad, and I don't think I'll ever like any home as much as the home we had with him. I will never get over this. I won't ever be okay with leaving home. I will never forgive you for this."

She swallowed the sob that seemed to come from deep inside, from a place that was so afraid that she'd just lost the biggest gamble of her life. Crossing her arms, she refused to give up, she refused to let those words sink inside her. She took a step closer to him and resisted the urge to throw her arms around him and hug him, because rejection from him at this point would be her undoing. "I know it feels like that. But give it six weeks. Actually try. Like, true effort."

He straightened his shoulders slightly. "What's six weeks?"

She lifted her chin. "Christmas."

He glanced back at the SUV. "So if I still hate it after Christmas, we can go back home?"

She nodded, her heart pounding. She had always been a lousy poker player, had always given away her hand. But she couldn't lose tonight. "Yes, if you hate it that badly, we can go back after Christmas."

He gave her a slight nod. "Deal."

Annie stood perfectly still as she watched him turn around and stomp to the SUV. Guilt stabbed her when she remembered that Maddy was still sitting in there. By herself, watching all of this play out. Her little girl must be sad. Worried.

Annie took a few deep, shaky breaths. She was furious at her sister for using and manipulating her child, and she was angry at herself for making an impossible deal.

She slowly walked toward the shoreline, her shoes sinking into the sand. She was losing control of everything. Of her family, of their happiness. She felt like both her kids were slipping away from her.

She glanced over her shoulder and, seeing that Adam was getting into the SUV, she let out a short, choppy breath. It was supposed to be a deep, cleansing breath but her chest was so tight, so clogged with the muck of the last four years that she couldn't seem to breathe through it. There wasn't enough room or enough air. The pain and the memories were too thick. She walked to the area in front of the benches and gazebo, so the kids wouldn't be able to see her.

She sank to the ground, the sand molding against her knees. She dug her fingers into the sand and then she let the tears fall. The ones she hadn't let herself cry in way too long.

She cried, telling herself that she would feel better once she got it all out. When she stood up again, she would be calm and collected. She would be the mom those kids needed her to be. But she couldn't stand just yet.

She closed her eyes, the drizzle misting over her, and she waited for something.

She wanted to believe in signs again, magic. She wanted to believe in happily-ever-afters. She wanted to believe that the jingling bells she'd heard at midnight on Christmas Eve when she was six were really Santa Claus. But she was too scared to believe in any of those things anymore. There wasn't an ounce of Christmas magic anywhere. And she was losing hope that they'd ever find it again.

She grabbed a fistful of the sand and cried for Cam and for herself and all their broken dreams. Just for a minute. She'd give herself this minute.

But when she felt control slipping further away instead of coming closer, she prayed for a sign.

Instead, she heard a car horn.

Angry kids. *Not* the sign she wanted. *Not* a sign that this Christmas could be better.

She slowly stood, brushing the sand off her knees, forcing herself to get it together. And then her phone vibrated in her pocket.

She pulled it out of the back pocket of her jeans. If it was Valerie, it was a sign that she was doomed. She held her breath as she read the text.

Hey, Annie, just checking in, making sure you guys are okay. Send me a text letting me know you haven't had a run-in with a moose, lol. I can't wait to see you guys.

The tiniest ounce of hope filled her soul at Matt's message.

She shut her eyes, her hand clenched around her phone, around his words. Matt had been their rock. He'd stayed with her and the kids for three weeks after the funeral. And on that last day, when he'd stood in the driveway, ready to go home to Prince Edward Island, he'd hugged her and whispered words that had offered her comfort, late at night when she worried about how she was going to go on . . . *Annie, if it all falls apart and it's too much, come to the island. My family and I are here, we will be your family.*

Even after four years, those words were vivid in her mind. The look in Matt's eyes was still as real to her as the island on the other side of the water now. Christmas could still be a time of miracles. They needed one.

She had to believe this was the right thing for all of them. That she could get back to the woman who believed in miracles, in the power of love.

Prince Edward Island was a new beginning for herself, for the kids, for the three of them as a family. Prince Edward Island was just across that expanse of blue water.

Their new lives were waiting for them, whether or not she was ready; she had made this decision and she was going to have to carry it out.

She had to believe that there was better out there for them.

That she could turn all of this around.

That she was not too broken to be put back together.

That she would pick herself up, piece by piece, until her family was restored.

And she had six weeks to do it.

CHAPTER THREE

Forty minutes later, Annie stared at her GPS screen one more time and then looked through her dash. The map indicated there was a road on the left but all she saw through the window was an empty field covered with a thin layer of snow. Not even a dirt road. Maybe if she really squinted, she could sort of make out the thinning of the grass at the edge, but still. This was *not* a road.

Dusk had turned to night faster than she'd anticipated and Annie was desperate to find their new house before it was pitch black out. This wasn't exactly how she'd hoped their first drive through Prince Edward Island would go.

Back in Toronto, she'd imagined the sun shining on them, the rolling green hills, the sparkling blue of the Atlantic, an almost cathartic welcome. A rebirth of their family. Instead, torrential rain had started halfway across the Confederation Bridge, the grass wasn't exactly green because it was November, and Adam had been despondent after their argument. Frankly, she'd been almost happy because she'd taken that time trying to calm down and come up with a way to make all of this okay in six weeks. Now, thanks to her impulsive promise and fear that her son would leave to live with Valerie, she was operating with a ticking time bomb.

But it hurt. Deep inside. It hurt and it filled her with anxiety to know that her sister was a threat to her family, that she would actually try to lure one of her kids away. Losing her kids was her greatest fear. To hear her son say he'd rather live with the aunt who'd never cared for them or spent more than a couple of hours at a time with them would keep her up tonight.

"Mom, turn left," Maddy said with an exasperation that Annie felt herself. This had been a road trip to end all road trips. Never again would she be trapped in a car, the sole driver, for longer than an hour at a time. She wouldn't be surprised if she developed some kind of PTSD from this trip. Seven hours on the Trans-Canada Highway from Quebec, through New Brunswick, and then into PEI had almost broken her. The moose signs had almost done her in. The gorgeous landscape, where there was nothing but vast expanses of green trees and rivers and lakes, had been breathtaking. For the first hour. Then the lack of rest stops, the lack of traffic, of civilization had started to haunt her. What if their car broke down? There wasn't even cell reception. What if they *did* run into a moose?

But now they were here. Almost. Except there was no indication that there was a road. Or a house anywhere. "Left? As in drive through a field?"

"I'm sure it's what people in the country do," Adam said with a dispassionate glance out his window.

She stared at the wet farmland in front of her and then back at the GPS screen. The only sign they were anywhere near the ocean was the fact that half the screen was blue. "I don't know, maybe I should call Matt and double-check this is the way to the house."

"Mom, just drive," Maddy said, clutching the back of her seat now.

It was rare that both her kids were in agreement about anything. This was how they used to be. She glanced at both of them and then turned her left signal on, even though it felt ridiculous since there was literally no one around, and then there was the fact that she wasn't even turning onto a road . . . she took a deep breath and turned, grateful she had four-wheel drive as she navigated through the field. She could see now that there were very faint tire marks, so she kept to those, until about a minute later they led her to a cornfield.

"Keep going," Adam said, the laughter and excitement in his voice making her smile. Maddy squealed with glee and Annie could have cried with joy at the happiness in her car. She would cling to this. She pushed aside all other thoughts and worries and basked in the first joy she'd felt in . . . years. All it had taken was driving off a road and now . . . through a cornfield.

She was actually smiling as she spoke. "Guys, hold on. This can't be right. And look at all that mud . . . well, red clay. We could get stuck."

"Then gun it," Adam said, sounding like a seasoned driver, sounding like the old Adam.

"*Gun it!*" her sensible, level-headed child yelled from the back seat.

So, in the name of family preservation, Annie did just that. She fishtailed her way through the opening in the cornfield, smiling as her kids hollered, then white-knuckling it until they made it to the clearing. She felt wild. Free. She felt laughter bubble up as her SUV tore over the clay and onto a new patch of land. Farmland. Green. And then blue. And then all of them were silent.

Straight ahead was the Atlantic Ocean.

Rough. Choppy. Invincible.

Filled with so many broken dreams and maybe so many unfulfilled dreams waiting for them.

"That's the house! From the pictures Matt sent, that's it!" Maddy yelled, pointing to the left.

She and Adam turned and sure enough, there in the distance was the little house, with blue siding and a big wraparound porch facing the ocean. It was their new beginning. Their new home. She blinked rapidly, faster than the quick succession of the windshield wipers, as the enormity of what she'd done stared her in the face.

She'd driven through four provinces, with a trunk-load of their most treasured belongings, with the two people in the world she would do anything for, based on a promise Matt had made. And now she had six weeks to make it work.

The gamble of it all was spiraling through her. She had taken her kids away from everything they'd ever known, to a tiny island. They had no family here, just the promise from her husband's best friend that they would be okay here, that they would be welcome.

But as the three of them sat in the car, the late November rain tapping against the windows, she wished there was a porch light on. She knew it was unfair to think that Matt would be able to take the night off to welcome them. His work was demanding, they were short-staffed. They would see him tomorrow, that was good enough. They had made it this far on their own. What was one more night?

And yet, she yearned. For *something*. Something that gave the tiniest inkling that they had made the right decision. That *she* had made the right decision. That maybe they weren't alone. That maybe she could win her son back in six weeks. That maybe this would be the Christmas she made her family whole again.

CHAPTER FOUR

"You look exactly like you did when you were six years old, peering out the window, looking for Santa Claus on Christmas Eve!"

Matt Williams grinned at his grandmother's comment. He turned to her and made room at the window overlooking the front of Annie's new house. "I guess that's how I feel. A little worried too, if I'm honest. It's a hell of a drive from Toronto and that stretch in New Brunswick, especially this time of year, is pretty daunting. I'll feel better when I see them. I'm excited for all of them to be here. They deserve a great Christmas and a fresh start."

She patted him on the arm, her touch a reminder of the security that came from a loved one who could always be counted on. Grandma Lila was exactly that. She had been a rock for all of them. He knew a lot of that came from the trials she'd dealt with in her own life—being divorced and a single mother of three children at a young age. But she was made of steel.

He placed his arm around her thin shoulders and the two of them stood there, keeping watch for Annie. With his grandmother, the silence was comfortable. She had never been one to fill silence with needless chitchat, and neither had he. He was thankful for that, right now especially. His feelings were complicated. He was happy Annie and the kids were coming to live here, but he also knew that there was a lot riding on this.

If they weren't happy, they could pack up and head back to Toronto at any time. And then he would have failed Cam and he would have failed Annie. He wouldn't be able to live with that outcome.

"I agree. Sometimes a fresh start means moving. Annie is a wonderful mother. I hope that we can give her the support she needs," his grandmother said.

He let out a rough breath, his gaze straight ahead. "Me too."

"Good. Excellent. I was thinking of giving her my magical recipe book."

He coughed. "Grandma, with all due respect, you can't actually believe that old book is magical. It's filled with your recipes. I mean, don't get me wrong—your food is legendary. But not magical."

She poked him in the side. "Matthew, if I say it's magical, it is. And I don't mean magical the way you're thinking, it's just brought me a lot of peace and comfort. It's also filled with my island-famous advice. I bet Annie would love it. It's hard being a single mom, especially when she doesn't have her own mom around anymore. Maybe she needs some help planning things. Maybe I can even help her some. And maybe it's slightly magical."

He swallowed against the panic rising inside. His family was way too involved in his personal life, and if his grandmother started meddling, it would only complicate things.

Not that things were complicated per se, but for him they were. Annie coming here was the right thing. He had promised Cam, those last days in the hospital, that he would look out for them. He had taken that promise seriously, and even if Cam hadn't asked him to, he would have. Obviously, he knew Annie could take care of herself and her kids, but it was the stuff beyond the everyday. It was knowing someone had your back, knowing you had someone to call in the middle of the night with an emergency, having someone to help on a deeper level than just childcare. As much as he had tried to be there for Annie and the kids, the last few years had gotten away from them both. They both had busy work lives as veterinarians as well as her with the kids. He felt as though he hadn't been keeping up his end of the deal. And this last year something had changed—her voice had sounded different on the phone. She sounded tired—not the exhausted at the end of the day tired, but more a weariness, a loss of faith and hope. That gutted him.

Her concerns for Adam were real, and when they had started toying with the idea of moving to Prince Edward Island, he'd had to make sure he wasn't projecting what he wanted. She needed to make the best decision for herself and her kids and not have him influencing that in any way. The fact that her sister actually caused her more problems than she helped solve made the decision to leave easier because Annie felt there was no family she could count on.

So he promised he was family. That his family could be her family.

And now, standing here, waiting for them, with his grandmother ready to hand over her legendary cookbook reaffirmed how grateful he was for such a supportive, if nosy, family.

The only complicating factor was his feelings for Annie. He had always been able to deny them when she lived halfway across the country. He would never act on them. She was his best friend's wife and somewhere along the way she'd become a best friend to him too. He valued their friendship, her trust, too much to ever break that. He had also had a long-term relationship that had ended badly, and he wasn't going to go down that road again. He was an expert at compartmentalizing. He would just have to remind himself of that as much as needed.

"Well, you can definitely ask her. I'm sure no matter what, she'll be touched by your offer. She has a lot on her plate," he said, finally getting back to his grandmother's comment.

She let out a long sigh, her eyes straight ahead, looking for a sign of them. "She does. I remember those days. They can be lonely and stressful. And this drive out here, being the only parent, had to have been a trial."

He knew it must have been. He stood a little straighter as he thought he caught a glimmer of headlights. "Annie's tough. At least she can rest up this weekend."

"Matt! I see headlights!"

"They're here!" Matt yelled so that his mom and sister, who were in the kitchen, could hear. They were busy with last-minute preparations but came bustling over now. His gaze was fixed on the slow-moving Mercedes SUV. He bit back a grin because he'd half expected a call from Annie about the fact that there was no actual road that led to the house. He had to hand it to her, though, for finding her way through the cornfield.

He'd always known Annie was a force to be reckoned with. She was the strongest woman he knew outside of the women in his own family. But he also knew everyone had a breaking point and, this last year, he'd sensed hers. She hadn't opened up to him about all the details, but he could sense it in her tone, in the way her voice either trailed off or was speeding a mile a minute as she darted around the city shuffling kids from one activity to another.

He took the promise he'd made to Cam seriously, though he'd never actually admit that promise to Annie. He would never want her to think he saw her as a burden or worse, think that she couldn't take care of herself. But it was more that he thought of her as family, and he was raised to believe that family helped family. That's what he was doing now. It didn't need to be more.

He held his breath as they stepped out of the vehicle, his chest tight, his muscles tense.

"Oh my goodness, those children are all grown up," his grandmother whispered. It was a slight exaggeration because Maddy was only eleven and Adam fourteen, but he understood what she meant. How did kids change that much in four years? FaceTimes had gotten less frequent in the last year, but still. He wasn't prepared for this, how much they'd changed in four years. The last time he'd seen them they'd been like little kids. Now, Adam was almost as tall as he was, and little Maddy wasn't so little anymore.

Hell. A lump formed in his throat because he wished his best friend was here with them. He'd give anything for Cam to be getting out of that SUV too. He'd give anything to be sitting on the back porch having a beer with him. No one had been as close as Cam, no one had felt more like a brother to him, and he missed him every damn day.

But when the three of them rounded the corner and Matt caught a glimpse of Annie, he knew this had been the right decision. The expression on her face in that moment—the fear, the exhaustion—made him vow to make them all happy again.

He couldn't let them stand out in the rain and fish around for the key he'd said would be under the rug. He swung open the door and flung the light switch on as everyone yelled, "Surprise!"

The three of them stood still for a moment, and then it was as though everyone in the house sucked them in, and soon the laughter and hugs were the only thing that could be heard. The mudroom was suddenly filled with boisterous conversation and jackets and boots being tossed around.

"Annie," he said, as she was finally released from the grip of his mother, grandmother, and sister. She looked up at him, the smile gracing her face reassuring him that this surprise welcome had been the right choice.

She paused for a moment, a few inches from him, and everything stopped. He took a moment to really see her again. She was as beautiful as he remembered. More, even. Her long dark hair was in a low ponytail, more pieces out than in, but she still managed to look pulled together. Her cheeks were flushed and her blue eyes were glistening with emotion. She was Annie.

The last time he'd seen her had been for Cam's funeral when Matt had stayed with them for three weeks. They'd sat together, late into the night, almost every night. They'd cried together. Drank together. She'd been the only person he'd cried in front of in his adult life. She'd held onto him, and he would never forget the trust she'd had in him.

Annie took a first step toward him and he completed it, putting his arms around her. She held onto him tightly, and he felt her shaky breath. She was home. Voices and laughter floated around them, but they stood together silently. He was vaguely aware of the kids running down the hallway with excited chatter. But Annie didn't move and neither did he. Annie was the only woman he'd ever felt a deeper connection with, and she would never know that. He held onto her as tightly as she held him. "I'm so glad you're here. It's all going to be okay, Annie," he whispered gruffly.

She nodded against his chest and then pulled back a moment later and looked up at him. "I know. Thank you for this, Matt. I can't even . . . we almost didn't make it because, uh, you failed to mention that I'd be driving through a farmer's field and then a cornfield."

He laughed, enjoying the sparkle in her eyes and the smile on her face when she spoke. "I thought you'd figure it out. Welcome to the island."

She shook her head, still smiling. She'd always had a smile that made him want to smile along with her. "And this house . . . I can't wait to look around."

"I can give you the grand tour," his sister Kate said, appearing out of nowhere, putting her arm around Annie's shoulder.

"Omigosh, please. I'm sure the kids are dying to look around."

"Too late, they're already upstairs, bedrooms claimed," Kate said with a laugh.

"I shouldn't be surprised. But that's a good sign that they're so interested. Okay, I can't wait to see what you've done. Start right here because I need to take this all in," she said, looking around the mudroom.

"I hope you love it. I went off all the pictures you sent me. And really, it's all the stuff you saw during our FaceTimes, but now it's just put together. Of course, I had to add a bunch of extras to make it feel like home. But there's still plenty for you to do to make it your own . . . if you decide to stay after the year is up," Kate said with an impish smile.

Annie's face turned red and she averted her gaze. "That's the dream. This is perfect. And I'm sure you'll have no trouble renting this out if we don't. That deal is still good, right?"

Kate nodded. "Of course it is. No pressure. This will be another great property to add to the vacation rentals I have. Seriously. We just want you all to stay. *Oops.* There I go again. Seriously. No pressure."

Annie smiled. "Thanks. Honestly, that does take some of the pressure off. I can't wait to hear all about your business. Sounds like you're growing fast."

"Let's do coffee this week and catch up," Kate said.

He knew that Kate and Annie had gotten closer as they'd worked on this house together. His sister's business had taken off in the last couple of years, and it had worked out perfectly that she could help Annie with this house. Private vacation homes on the island had become a booming business, and Kate had gotten in on it at the perfect time, scooping up oceanfront land and then building homes and renting them out as luxury vacation rentals.

Annie nodded. "Perfect."

Kate linked her arm through Annie's. "Okay, then let me show you around your new house. I tried to design this so it would be really functional for kids and all the mess and chaos. This is the mudroom; the tiles are super-hardwearing and indestructible. The bench is built in, with storage cubbies underneath for each of you, and the powder room is through the pocket door. I kept the tiles the same," his sister said as Annie looked around.

"Kate, this is gorgeous. Way beyond what I could have imagined. It's the perfect size too. And I love these tiles. And this white vanity and mirror," Annie said, poking her head into the powder room.

His sister gave a little clap and then swung open the double doors that led to the small laundry room. "Ta-da! Hidden laundry room! The quartz counter on top of the washer-dryer is enough space that you can fold here too. Storage cabinets above, and then you can just shut the doors and be done with it."

Annie gasped. "This is perfect. I can't believe you fit so much storage in such a small amount of space. Um, and I totally love the seagrass laundry baskets on the wall."

Matt wasn't going to burst anyone's bubble, but it looked like any laundry room. And he had no idea there were different types of wicker baskets, but whatever, because Annie looked as though she'd just won the lottery, and she deserved that.

"Okay, then come this way. I will say this space was one of my favorites ever," Kate said, giving a theatrical sweep of her arm as she led them to the great room. Annie clutched Kate's arm like she was hanging on for dear life. His grandmother and mother were in there, by the island with the platters of food they'd set out. His grandmother's eyes had a sparkle in them that had him on high alert, and his mother was fussing with the arrangement of food while looking up here and there to see what was happening. When Annie didn't speak, he glanced over at her. Her eyes were filled with tears, and her hands were covering her mouth.

"I can't believe this. You've all made it feel like home already. Thank you, for all of this . . . I never would have expected a welcome like this. I'll never forget your kindness," she whispered raggedly.

His mother blew her nose and his grandmother was watching him like he was the view and not the ocean. "This is what family does," his grandmother said.

Annie gave her a wobbly smile and nodded. He knew that comment was from the heart, but he thought of Annie's sister and her lack of family and wondered if that's what she was thinking. Hell, the mood in here was getting too heavy, because even he felt a lump in his throat as he witnessed the raw emotion on

Annie's face. "Frankly, I'm just surprised Kate managed to pull this off," he said.

Kate poked him in the stomach, and the lightheartedness returned. He shoved his hands in his pockets and stood still, taking in the room as Annie did. He'd been here over a few dozen times during construction and he had to admit it was pretty spectacular. His sister was a talented designer and she'd really put her heart and soul into the place, determined to give Annie the house of her dreams, all on budget.

The high ceilings made the house seem bigger than it was, as did the open-concept kitchen and great room. The kitchen was all white, with built-in appliances that made the fridge and dishwasher look as though they were part of the cabinetry. The island was huge, with four counter stools. The eating area had a large, rustic farmhouse kind of table that he knew she'd picked up from one of the local woodworkers. The built-in bench with pillows on one side was framed by the massive box window that overlooked the ocean. The rest of the chairs matched the table.

"This kitchen," Annie whispered, her finger trailing along the white quartz counters.

"It's a dream kitchen, for sure the perfect place for cooking up a storm!" his grandmother said, beaming at Annie. He imagined this was his grandmother's attempt at laying down the foundation for her magical cookbook presentation later.

"Well, I'll definitely have to brush up on my cooking skills to be worthy of a kitchen like this," Annie said with sigh.

"Oh, don't you worry about that, my dear," his grandmother said, the smile on her face practically bursting with excitement.

"Thanks. And all this food. My goodness, you've all worked so hard. The kids are going to love all this too," Annie said, her voice catching as she spoke to his mother and grandmother.

His mom came and put her arm around Annie's shoulders. "We are happy to do it. Now, we'll be waiting here once you've looked at the house. Enjoy taking it all in. We already snooped around before you got here," she said with a laugh.

Annie smiled. "Thanks. I will."

"We'll hurry up because you must be hungry too," Kate said.

Annie slowly turned, taking in the entire room. "I am, and I think we've eaten enough fast food to last us a lifetime. I just can't get over this house, Kate. These floor-to-ceiling windows are gorgeous. I can't believe I get to wake up to that view every morning. And the furniture, Kate . . . this looks so amazing. I'm just going to keep gushing all night."

"Gush all you want. I'll give you the quick tour and then come and eat, and then we promise to leave you all alone. You must be exhausted," Kate said.

Annie walked over to the great room, her gaze moving from one area to the other. "I am, but I'm so wired now and I just can't get over all this. Even this fireplace looks nicer than in the pictures you sent—and I already thought it looked gorgeous. And the built-ins and the couches. Honestly, I feel like I'm on HGTV and just won my dream house."

Matt shoved his hands in the front pockets of his jeans, needing something to do with the emotion that seemed to hit him out of nowhere as he watched Annie. He had no idea how she managed to look so gorgeous, even after hours on the road with her kids. Her navy hoodie and dark skinny jeans hugged her curves beautifully, not that he should be noticing, but he did before a stab of guilt hit him. So he focused on her eyes. Her blue eyes were alive and filled with wonder, and it made him so damn happy to see.

"You deserve this fresh start, Annie. All of you do," his sister said.

The fireplace mantel matched the kitchen cabinets, and there were two overstuffed white couches facing each other and a big ottoman-style coffee table. His sister had picked out a large tray and placed a lantern on it along with a pot of mums.

"Thank you, but you really have gone above and beyond," Annie said as his sister led them upstairs.

There were more gasps and thank yous as they all stood in the bonus room. It had another fireplace and a large sectional couch and a games table area. The ceilings were vaulted and there were windows on three walls that faced the ocean. A large, wraparound deck could be accessed through patio doors and his sister had Adirondack chairs and pots filled with mums outside. "You've thought of everything, Kate," Annie said, touching one of the throw blankets on the back of the couch.

"I'm glad. Now let's go see the bedrooms," she said, giving Annie a playful shove down the hall.

The first bedroom was Maddy's room. Matt smiled as soon as they entered the room. He'd been in here before, but now it was all real. Maddy was sprawled across the white double bed of the pink room. Matching white nightstands and a dresser and desk made up the rest of the room. There was a window seat that overlooked the ocean.

"Aunt Kate, this is the best room ever. I can't believe I even get my own bathroom!"

Maddy reached out to hug Maddy. "I'm glad you love it. The bathroom was a little surprise your mom and I thought you'd like."

Maddy looked at Annie, her eyes dancing, her smile easy. "Thanks. It'll be great not having to share a bathroom with a boy anymore . . . no offense, Uncle Matt."

He laughed. "None taken."

"Yeah, don't worry, Maddy. I had to share a bathroom with him and he's a total slob," Kate said, giving him a shove in the doorway as she passed through.

Annie leaned down to give Maddy a kiss on the head. "There's lots of food downstairs. Why don't you head down there in a minute, okay?"

Maddy nodded. "Sure."

Matt gave Maddy a wink before leaving the room. The next room in the hallway was Adam's, and the door was shut. Annie knocked and Matt heard a grumbled, "Come in."

A heaviness settled in Matt's chest as they walked into the room. The space was beautiful, almost identical to Maddy's with the window seat and peaked ceiling and en suite bath, except the colors were navy and gray and white. Adam was lying on his bed and Matt couldn't read his expression, but there was a closed-off vibe there that he didn't remember seeing before. Granted, Adam was a teenager now and those good memories Matt had with him were from when Cam was still alive. They'd gone fishing together and played catch and gone on hikes. But those days were long gone now. Matt would have given anything to see this boy smile the way he used to.

"Hi, Aunt Kate. This room is great, thanks."

At least he could still be polite. That counted for something.

"You're very welcome, I'm glad you like it. This place will feel like home before you know it," Kate said before turning and leaving the room with Annie.

The stare exchanged between Adam and Annie was something that made him pause. "So how was the road trip?" Matt asked, leaning against the doorjamb. It didn't feel right to just walk out without at least trying to have a conversation with him. He'd given this kid piggyback rides and made smores with him.

He'd held his hand at Cam's funeral. He'd do anything for him. For all of them. And not just because he'd promised Cam, but because they were family.

Adam shrugged. "Long."

"See any moose?"

A smile tugged at one corner of Adam's mouth. "Unfortunately, no. Mom was worried we would, so that was kind of funny. But not as funny as when she had to drive through that dirt road and cornfield. Maddy was pissed because she has a collection of stuffies from every province, but we didn't find a moose at any of the rest stops in New Brunswick."

Matt made a mental note to get her a stuffy for Christmas. But he was also thrilled that Adam was making conversation with him. Annie had been so worried about how despondent he'd been lately. Adam wasn't so naïve as to think that a change of scenery would change everything so quickly, but maybe things weren't going to be so difficult anymore. "Well, I'm glad for your mom's sake you didn't have a run-in with any moose. They can be pretty scary in real life. Especially on that highway. As for the cornfield, thanks for letting me know, I'll be sure to tease her about it. How do you like the new room?"

Adam leaned back against the headboard, stretching his legs out as his gaze roamed the room. Matt was again reminded of how big he'd gotten. He wasn't a kid anymore. He looked so much like Cam. Looking at him was like witnessing a painful miracle. "It's awesome. This whole house is."

"Glad you like it. Hey, my mom and grandmother have a whole bunch of food waiting downstairs if you're hungry," he said.

Adam surprised him by swinging his legs over the bed. "I'm starved actually. I think I'll go down. You coming too?"

Matt walked out into the hallway with Adam. "I'll join you in a minute. I'm just going to finish the upstairs tour. Enjoy. They've been working on it all day."

A look flashed across Adam's eyes that Matt couldn't quite figure out. "Sounds good." He turned toward the stairs.

Matt stopped in Maddy's doorway when he noticed she'd fallen asleep. She was sprawled out in the middle of the double bed, a lobster stuffy tucked under one arm, her dark hair fanned out around her face. His heart ached as he walked forward and picked up one of the pink throws sitting on the window seat and placed it over her small frame. It should be Cam doing this. Not Matt, the single guy who'd never wanted kids or a family of his own.

He crossed the room quietly and shut off the light. He left the door slightly ajar so that the hallway light would filter through in case she woke up in the middle of the night, before heading downstairs. Judging by the laughs and squeals, Annie was loving her room.

He joined Adam and his own mother and grandmother in the kitchen. Adam was currently sitting at the island with a plate filled with so much food that it was toppling over the edges. That didn't stop his grandmother as she added one more cupcake. "Grandma, I don't think Adam has five hours to sit here and eat," he said with a laugh.

His grandmother waved a hand and then approached him with a plate containing almost as much food. "This one's for you."

He leaned down and gave her a kiss on the cheek. He knew better than to argue with her. "Thanks."

She patted his arm. "You're welcome, and you're too skinny and you work too hard."

It was her classic line. It could be worse. At least she didn't have the heart to tell him what he knew she probably thought was his biggest problem—his lack of commitment. Or maybe because she knew that he didn't view it as a problem. Grandma Lila was tough as nails and sweet as icing. She had been a strong presence in his life, especially after his father left. The women in his family were the strongest women he knew, aside from Annie. He owed them a lot; when he'd faced hard times as a teenager, they'd reeled him in. He'd been bitter and jaded for a long time, much more than Kate. Maybe because he was five years older and he remembered their dad vividly. He wasn't so sure it was a good thing. It was one thing to be angry with a dad who was an ass and then left, and entirely another to think your dad loved you to pieces and then left to start a new family with better kids. "Thanks, Grandma."

"So how is Annie liking the house?" his mother asked, as she wiped down the counter.

He took a bite of a lobster roll. "I'm pretty sure she loves it. What do you think, Adam?"

Adam nodded; his mouth full.

"I absolutely love it. This was all way beyond anything I could have ever expected," Annie said as she and Kate came down the stairs and joined them in the kitchen.

His grandmother beamed and immediately filled a plate with a lobster roll and salad. "We're glad. And we're so glad you're all here. This place will feel like home in no time. Now, we're going to get going because I know you all must be exhausted. Your fridge is stocked with the essentials and there's enough lobster rolls and salad and fruit that you won't have to worry about breakfast or lunch tomorrow for yourself or the kids."

Annie reached out to hug his grandma before accepting the plate. "This is all so thoughtful. It already feels like home thanks to all of you."

48

"Poor Maddy is wiped and in deep sleep," Matt said.

He glanced over at his mother, who was blotting the corners of her eyes with a tissue. He knew she adored Annie and her kids. "That poor dear. You all need a good night's sleep. We'll be on our way then," his mom said, giving Adam, who hadn't come up for a breath, a quick hug.

They all walked to the front door as everyone said their goodbyes.

"I'm going upstairs too. Goodnight, Mom. Goodnight, Uncle Matt," Adam said before walking back into the house.

Annie let out a long sigh and turned to Matt. The rain had turned to drizzle and the ocean waves filled the silence. She huddled further into her sweater before looking up at him. It was strange, standing there, just the two of them. He met her gaze and he had a flash of a memory, a long-ago moment they'd shared, back in university, when they were both different people. God, it felt like another lifetime. A time before marriage, kids, adulthood. They'd been free, with only hope in front of them. But he pushed the memory aside, feeling uncomfortable just remembering it. There was something in her blue eyes that made him wonder if she ever thought of it. Or how she remembered that moment. He shoved his hands in the front pockets of his jeans. "You must be exhausted."

She shot him a smile that was both beautiful and rueful. "I think I hit exhausted in Quebec, now I'm just running on empty. But this welcome was just . . . it was exactly what we needed. And your family is amazing. Things were pretty rough there for a while with Adam, and I was questioning all of this."

His chest tightened. "Like moving here, you mean?"

She tucked a strand of hair behind her ear. "Yeah . . . I . . . it was bad. A total low point and I kind of broke down. Honestly, I don't even think I can retell the story while I'm sober."

He smiled, resisting the urge to reach out to hug her, because she sounded like she needed one. "You made it, that counts for everything. I won't push. You don't owe me any explanations, but if you need someone to talk to, you know I'm here."

She looked away for a moment. "Thanks. I appreciate that. I'll fill you in later, but the biggest problem I have right now is that, in a moment of utter weakness, I promised Adam that if he hates it here, we can move back to Toronto after Christmas."

His stomach dropped. "Hell, that's a lot of pressure."

She nodded. "It was so stupid of me. I'm still kicking myself. But it was Valerie."

He tensed. He'd already been warned about Valerie—by Cam and then by Annie over the last few years in their phone conversations. Just listening to half those stories made him appreciate his family even more. "What did she do?"

Her hand was shaking as she tried to grab the strands of hair the wind was blowing around. "She contacted Adam on our road trip and told him he could go back to Toronto and live with her. That he could take a bus back."

Anger slashed through him. "Are you kidding me?"

She shook her head. "I wish. I knew she was mad we were moving here. I should have seen this coming, in retrospect. Maybe I could have prevented it. There were a few hours on the drive when I had to ignore her calls and texts and I bet that set her off."

The waves crashed harshly in the distance and he felt the same turmoil as he listened to her. He wrestled with what he wanted to say and not wanting to hurt her feelings. But in the end, he knew he couldn't lie. "You can't possibly think that this is your fault. What, you didn't answer a text or phone call while on a road trip with your kids so your sister has the right to go behind your back and manipulate Adam?"

She groaned and covered her face for a moment. "You're right. You're right. I know you're right. But I've always managed Valerie by . . . doing what she's wanted. I have to stop. I know I have to stop."

He took a step forward and then stopped himself when he realized he wanted to pull her in for a hug. It would be awkward. But she looked so tired and lost and he just wanted to comfort her. He stood still. "For the record, I'm not criticizing your strategy. I get that you have to do what you have to do. I'm just angry on your behalf. And Adam's. But sometimes it's good to tell people this stuff so they can remind you what a normal, healthy relationship looks like. And your relationship with Valerie is not healthy."

She nodded. "I know. I know. You're so easy to talk to. I almost lost it when Adam told me what she did. She used his vulnerability against us. She's trying to undo everything I'm trying to build here. It's completely overstepping. The saddest part is that she doesn't truly love my kids. They're just objects to her. She doesn't even have full conversations with them."

He ran a hand over his jaw. "What are you going to do?"

She turned her head toward the ocean. "I don't know. He's my first priority—I'm hurt that he would even think of leaving us, but I'm trying to be rational. I know he's heartbroken and he's scared and vulnerable. It's not his fault. He's being played by his aunt. That's . . . ugh. Your family is so normal, and that's just what we need right now.

"But Matt, I made a commitment to work at your clinic and I'm so grateful that you've given me this job, so I don't want to leave you high and dry, and I don't want you to think I don't take that seriously. I made that stupid agreement in a panic after I found out what Valerie did."

He reached out to put a hand on her shoulder. "Hey, hey, we've got your back, okay? Whatever you need. I still think you made the right decision, and I'm too stubborn to give up without a fight. I have a feeling that, in six weeks, Adam is going to be begging to stay here."

"I'm almost afraid to hope that this will work, that I can really have a fresh start."

"Of course you can. And if you want the week to settle in with the kids, take it. Maybe starting on Monday is too aggressive. For the kids too."

She took a deep breath. "Thanks, but I think we should just rip it off like a Band-Aid, so to speak. I think if we're just hanging around the house it'll only make things worse. It'll be more time for Adam to worry about his new school. I think he needs to just start. We all do. The sooner they make friends, the better it will be. It's already less than ideal, starting at this time of year, but it is what it is. I just want him to find a good group of friends and get back on track."

"He will. It's a fresh start for all of you. But if you do change your mind about work, don't hesitate to tell me. Everyone at the clinic is really looking forward to meeting you."

When her eyes watered and she gave him a nod, he vowed to be true to his word. He didn't want to lose her; he didn't want her to leave. He wanted so much more for all of them. He wanted to see them all smile and laugh. He wanted Adam to fall in love with this place like he had.

Annie had trusted him with her whole heart and he wouldn't let her down. And he wouldn't let Cam down. Somehow, he had to make this place feel like home to all of them by Christmas.

CHAPTER FIVE

The sound of coffee percolating was almost as comforting as the smell of the rich brew in her new house. It was barely six in the morning, but getting out of bed had been welcome because she'd tossed and turned all night. Worry had coiled a tight knot in her stomach. Or maybe it was the sense of betrayal or fear thanks to Valerie.

But as Annie walked down the hall that morning, pausing outside her kids' rooms, she'd pleaded and silently prayed that things would all work out for them. Now, with the fireplace on and pouring her first cup of coffee in her new house, she asked for a sign. A sign that this would be okay, that she was doing the right thing.

She added a splash of milk to her coffee and took a sip, letting out a sigh. It was a delicious blend from a local roaster, and she could tell it was freshly ground. Matt's family had all come through for her. Their welcome had been unlike anything she'd ever experienced. She had never had people take such good care of them. She felt cherished, protected. Her conversation with Matt had only reaffirmed that.

She lifted the lid on the frosted cranberry-scented, soy-based candle that Kate had left for her. It smelled like Christmas and home . . . and hope. It smelled like the kind of Christmas she wanted—the one she dreamed about, the one that didn't feel like it was going to happen this year.

She quickly placed the lid back on, a wave of anxiety crashing over her. She wasn't relaxed enough or happy enough to light it. She was afraid to hope, and this candle was all about hope.

She was going to have to deal with Valerie at some point.

Walking over to the set of patio doors, she peered through the glass to try and catch a glimpse of the ocean. Sunrise was almost an hour away, and she couldn't wait to watch it. Last night she'd barely enjoyed the view before night had settled. It was almost surreal to think this place could be theirs forever—or for six weeks.

She jumped as a knock at the door sounded as loud as a megaphone in the quiet house. Who could be coming here this early? She padded softly across the wide-planked wood floors, hoping the sound hadn't woken up the kids. The porch light was still on, and Matt's grandmother was standing on the other side of the door. She was waving and smiling.

Annie quickly opened the door and Lila, along with a gust of wind and a handful of flurries, came through the door. "Lila, what a lovely surprise! I just made some coffee."

Lila gave her a warm smile before patting her arm. "Thank you, dear, but I'm not staying. I wasn't even going to knock on the door, but I saw your kitchen light on and thought I'd quickly say hi and give you a little something."

"My goodness, you didn't have to do that. You've already done so much."

Lila gave her a little wink. "Nonsense. But I do hope you get some rest later today. After that drive, I would probably sleep for a week!"

Annie laughed softly. "Somehow, I doubt that. But I think I was too excited to sleep in. I'm sure exhaustion will set in at some point today."

Lila pulled out what looked to be a leather folder of some sort. "That's understandable with this house and this view. I will come back for a coffee one day. Now, my dear, I wanted to give this to you last night, but it has a kind of reputation in our family. Everyone wants it, and I only hand this out when I think it's going to the right person at the right time. So take this traveler's notebook and sit down with it when you're having coffee or wine and have a few minutes to yourself. It's filled with recipes and a little advice along the way. Not braggy type stuff, more like notes from the trenches."

Annie clutched the book to her chest. "Oh, Lila, I'm touched. Thank you so much for thinking of me. I will take good care of it and, when I'm done, I'll be sure to give it back in perfect condition. I'm not exactly the best cook or homemaker most days, so I'll take whatever advice and recipes I can get. This is so sweet of you, thank you."

Lila squeezed her hand. "I know the road can sometimes feel lonely, but I'm here to remind you that it doesn't have to be. Don't forget about Sunday night dinner tomorrow—I make a killer roast. Now, I'm off to sunrise yoga so I must jet. Text me and we'll do lunch next week when you have a moment. I know a great place, and we can even squeeze in some Christmas shopping!" She winked and opened the door.

"Sounds perfect! Thank you!" Annie called out as Lila bolted down the steps to her car.

She waved as Lila drove away and then locked the door and made her way back to the great room. Topping up her coffee for warmth, she made her way to one of the overstuffed chairs by the fireplace and sat down with a sigh. They had been here less than twenty-four hours and Matt's family was already making her feel like everything would be okay. When was the last time anyone had ever dropped something off for her?

Gingerly opening the worn, leather-bound notebook, she held onto it a moment, taking in the artwork on the first notebook cover. She realized that each of the four books represented a season. She ran her fingers over the first book. The cover was a watercolor illustration of a house with blue siding enveloped in snow. It looked like twilight maybe, with a yellow glow coming from inside. It was warm, evoking a sense of comfort and peace.

She flipped to the next notebook. The cover was a watercolor illustration of a woman on a bicycle with a large straw hat, on a road with the ocean beside her. The woman looked carefree, a smile on her face, wind tousling her long blonde hair. Annie stared at her, wondering how old she was, wondering if she'd ever been like her, or if she could still be that woman.

The next notebook depicted a young woman on the beach, staring straight ahead at the ocean. It was sunny and her beach blanket was red and white striped and there was a novel sitting on top of it. Annie couldn't remember the last time she'd sat on the beach like that. There was something about the brushstrokes, the colors, that was almost nostalgic.

The last notebook; autumn. The same young woman was standing in a pumpkin patch, and this time she wasn't alone. There was a man beside her, holding a pumpkin under one arm and holding her hand with the other. The colors were rich, warm, deep, evocative. She didn't know much about art, but she knew that these images stirred something inside her. Longing. Comfort. Home.

She took a deep breath, keeping her hand on the cover, not wanting to let go in case the feeling left her. When had their family home in Toronto stopped feeling like home?

Or maybe it wasn't that it didn't feel like home, maybe it was the safety of it that had been lost, the comfort. Life hadn't gone the way they'd dreamed.

Home hadn't remained a sanctuary at the end of a long day at work; instead, it had become a museum of days gone by without any hope for better days ahead.

How could these watercolor books induce a feeling of hope and home? They were just recipe books from a woman who'd raised a family, who'd lived her life.

Annie didn't need recipes, she needed hope and faith that they hadn't lived their best days. It was sweet of Matt's grandmother to hand over this book of treasured recipes. It was obvious from the dog-eared pages that it had been cherished. But Annie's problems were much bigger than any casserole recipe could solve. She was scared that if she did open these books, they would only add to the pressure. One more failed attempt at domestic bliss. Some days all she could handle was takeout, and even that was a big deal.

She tucked her feet under her body and wrapped her hands around her mug of coffee and closed her eyes. She was just going to appreciate this moment for what it was—the first day of their new lives. Solving all her problems didn't have to happen this morning over coffee. And if this recipe book was any indication, she wasn't alone anymore. Matt's family had come through, and Matt had come through.

When she had pulled up to the house last night, she'd felt so beaten down, but when he opened the door and everyone came running out of the house, she had been in tears. She wasn't alone. It wasn't just the three of them against the world anymore. It felt right. And when Matt had hugged her . . . something in her came alive again. Something deep inside. She knew that it must be the fact that she rarely hugged anyone other than her kids. Especially not another man. That was probably it. And talking to him outside last night had felt so right. He was so easy to talk to and . . .

Her phone vibrated on the coffee table and dread filled her stomach as Valerie's picture filled the screen. All her peace was interrupted.

She stared at the screen, the warmth of her thoughts draining faster than her emptying coffee. She really should pick up the phone and call her out for her deceit. But if she did, it would start a war. Annie had hoped that, by moving out here, Valerie would just become a distant relative, and she could keep the peace by lack of constant contact, but her sister was making that impossible. And Annie should address what she'd done to Adam. Ugh. No one could confront Valerie.

She took a sip of coffee, half relieved when her phone stopped vibrating. But no sooner did she swallow her sip of coffee than Valerie's face lit up her screen again. She sat up a little straighter and put the traveler's notebook on the side table. She glanced at it—those pictures so far from the life she was living. She had to answer the call. She had to assert herself.

"Hi, Valerie."

"Wow. I was wondering if I was ever going to hear from you again. So, I was at Starbucks this morning with Penelope and you wouldn't believe how many people stopped me because of her. She's like a celebrity! I think you're really making a mistake not even asking Matt about having a mural painted of her. Or you could do a poster."

Annie's heart raced, and she tried to keep her temper in check. Valerie was actually pretending she hadn't done anything. Not only did she not think there was anything wrong with approaching Adam behind her back, she was still pushing the Penelope idea. There was no point in arguing. Valerie would only get offended and would start all sorts of drama. Annie had long ago given up on actually having a two-way conversation with her sister. Or having her sister actually ask and then listen to what was going on in Annie's life or with the kids. Sometimes she would ask, but then when Annie answered, she'd already be talking over her about something else. But this whole thing about Penelope being the veterinarian celebrity mascot or whatever was so absurd she could barely contain herself. She couldn't even tell Matt about it; it was so embarrassing. "Like I said, it's not my vet clinic. I can't just tell them to make Penelope the star of the practice . . . or whatever it is that she would be."

Valerie let out a huff. "Your loss. Penelope's face would bring you *so* much business. People literally fall all over themselves when she's around. You could ask Matt, you know. I'm sure it wouldn't cost much to do a mural on the side of the building. Labor is cheap out there—I'm sure there're lots of artist types who would work for next to nothing."

Annie pinched the bridge of her nose, not even believing this was an actual conversation with an adult, let alone someone she was related to. It was so bad that she almost forgot about the Adam situation. "I'm actually more concerned with what you said to Adam."

Silence.

Her heart pounded and her palms grew sweaty. It was a silly reaction, but it was a holdover from her childhood, she knew. When she was little, if she had dared question Valerie, she'd receive a major physical and verbal thrashing. Valerie had been older and larger and hadn't been afraid to hurt Annie when their father wasn't around. She hated thinking that Valerie could still evoke that kind of fear in her, but it was obvious she did. She took a deep breath and pushed. She was not the same little girl anymore. "Hello? Valerie? You told him that he could take a bus back to Toronto and live with you?"

"Uh, wow, that's the thanks I get? Be a team player, Annie."

Annie wanted to pitch her mug of coffee across the room. She would never, of course, it was too nice a mug, and too gorgeous a house, but still. "What does that even mean? Be a team player? That has nothing to do with what I just said."

"You should learn how to have peaceful relationships with your family."

Annie's mouth hung open as her sister ended the call. Her stomach burned with acid. She should learn how to have peaceful relationships? Be a team player? Had her sister seen that line on the back of a cereal box? Annie wanted to pull her hair out. If her parents were still alive, Valerie would have spun some kind of tale and made herself the victim and created all sorts of problems. Then her mother would have called Annie and questioned her and tried to spin Valerie as misunderstood and concerned about Adam. But their parents weren't here.

Annie couldn't keep doing this.

This wasn't how she wanted to live. She didn't want her kids to be pawns in her sister's game. She didn't want to be distracted from the people who really mattered—her kids. She didn't want to be angry and trying to hide it. She just wanted to live again. She wanted to enjoy this Christmas, this house, this new province . . . Matt . . . and his family.

"Mom?'

Annie started at the sound of Adam's voice; she hadn't heard him walk down the stairs, and now he was sitting opposite her on the other chair. His hair was all disheveled and he looked rumpled. But his eyes were filled with the soul of the boy she'd raised, the spirit she rarely saw anymore. "Good morning, sweetie. I didn't even hear you come down. Did you sleep well?"

He leaned forward, running a hand through his hair. "I'm sorry."

The match that lit her soul was alive again. Valerie and her games didn't stand a chance against the love between her and her kids, she had to remember that. It wasn't too late. She would do whatever it took.

She looked deep into his eyes, grateful that no matter how mad at her he was, her boy knew right from wrong and that he could actually humble himself enough to apologize when needed. "For what, honey?"

"For agreeing to that crap with Aunt Val. I feel like a traitor. I should have shut her down right away. I was just pissed that we were coming here and . . . I don't know."

She swallowed past the lump in her throat. "You are not a traitor, and I would never think that. But I get it. Thank you. That means so much to me. I just want you to know that, as an adult, Valerie shouldn't have done that. It was inappropriate. It was an awful situation to put you in. But today is day one here, and I think it's going to be a good one. Look over there," she said, pointing to the patio door in the kitchen. "The sun is rising. Have you ever seen anything so gorgeous?"

They sat in silence for a few seconds. "That's so cool," he said, his gaze fixed on the glowing sun, which seemed to rise straight out of the red sand cliffs on the beach.

"How do you like your new room?"

He turned back to her, smiling a bit. "It's amazing, to be honest. Like, I never expected that. The bathroom is cool too."

She was barely able to contain her own smile. This was better than she'd hoped. "Good. I think so too. This entire house is gorgeous. So, I was thinking that today we could just get settled in and unload the car and unpack and stuff. Matt offered a few times last night, but I told him we'd take care of it today."

He nodded. "Sounds good. He asked me too but I promised I'd help."

"Perfect. Oh, I spotted cinnamon rolls in the fridge, so when Maddy wakes up, I'll pop them in the oven to warm up."

"Sure. I haven't even looked inside the fridge yet."

"Well, get acquainted. The fridge was your favorite place in our last house," she said, barely holding back her smile.

He stood, shooting her a grin, "Ha ha."

She wished every morning could be like this—minus the call from her sister. But she considered it a good start. This little step with Adam also reminded her, though, of where her concentration needed to be. She needed to be fully present in her life, for her kids. Not caught up in whatever schemes her sister had going on. Those were distractions. Those were the things she'd regret when her kids were all grown up and she looked back on her life.

She had forty-three days left to convince Adam that they could have a fresh start here, that they could build a life here. Forty-three days until Christmas.

*   *   *

Matt pulled up in front of Annie's house and again contemplated calling instead of just showing up this early in the morning. But in case she was still sleeping and left her ringer on, he'd hate to wake her. He'd just knock softly on the door and, if she answered, great, and if she didn't, at least he wouldn't have woken her.

She and the kids had looked wiped last night, so he wouldn't be surprised if they were all still sleeping. But this was for a good cause. A mutually beneficial cause, really. He wasn't taking this six-weeks-to-Christmas deal lightly. Last night, after their conversation on the porch, he knew he was going to have to go out of his way to make their time here special. He was going to have to win over the kids.

He glanced over at his passenger. At least this was for a good cause. "You wait here," Matt said, before hopping out of the truck and jogging up to the back door.

He tapped lightly and waited. Flurries swirled around, and the wind coming off the ocean was crisp and fresh. A few moments later, Annie appeared, wearing red and green flannel pajamas, her hair in a heap around her shoulders, but a gorgeous smile on her face when she saw him.

She swung open the door. "Does your entire family do drop-ins on the weekend before eight in the morning?"

He ran a hand over his jaw. "Let me guess, my grandmother came before sunrise yoga?"

She laughed. "Yup. And I'm just teasing. I've got a pot of coffee and cinnamon rolls coming out of the oven."

His stomach growled. "That sounds perfect, but, uh, come outside for a sec," he said, lowering his voice.

She frowned but nodded and shut the door behind her. She shivered visibly and crossed her arms over her chest. "There has to be a good reason you're making me come out here when it's this cold."

"I have a twenty-pound reason."

She frowned, hopping from one foot to the other. "Now you're scaring me. I'm not good at cooking turkeys, Matt, and I have barely cracked open your grandmother's cookbook."

"You got the cookbook?"

"It was delivered this morning."

He let out a low whistle. "My grandmother adores you. Just don't tell anyone at dinner tomorrow night—my sister hasn't been given the cookbook and my mother only gets it for one-hour loans."

She burst out laughing and he found himself smiling at the sound, at the way her eyes sparkled. He hadn't seen her laugh like this for as long as he could remember. He also recalled the sound of her laugh having the same effect on him back then. "You're kidding."

He made an "X" over his heart. "Nope. But that's not why I'm here. Back to the twenty-pound, *live* reason I'm here: how do you feel about taking in a cat?"

Her eyes widened. "Like, fostering?"

"More like permanent. His owner is elderly and is in the hospital. She won't be going back home. Her daughter called me in a panic, not knowing what to do with the cat. He's been a patient at the clinic from birth. He's now three and he was really pampered and treated like royalty. He's one of the nicest cats I've ever had as a patient."

She chewed her lower lip, and he could tell she was wavering. "I did want to get another pet after our dog died, but it's been so hard to find the time. Maddy would love a cat . . . Adam, I'm not so sure. But then again, he doesn't like much right now."

He chuckled. "This cat would win over even the toughest cynic. I know you just got here and have to unpack and get settled, but I'll help you out. And . . . he's a Maine coon."

She slapped a hand over her mouth. "Really?"

He nodded. "Pure bred. He's a real ham, actually, puts on a show for new people, guests. He will not stop performing until he wins people over. Orange haired, some tiger stripes, white belly and paws. Handsome. He's very stubborn in his determination to impress people. Possibly more stubborn than Adam."

She cupped her hands and blew into them. "He does sound lovely and you know that's my favorite breed . . . It's so cold out here . . . okay. Maybe this is what we need. When would we get him?"

He cleared his throat. "Uh, how about now? Jingle is sitting in my truck."

"Jingle?"

He nodded, barely keeping a straight face. "Jingle. Your new cat."

* * *

An hour later, they were sitting in the great room. Maddy was Jingle's number one fan.

"Jingle is the cutest cat in the world," Maddy said, eating a cinnamon roll and watching as Jingle familiarized himself with his new home. True to form, he had sniffed around the house for about half an hour and then started his performance. He brushed up against everyone until they petted him, he rolled around on the ground, jumped on the counter and table, and had Maddy laughing hysterically. Maddy and Annie gave him a great reaction, but Adam was more aloof.

Luckily, Jingle wasn't offended or easily deterred. He sprawled himself out on the coffee table in front of where Adam was sitting.

"He's very handsome," Annie said, stroking the cat's head.

"I love how orange he is and his white belly. And I love his whiskers. Oh, and the way that fur goes past the tips of his ears," Maddy said.

"That's a signature feature of the Maine coon," Matt said.

"He has a loud purr," Adam said.

Matt nodded. "Yeah, he's a male and he's pretty big. Seems to be happy right now, too."

"He does seem to be adjusting well. Thanks for bringing over all his supplies and stuff too, Matt. You didn't have to do all that," Annie said.

He took a sip of coffee. "Of course I did. I knew it would be an easier sell."

Annie smiled at him from the other couch. "Can't argue with that logic."

"So listen, guys, I know you're spending the day unpacking and stuff but I thought I'd mention that the Charlottetown Festival is happening a few weeks from now, and I was hoping you're all free."

Adam looked wary, but Maddy's face lit up like a Christmas tree. "What do they do there?"

"They have the Victorian Christmas Market. There are carolers, horse and wagon rides, live music, hot cocoa, firepits, live ice sculpting, local vendors, artisans, crafters, food vendors. It's amazing. We can spend the day. You'll get your Christmas shopping done, eat great food, and you'll see the capital of Prince Edward Island."

"That sounds amazing. Count us in," Annie said.

"I can't wait! I don't remember what Charlottetown looks like. And I can't wait for a wagon ride," Maddy said, doing a little dance.

Adam was silent. Matt knew it probably didn't sound that appealing to a teenage boy, but he also knew that there would be enough for him to enjoy himself and familiarize himself with Charlottetown. He needed to start thinking of it as home. Besides, Matt knew all the places Adam would like—especially the food. He'd take over Adam duty for the day. "So, anyone excited for school on Monday?"

Annie shot him a look before raising her mug of coffee and taking a sip. Clearly, it had been a while since he'd hung around kids. "All right, don't answer all at once," he teased.

"I'm kind of excited," Maddy said, giving him a sympathetic smile.

"There you go, I bet you'll make friends in no time. And I'm not sure if you know this, but you're going to the same elementary school I did. And Adam, you're going to my old high school," he said, trying to draw him into the conversation.

Adam picked up another cinnamon bun. "Cool."

Matt glanced over at Annie, who was watching Adam inhale the cinnamon bun. Her gaze was pensive, her blue eyes glistening slightly. He wanted all this to change for them. He wanted Adam to come around for his own sake, but also for Annie's. He wanted them all to heal.

He sat with them and ate cinnamon rolls and drank way too much coffee. He knew it was early days, but this house had to become their home. The island had to capture their hearts.

These were his people. This was Cam's family, and he had to make things right for them. For Annie.

He didn't have much time. Six weeks until Christmas. Six weeks to convince a teenager that this was home. Six weeks to convince Annie that she had made the right decision by moving here. Six weeks for this family to get a new start, one that was filled with hope. Good thing he had never been a quitter.

CHAPTER SIX

Monday morning, Annie stood in the lunch room at the veterinary clinic, squeezing the handle on her mug of coffee and trying to look as though she was excited and happy and confident. It was barely nine and Matt had most of the staff in here for quick introductions. The other two veterinarians were friendly and gave off very welcoming vibes, as did the two assistants.

The person Annie was currently having a problem with was the receptionist and office manager, Jessica. Actually, it was more like Jessica was having problems with Annie. Jessica was standing next to Matt and made a point of touching his arm whenever she spoke. It was a casual gesture of familiarity. But there was this other vibe about her that Annie detected. The one good thing that had come from having Valerie as a sister was being able to detect undercurrents in other people. Jessica was tall and slender, with gorgeous skin and perfectly applied makeup—almost like she had a real-life Instagram filter. She was almost Matt's height and she was constantly touching him. They had to be more than just friends.

Was he seeing her and he hadn't mentioned it to Annie? But he would have said something. Then there was the fact that he never made any gestures toward her. In fact, he looked stiff. Interesting. Matt never reciprocated Jessica's attentions, and every time she touched him, his jaw clenched.

If she were being completely objective, the two of them did make a good-looking couple. They were both tall and fit. The hard lines of Matt's athletic build were highlighted in the navy Henley and worn-in jeans. Jessica's blonde hair was a stunning contrast to his almost black hair. And Matt was undeniably handsome. Even though he was Annie's best friend, she couldn't deny the obvious. His green eyes were striking and his face was lean, with a strong jaw highlighted with dark stubble. His dark hair had a couple of strands of gray that hadn't been there last time she saw him, but only seemed to add to his appeal. Not that she found him appealing. Not in that way or anything.

"So, this will be a big adjustment from city life. Have you worked with a lot of large animals? There are *so* many farm calls out here," Jessica asked, a twinge of smugness in her voice.

Annie took a sip of coffee before answering. It was *way* too early in the morning for this. She'd already had to deal with two kids and first-day jitters. Or in the case of Adam—first day gloom and doom. But drop-off had been completed. At least they were both at school. If was a first day for all of them, and Annie was already looking forward to hearing about their school day that night at dinner. She was not looking for office drama or small-town politics. In Toronto, their clinic had been so busy, there wasn't time for drama. Everyone got along for the most part. No one had been really close, but she had preferred that in some ways. She had a hard time opening up to new people, and there wasn't really time for it these days. Just looking and listening to Jessica reminded her of why she didn't get close to people. Then again, if Matt was involved with her, she was going to have to make an effort.

Annie forced a smile. "I think it'll be a nice change, and I'm looking forward to learning whatever I need to."

"Annie was always at the top of our class. I have no doubt she'll be a quick learner," Matt said with an encouraging smile.

"I hope you're right," she said with a smile.

"How's Jingle settling in?" he asked.

She opened her mouth to answer, but Jessica interjected. "Jingle? As in Mrs. Ferris's Jingle?"

He nodded. "Yeah, Annie's adopted him."

"If I'd known he was in need of a home, I would have taken him in," Jessica said, crossing her arms.

Matt shrugged and glanced at his watch. "I thought he'd be a perfect fit at Annie's. He loves company and kids."

"He's getting tons of attention and slept on Maddy's bed last night, much to her delight," Annie said.

He gave her a grin. "Glad to hear it. Anyway, I've got to run, I'm late for a few farm calls. Annie, I'll check in with you later. Jay and Liz are here for the full day if you need anything."

She nodded. "Thanks. I'm sure I'll be fine. I'll be joining them on their appointments and getting used to everything. You, um, have a good day."

He nodded, glancing from her to Jessica. "See you both later."

She was about to head over to Jay and Liz because even her hot coffee wasn't warm enough to deal with the frostiness from Jessica. Right before she turned around, Jessica cleared her throat and stood in front of her.

"So, Matt said you have kids?"

Annie nodded, forcing a smile. She should have made her move, now it was too late. "Yup. Two kids. One's in grade nine and the other in grade six."

Jessica raised her eyebrows. "Wow, you don't look that old. What's your secret?"

Annie almost choked on her coffee. Was that a compliment or an insult? She stared at Jessica for a long moment before answering, trying to figure her out. "We had our kids pretty young."

Jessica raised an eyebrow. "Hm. That's nice. I guess at least you got it all over with and now you're done with kids."

Annie blinked a few times, trying to focus. Was she a magnet for people like this? Sometimes it felt like she was. Being spoken to like this by her sister was one thing; she didn't need to take this from a stranger. It was time she started asserting herself. And there was no way she was going to discuss family planning with a woman she'd met ten minutes ago, who clearly had a whole other agenda. "Better get to work. Lots to do on the first day."

Jessica pursed her lips. "Right. I guess making a good impression on Matt is important to you. I don't think you'll find it very busy compared to Toronto. We're pretty laid back here."

Annie squeezed the handle on her mug. "That sounds perfect. I'd better get to work."

Four hours later, Annie felt like she had a handle on the office and procedures. They ran very similarly to her clinic in Toronto. At least something was going smoothly—that and the fact that she hadn't received a call from the high school, so at least that meant Adam was making it through his first day as well.

The two other vets she was working with, Jay and Liz, were so friendly and open to answering all her questions. The day was flying by, and Annie had one hour left before she had to pick up

Maddy. At least she didn't have to worry about Adam getting home and staying by himself if she was running late. But she didn't feel comfortable with Maddy getting off the bus and walking half an hour through a cornfield by herself to get home. The cornfield—a question she needed to remember to ask Matt about later. Something she'd never ask in front of Jessica.

Jessica poked her head into the exam room. The space was empty, but Annie was just finishing updating a chart. "Annie, there's a family out here who needs to put their cat down. They've been with us for years. We knew it was a matter of time. Here's Casper's chart."

Annie's stomach turned. This was one of the worst parts of her job. "Um, okay, I'm going to talk with Jay or Liz and then I'll meet them in here."

Jessica gave her a nod before walking out.

Annie left down the back hall to the other exam room to find Liz. After speaking with her for a few minutes, Annie felt confident enough to handle the appointment. She walked down the hall that led to the waiting room, already bracing herself to face the family's heartache. This was never easy. She drew a deep breath and, just as the waiting area was about to come into view, she heard Jessica speaking. "She's a new veterinarian. It's really sad. Her husband died, leaving her widowed with two kids and no job. Matt has such a big heart that he hired her even though we had no need for any more veterinarians."

Annie quickly slipped into the empty supply closet, her hand over her mouth, her heart racing. She was too stunned and blindsided to know what to feel. Her heart raced and her stomach turned. There was so much there. First of all, who was Jessica to be recounting Annie's life story and then . . . the worst, though, was the part about the job. A pity job.

Before she could even get herself together, Jessica poked her head in. "Um, this really can't wait. These people are really suffering. Can you get to exam room three, please?"

Annie snatched the chart from Jessica's hand, seething at the patronizing, impatient tone with which she spoke. This was not how her first day was supposed to go. If she didn't know better, she'd think her sister had hired Jessica.

She had no interest in engaging in some kind of petty office drama or whatever this was. She also had no time. She had to help this family say goodbye to their beloved family pet and then race out to pick up her daughter and then deal with her son and his perpetually bad and resentful mood. Oh, and then think about dinner. All the while trying not to be mortified or panicked that Jessica was right about Matt only hiring her out of pity. He wouldn't do that, would he?

She wanted to cry. That wasn't an option, obviously. So she slapped on the smile that felt like a worn T-shirt at this point, it had been used so often, and walked out of the supply closet.

* * *

Three hours later, Annie lifted the covers and tucked them under Maddy's chin. Not that it was bedtime. No, that would have been too easy. Maddy was in bed at seven o'clock at night because she'd just thrown up. Repeatedly. It appeared she had a stomach bug. She smoothed the hair back from her daughter's face and forced some kind of optimism into her voice. "You rest, sweetie. I'm sure you'll wake up tomorrow and feel so much better. I bet it's a twenty-four-hour thing. At least Jingle is here with you."

Maddy gave a faint smile and put her hand on Jingle's back as the cat purred and rested on the bed beside Maddy. Jingle had won Maddy's heart, and Annie was extra grateful for their new family member.

"I'll be right downstairs if you need anything, okay?"

Maddy nodded. "Thanks, Mom."

Annie smiled, this time for real. "I'm always here for you. And hey, at least your first day of school went well. And now you know everyone and what the school is like. At least you don't have to be nervous about that again."

Maddy nodded slowly, her eyelids closing.

Annie's heart squeezed. She pulled the white curtains shut and left the light on in the en suite bathroom in case Maddy woke up again. Walking across the room quietly, she picked up the clothes strewn about the floor and dropped them in the hamper before closing the door behind her. What were the odds Maddy would pick up a stomach bug on her first day of school?

It was a day that made her wish she could just stay in this house and never leave. When she entered the kitchen, Adam was sitting at the island looking slightly less sullen than that morning. But as soon as he saw her, his expression went to extra-sullen. She wondered if he was trying to make her feel bad on purpose. "Well, looks like Jingle is going to be keeping Maddy company. How was your day?"

He shrugged. "Could be worse. But it was bad. At least I'm not puking."

She started a pot of coffee because she had laundry to do and she wanted something warm and comforting. Luckily, it never kept her up at night. "Very true. Meet any new friends?"

He nodded. "Yeah. Sort of."

She leaned against the counter, trying to look casual, desperate to keep the conversation flowing even though she was exhausted. The more he talked, the better insight she'd have. It was also hopeful that he acknowledged that Maddy had it worse than he did and very hopeful that it sounded like he'd made some friends. She'd cling to even the smallest victories with him. "How are your classes?"

"Boring."

"How are your teachers?"

"Weird."

Ugh. Why did she even bother? She stared at his face, already knowing her answer: because she loved her kids more than anything in the world. Even like this. If there was anything to be learned, any lesson from Cam's death, it was that life was fragile. She had no control over it. There would never be enough time together. A hundred years would feel too short with the people she loved. And so she'd take her kids in any form. She knew Adam hated change, he hated that they were here. He had been struggling, and she was going to be here for him. She was going to believe that the little boy with the heart of gold, with the smile that could melt her heart, was still somewhere inside this young man's body.

She wouldn't give up until she saw his heart again. "I hated meeting new people too. I was so shy that it took me a full year once to make a friend at a new school. At least you and your sister are outgoing."

"I guess. Do we have any Goldfish?"

She wasn't surprised by the abrupt change in topic because it was a tactic when he wanted to put up walls between them. That was fine. She was patient. "I put them on my grocery list. I was supposed to go after work, but I didn't get out on time."

Adam groaned theatrically and put his head down on the counter. "Can't you just order groceries?"

"Don't I wish . . . there's no grocery delivery out here."

He lifted his head with a start, his eyes wide. "Is this 1995?"

She burst out laughing and poured her coffee into her favorite Christmas mug and added a splash of milk. "It'll be okay. I just need to get a routine going. Today did not go as planned. Hence the pizza."

He looked down at his phone but didn't pick it up. "How was it?"

She shrugged, not knowing how much to reveal. But she did take it as a good sign that he was talking more and asking about her day. "Meh. It was really great in some ways and really bad in others. I ended up with a last-minute patient and didn't get out until later than expected. Then I had to race to pick up Maddy. Luckily there were other kids still in the playground, but it was stressful. But . . . there is no traffic on this island compared to Toronto."

"'Cause like, five people live on it."

She smiled before taking a sip of her coffee. "Yeah, it kind of feels like it."

"Did you get to work with Uncle Matt?"

She shook her head. "No, he was busy with farm calls all day and hadn't come back by the time I had to leave to pick up Maddy."

He nodded and stood. "I guess I'd better get started on my homework. I hope I don't catch whatever Maddy has."

"Ugh, you and me both," she said with a short laugh.

He picked up his backpack and headed up the stairs while she grabbed the empty pizza boxes and put them in the recycling bin. She had missed the sunset on the ocean, and dusk had almost given way to night. What a day. She turned on the gas fireplace, weariness hitting her all at once. How was she going to pull this off? The animosity from Jessica, the fact that she was a pity hire, a sick kid . . . at least Adam had been neutral enough tonight.

She set her coffee down on the end table and sat on the couch with an audible sigh. Her gaze stopped on the traveler's notebook and guilt shot through her. She needed to look at this. Last night at Sunday dinner, Matt's grandmother had asked about the cookbook and Annie had to confess she hadn't had a chance to get into it beyond looking at the gorgeous covers. Maybe now was the time, especially in case Maddy woke up again and needed her.

One of the tabs caught her eye: *Systems.* That was interesting. She thought this was a cookbook. She reached forward and picked it up. Tucking her legs underneath her body, she grabbed one of the sherpa-backed, plaid throws and settled in. Her gaze scanned the tabs of the journal:

Sick kids.
A Comforting Home.
Bread to save your family.
Sunday Brunch with Heart.
Food to save your sanity.

What was all this? Since she was most in need of systems at the moment—something she'd never been good at—she flipped to that tab first. Matt's grandmother's handwriting was perfect, and the ink was red and still vibrant. This clearly wasn't just a recipe book . . . these notes were personal.

Notes to Self:
Claire is a very picky eater and John will eat up my entire paycheck.

Never put off for tomorrow what you can do today.

Do laundry in some form every day. Day one—wash clothes. Day two—fold and put away.

Clean your kitchen every night, Lila. No excuse. Then you won't hate your family in the morning.

Sundays are for church and resetting. Do some meal preparation. Tidy the house. Make sure you are ready for the school and work week. Get school lunches prepared the night before. Sundays are for family and faith—it's sacred.

Fridays are for groceries. Make your meal plan in the morning and make your grocery list at the same time. Get them done after work so that you've just freed up a Saturday chore and you can have a relaxing cup of coffee in the morning. Kids will be happy the fridge is stocked when they wake up.

One night should be slow-cooker meal. One night should be a homemade frozen meal. One night should be from a restaurant. One night should be leftovers. Now you're only cooking three nights and everyone thinks you're a star.

You need to bake. See baking section. Don't worry, you can do this.

Annie looked up from the pages, the book still on her lap. This was the best advice she'd ever had in her life. While she didn't consider herself to be disorganized, juggling family and work had always been challenging. Her mother had never had systems or regimented days of the week for things, but she hadn't worked outside the home. Her mother had taken pride in her home, in her cooking, but it had come naturally to her. Annie had never been able to find balance between work and home. She knew her home skills were lacking but she never thought she'd be able to achieve the idyllic comforts of home between work and single parenting. But Lila broke it down so simply. It was almost doable.

These pointers, while intimidating, also seemed to offer a sense of freedom. Like, if she took these steps, life might actually fall into place. All she'd been missing were systems.

The knock on the door startled her. She felt as though she'd just been pulled from the most engrossing thriller. Gingerly setting down the journal, she made her way to the mudroom, assuming it was probably Matt. Sure enough, he was standing on the porch.

An unexpected wave of anticipation swept over her as she opened the door. It was unsettling. If she was completely honest with herself, she'd felt it the moment he'd hugged her on their first night here. She had blown it off, thinking it was just comforting to be held by anyone again. Really, she'd had no physical contact with anyone other than her kids. She was probably reading too much into this. Matt was . . . family. She'd known Matt forever, they had talked on the phone and texted at least a dozen times a month in the last few years. But every time she saw him, she felt it.

He stepped inside the house and seemed to swallow up the small mudroom space. She pushed those thoughts aside, desperate to attribute them to exhaustion and vulnerability. What she was probably feeling was relief that she had someone on her side. She wasn't alone anymore, not with Matt and his family.

In the last four years without Cam, she'd learned how to deal with the world all on her own. It had taken so much out of her—there were some weeks where every single day was a fight. A fight to make her kids happy, to make her patients happy, her coworkers happy, her sister happy, and finally, at the end of it maybe do something for herself.

But in the last year she hadn't done anything for herself—oh, except the Le Creuset pot. She'd done that for herself. But she hadn't even gotten a haircut because taking an hour out of her day had felt too stressful when there was so much else to do. So she'd been tying it back in a ponytail or putting it up in a clip. She was a veterinarian and pulling her hair off her face was normal. But last week she could have sworn she saw a gray hair somewhere in that rat's nest she sported in the morning before showering. She quickly shoved her hands in her pockets now because she had suddenly realized her nails were also a disaster. When had she stopped caring? These were basic grooming skills. It's not like she had done all those things like haircuts and nails to impress Cam . . . but she'd also stopped impressing herself.

The image of Jessica popped into her mind, much to her horror, because she didn't need to be comparing herself to her. Jessica was a single woman who had much more time. It wasn't a fair comparison. But Jessica *did* have great hair. And makeup. And nails.

Maybe she was noticing now because Matt was . . . well, Matt was a very attractive man. She'd always known that, and when she first met Cam and Matt, she'd found them both equally good-looking and appealing in their own ways. And very early on, before she and Cam started dating, there had a been a moment, minutes, where she thought she was falling for Matt. It seemed silly to even think of that now, over a decade later. She was pretty sure he'd never thought of it again.

But none of that explained why things suddenly felt different. Maybe she just wasn't used to being alone with men who weren't coworkers. Or having men in her house. That was it: lack of a life. That was a far more reassuring explanation than whatever was going on in her head.

"Hi, come on in."

"Hey. Sorry for not calling. Just thought I'd drop by to check in on you guys," he said.

"Oh, we're good; except for the fact that Maddy is in bed with a stomach bug."

He winced. "Poor kid. Those are the worst."

Annie nodded. "Tell me about it. But Jingle is being a loyal companion and hasn't left her side."

"Glad to hear it, though I'm not surprised." He ran a hand through his already disheveled hair and smiled at her.

Feeling a wave of jitters float through her, she flashed him a quick smile and led the way back to the great room. "Can I get you a drink? Something to warm up? I have the fireplace on."

"I'll have a coffee if you're having one," he said, standing in the middle of the room. She tried not to pay attention to how handsome he was again Anyone with eyes knew that. But suddenly things felt different. What was wrong with her? His navy and hunter green plaid flannel shirt seemed to highlight his broad shoulders and fit upper body. His jeans were worn and fit him like he was some kind of model. Stubble only accentuated the hard lines of his face, and his green eyes were filled with worry. For her? Maybe it was the eyes. Kind eyes. Maybe this was just as awkward for him. Like, maybe he was wishing his best friend was here.

"I have one already. I have a serious question for you, though," she said, pouring him a mug of coffee.

He gave her a quick nod, a flicker of worry passing through his eyes as she handed him a mug. "Sure. Ask anything."

"How the heck am I supposed to drive through that cornfield this summer when the stalks are like twelve feet high without dying of fear that one of those creepy kids from that *Children of the Corn* movie is going to come out and snatch me?"

His eyes widened for a moment and then he threw his head back and laughed. She smiled at the sound of his deep, rich laugh. But she was only half joking and anxiously awaited his laughter to die down. Which wasn't any time soon. When he finally swiped his hands over his eyes, she started tapping her foot. It was a valid question.

"That was the best thing I've heard all day."

She crossed her arms and looked up at him. "It wasn't supposed to be funny."

He closed his eyes for a moment and gave a slow nod, like he was trying to compose himself. Clearing his throat, he made eye contact with her. But his lips twitched, like he was barely containing his laughter. "Okay. Legit question. Just put your high beams on and follow the tire tracks."

She frowned. "That's not helpful."

His eyes sparkled. Watered even. "Right. Because the children of the corn."

She raised an eyebrow and tried not to smile. "Exactly."

He grinned. "Then I suggest locking your doors."

She rolled her eyes. "Great. I'll be sure to do that. Hey, have you eaten? Can I get you some food?"

He sat on one of the couches and placed his mug of coffee on the side table. "No thanks, I already ate."

She sat opposite him. "Well, I'm glad you stopped by."

"I just wanted to know how day one was. For you, the kids? I'm sorry I didn't make it back to the clinic before you left. I heard you had a tough final patient."

She waved a hand. "You know how it is; never easy to put down an animal. But the family took it as best as they could. It's tough, so close to the holidays. Part of the job, though. As for the kids, it seems like Adam actually had an okay day. The rundown was: boring classes, okay kids, weird teachers."

He choked on his coffee. "That's pretty good."

She wrapped her hands around the mug of coffee and settled into the plush couch. It felt good to talk to him about the day instead of sitting here rehashing everything by herself. "Agreed."

"Hopefully he'll meet some kids who are a good influence on him and he'll feel welcome really soon."

She nodded. "That would be amazing. But of course, Maddy is sick. I feel so bad. Her first day too."

He frowned. "Maybe it was something she ate?"

She shrugged. "I'm hoping it's a twenty-four-hour bug."

He leaned forward, resting his forearms on his legs. "You should stay home tomorrow."

"I'd hate to do that, Matt. I mean, I just started. I'm supposed to work Tuesday and Wednesday."

He took a sip of coffee. "And it's not a big deal. If she's better by the end of the week, then trade your days. No one would care, if that's what you're worried about."

She thought of Jessica and shifted on the couch, pulling a pillow closer. How much did she want to tell him? She didn't want him questioning Jessica and making things worse for her. And then if she told him about what she'd heard about the pity hire, it might make things even more awkward. But she had to know the truth. She drew a deep breath and looked him in the eyes. "Okay, but you have to promise that what I'm about to tell you stays in these four walls."

"Who would I tell?"

"An entire office? Your family? I'm the one who can say that since I have, like, no friends here. You could tell the whole island."

His lips twitched. "Fine. I promise. Tell me."

She clasped her hands together, suddenly nervous. She didn't want to offend him if he was interested in Jessica, and she didn't want to look like she was asking for help. "Okay, but it's just little things. Nothing horrible. Nothing I can't solve on my own."

"All right, Annie, out with it."

"Jessica."

He grimaced. "I should have known. I should have prepared you. I mean, it's complicated. It shouldn't be, but it is. I'm sorry."

Her stomach dropped, but she reminded herself that this wasn't really her business. She shouldn't have emotions about whatever he was going to reveal. This was just for work relations. "Oh no. Prepared me for what? Are you guys together? Is she an ex? And why are you apologizing?"

"No. Not really an ex. And I'm apologizing because I have a feeling she made it awkward."

"What does that mean? No, not really?""

"A long time ago . . . we dated. Once or twice."

"Oh . . . *no*."

He nodded grimly. "Yeah. It was definitely an *oh no*. But that was it. I thought it was ancient history for the most part, but when she started working for me last year . . . let's just say she became very invested in what I was doing on the weekends and who with."

Annie tucked some hair behind her ear. What exactly was he doing on weekends and who with? She wasn't about to ask that. As close as they were, they didn't discuss their romantic lives. Well, she didn't have one, and he did, but they didn't discuss it. Which was probably for the best. "You went out once or twice, like when she was working for you?"

He shook his head. "Nope. But I'd run into her a lot and she mentioned she was out of a job; we were looking for someone, and so I felt bad and hired her. I had no idea she was going to be this interested still. I mean, we went out and . . ."

Her stomach felt strange. She didn't want to think of him in any sort of "brief" situation with Jessica. She could analyze why later. "This feels like something I don't really want to know about. Like, maybe this is something Cam would have been interested in hearing . . . me? Not so much."

He let out a short laugh and looked down for a moment. "Fine. We knew each other through friends. It was a very casual, very noncommittal type of thing. It was mutually understood that it . . . would go nowhere permanent. I had no idea she'd one day be working for me. And before we even went out, I have sort of like a verbal contract women must commit too."

Annie choked on her coffee and it took a few seconds for her to gather her thoughts and composure. This was venturing into very new conversational territory for them. "A verbal contract?"

He was staring at her as though he had no idea why she was having trouble grasping what she was saying. "Yes, very simple so all parties know what they're getting into."

She couldn't look away from him. A part of her was dying to know the terms of this contract, and the other part of her was a little nervous that she had no idea he had this side to him. "Which is what exactly?"

He placed his feet on the coffee table, linking one ankle over the other. "Basics. No feelings. No wishing for feelings. No phone calls longer than ten minutes. That kind of thing."

She placed a hand over heart, only half joking. "You have shattered all my illusions about you."

A look flashed across his green eyes, something she wasn't used to from him. She didn't know what it was, she didn't want to know what it was. "I hope I haven't misled you then."

Her heart pounded against her chest, and it was like the room shrank around the two of them, pressing closer. What was happening? His tone. His demeanor. He wasn't friendly, jokey, Matt. Now he was . . . his voice had gone down a notch, seeming to scrape against her insides in a way she'd never expected. His eyes were glittering. *Oh, Annie. You're in way over your head.* She needed to bring this right back to where they were before. Back to where they were before she arrived on the island. When he was just Matt, her best friend. She was probably just imagining things. When was the last time she'd sat down with a man and had any kind of face-to-face, personal conversation? It was with Matt, four years ago. Clearly, she was out of practice. She did not want to embarrass herself.

She took a sip of coffee, grimacing because it was now cold. "Of course not. I'm just teasing."

He tilted his head. "Seriously. I'm doing the right thing. It's a good policy, and it's always worked for me. No broken hearts."

She lifted a brow. "So, these women all just have their hearts broken and want to profess their undying love for you and hope that you'll carry them off into the sunset?"

He gave her a deadpan stare. "I had no idea you were this sarcastic and cynical either. It's a mutually beneficial agreement."

She raised a brow. "I see."

"You clearly don't. It's to protect myself too, Annie. I've fallen . . . once. But back to Jessica, because I think that's how this interrogation started, right?"

Her head was spinning, trying to process this. There *had* been someone. And it had ended badly and she'd had no idea.

Was this before or after Cam? Ugh. She couldn't ask him and he clearly didn't want to talk about it anyway. "Right. Jessica. I get the sense she might not be thrilled with me."

He frowned. "I can talk to her. I mean, she's been out with dozens of guys since we were together, so I don't know why she'd be threatened by you."

She didn't know whether to be offended or flattered by the idea that Jessica would be threatened by her. But there was an even more pressing issue that she was almost too embarrassed to bring up in case it was actually true. "I can deal with her. I'm sure it'll be fine and we can smooth things over . . . because this entire thing is ridiculous and juvenile. You and I are friends, so she has nothing to be worried about."

"Yeah, but if we weren't just friends, that still isn't her business. I have done nothing to lead her on. I never ask her about her personal life."

She stared into her coffee cup, trying not to be affected by that. He was just making a casual statement, and he was right. She put her mug down, needed to get to the real point of this conversation. "Fine. But also, I overheard her telling patients that you only hired me because you felt sorry for me. Like, you're not actually short on vets?"

When he opened his mouth and then shut it, taking a drink of coffee first, she had her answer. "That's ridiculous. Jessica has no idea what the office does or doesn't need."

Annie let out a breath and blinked past the unexpected moisture in her eyes. She didn't know if it was humiliation or emotion. "Matt, *please* tell me you didn't hire me out of pity."

His jaw clenched, and he looked her squarely in the eyes. "I didn't hire you out of pity. But there might be some truth in that we didn't actively need another vet—but it is welcome because we do work long hours. But make no mistake, there is no pity. There is no vet on the planet I'd want to hire before you. You are talented and dedicated. We are fortunate you chose to join us."

She covered her face and groaned. "I can't believe I just drove for days to an island for a pretend job offer."

"Hey," he said, walking over to sit on the ottoman in front of her. He pried her hands off her face and held them. She suddenly felt flushed, like she couldn't quite catch her breath and she didn't know what to do with her hands. Should she leave them in his? He was holding onto them, so it would probably be weird if she just pulled back. But then again, it felt . . . strange to have his large hands wrapped around hers. Strange, but a good strange. A comforting strange. Maybe thrilling strange too, which would explain her runaway heartbeat. But that was also a ridiculous reaction. He was holding her hands like good friends did. They had been through so much. He would hold his sister's hand if she needed comfort. That's what this was.

It was too bad that he smelled so good. Like citrus and pine. And up close, she realized she'd forgotten there were lighter flecks of green in his eyes. "It wasn't a pretend job offer. It wasn't pity. It was me helping out my best friend's wife. You guys were struggling. Adam was struggling. How many conversations did we have about this move? And don't tell me that if I needed a job, you wouldn't have found me one in Toronto?"

She held his gaze, reading sincerity in those green depths. Reading . . . so much that she broke his gaze. "Okay. I can't argue with that, because if you had ever told me you wanted to move to the city, I would have called all my connections and contacts and had you set up with a clinic. But still. I'm so embarrassed. I don't want to be a charity case. Now it feels weird because I'm getting paid for something that you don't actually need."

He squeezed her hands briefly. "Trust me, I need you. The clinic needs you."

She looked away because she was finding it difficult to breathe with him this close. What was going on with her? "Okay, but if you ever decide that it's too much, I can get a job somewhere else."

He rolled his eyes before letting go of her hands. She felt the emptiness immediately. Like shutting off a faucet of warm water on a cold day. "Sure. Okay, so what else happened?"

As if on cue, her phone vibrated on the couch beside her. Valerie's face illuminated the screen and Matt's eyes widened. "I forgot to ask about Valerie. Do you need to get that?"

"I can't. She will rob me of the little energy I have left."

He let out a laugh. "Okay. So, listen, is there anything you need me to pick up for Maddy? For her stomach or anything?"

She shook her head. "I came prepared. And besides, I do not want to be driving through that corn maze at night."

His eyes filled with laughter. "You will have to leave this house at night sooner or later."

She rubbed her temples. "I was hoping to make it to the time change in the spring."

He laughed out loud this time, the sound of his rich laugh making her smile. "Seriously. You'll be fine. No creepy kids will jump out at you."

"No, just your exes trying to take me down."

"No, that won't happen either. But on to more pressing matters, I was making a list of possible things I could do with Adam. Things to show him around the island."

"Really? Okay, that's great. To be honest I haven't even had a chance to think of anything. I was planning on doing the Anne stuff next weekend that Maddy has been asking about. Like, the museum, the house, and then Cavendish."

He pinched the bridge of his nose. "No fourteen-year-old boy wants to go to the Anne stuff on the weekend. That will make him want to cross Confederation Bridge on foot."

She rolled her eyes. "I wasn't going to drag him along with us. But I was going to see if he'd want to come along for the food. I hear there's a great lobster roll place and burgers. Then ice cream."

"Getting a little better, but still. Maybe we can split the day up with things they both like? I know some good places to eat that we'll all like too."

"Okay, that sounds amazing already. We'd all love it if you came along. Oh, also, Maddy was asking about going to the hotel from *Anne of Green Gables*? I think it was called the White Sands Hotel? Every time we watch the movie, we keep saying that we have to go there."

He chuckled. "Perfect, we'll do that one day too. Then the weekend after that is the festival."

She smiled. "Great. All I need to do is get through this week and make it to the weekend. He won't know what hit him."

CHAPTER SEVEN

Five weeks until Christmas

Matt knew himself well enough to acknowledge that what he felt for Annie was more than duty, obligation, and friendship. But he was very good at compartmentalizing. He was a master at self-control and discipline, and that was perfect because Annie would always be his best friend's wife. And Matt was not the douche "best friend" from *Love Actually*.

Yeah, Cam was gone, but he couldn't shake the guilt because he'd had feelings for Annie from day one. So being alive when Cam wasn't dug a hole in his chest that refused to be filled. Maybe that was why he'd been able to let the woman he'd been engaged to just leave. He hadn't been heartbroken; he hadn't been devastated. He'd just gotten up and gone to work the next day. She had asked him to leave the island with her, and that had been a deal-breaker for him. She had accused him of not loving her enough, and he agreed. Not quite so callously, of course, but he couldn't lie. He hadn't realized that he didn't love her enough until then. He regretted hurting her, and he never wanted to cause anyone that kind of pain again.

Spending the day with Annie and the kids was the best thing he'd done on a Saturday for as long as he could remember. He'd had an emergency call on a farm and had taken Adam with him. It wasn't how he'd planned on spending the morning, but Adam had shown so much interest in coming along that he took him. After, they'd picked up coffee for him and hot chocolate for Adam along with breakfast from the drive-thru before picking up Annie and Maddy.

They were currently wandering around Avonlea village. Snow flurries tumbled from the sky at a slow enough rate that they weren't too irritating. Maybe even just right. The old wood-framed buildings were decked with cedar boughs and garlands with twinkling lights. Annie and Maddy had gotten a kick out of it as soon as they arrived. The two of them kept ducking into the shops and disappearing for what seemed like forever. But he didn't mind because it gave him a chance to hang out with Adam. He hadn't been to the village in years. Since tourist season was long gone, at least they didn't have to contend with any crowds. "So, you hungry? I think it's about lunch time."

Adam turned to him, his posture suddenly improving. "Starving."

He almost laughed out loud. Adam had ordered enough at breakfast that he had no idea how the kid could be starving this soon. "Me too. Burger?"

"Yessss. I can't take any more stores, and if I have to look at another Anne doll, I'm going to go crazy."

Matt laughed out loud and gave him a pat on the shoulder. "Great. There's an amazing burger place in that old church. So good that you'll forget all about Anne dolls. I'll just tell your mom where we'll be."

He opened the door to the artisan gallery he'd seen Annie and Maddy enter. Maddy was looking at one of the *Anne of Green Gables* displays, and Annie was standing with her back to him. "Hey, Annie?"

She turned to him and her eyes were all misty before she blinked a few times. Her hair was down today, shiny and wavy over her shoulders. She usually wore it back, especially at work. Her blue eyes were filled with something he couldn't pinpoint. She didn't look upset . . . more . . . hell, he had no idea. Annie wasn't overly emotional as far as he could remember. In some ways, she wore armor around her, like he did. He respected that and he understood it. She pointed at a large wooden sign. It looked like a quote of some sort. "I have to buy this. For the house."

He nodded. "Sure. You want me to bring it to my truck?"

She hesitated for a moment and then nodded. "That would be great. I'll just go buy it and then you can take it. I'll check in to see if Maddy wants anything. How are you guys doing?"

"Better now that I told Adam we're going for burgers."

She smiled. "Thanks. He's actually looking like his old self today, despite the Anne stuff. I think having you around really helped."

"It's my pleasure. This is what I'd hoped for, having you guys back here. I remember what it was like being a teenager, and there's just so much to process, let alone the loss of a parent and moving to a new place."

She pulled her purse further up on her shoulder and looked down at the ground for a moment. "I know. This is what I wanted for them too—I wanted them to have people they could count on, especially now that my parents are gone. My sister is family, but she makes and breaks promises without ever saying sorry or making it up to them. And then when Adam started hanging around those guys and getting in trouble and skipping class, it just became too much. Too many hours for me at work and, as much as I love my job, it can also be an excuse to escape from all the drama at home. That and the cost of living in Toronto made it impossible to keep up our way of life without working all those hours.

"And I need to be there for them. I need to be around, now more than ever. I feel it. They need me—whether or not they want me or know it, they need me around more. I have to turn everything around. I have to get my family back."

He felt the weight of her words, even though she said them almost matter-of-factly. Annie had never been into self-pity or drama or woe is me. In fact, other than those weeks after Cam died, he'd never seen her break down, cry, or panic. But he saw it now that she was here, in her eyes; hidden between the lines of her words; she had the weight of the world on her shoulders.

"Hey, you haven't lost them. They're great kids and that's because of you and Cam. And you held it together after he died. You were there for them. Adam hit a rough patch, that's all. And this morning, on the farm, that kid was completely present and engaged. You haven't lost him. I'm here for you, Annie. We all are. You're not alone anymore, okay?"

She rolled her lips in and nodded quickly. "Thank you. I know you're right."

If she'd been anyone else, he might have reached out to hug her or put an arm around her shoulder, but with her it would be too intimate. It wouldn't be a simple hug between friends, because he would want more. But he couldn't want more without feeling like he was betraying his best friend.

He also couldn't jeopardize his relationship with Annie. Hell, she had so much to deal with. If she had any idea how he really felt about her, it would only further complicate her life and he didn't want that for her. So there was nothing to do except be the good family friend. That's what Cam would have wanted. Cam wanted him to be there for her, not be with her. He forced a smile, trying to keep things lighthearted.

"Thanks. I rarely hear those words. Okay, so I'll bring this thing out to the truck for you and then head over to the burger place. Do you want to meet us there when you're done?"

She nodded, walking up to the cash. "Perfect. I can't wait to try those burgers. I'm actually starving right now. Oh, and then the coffee shop next door looks great."

And just like that the mood was lifted. She was like that, always pushing through, never staying in a place of sadness for long. That took resolve. He left the store with Annie's canvas to find Adam waiting for him outside.

Once he and Adam put the painting or whatever it was Annie had purchased in the truck, they headed over to the old church that had been repurposed into a burger joint. "What do you feel like?" he asked as they stood at the cash and read the menu items on the blackboard sign.

"Everything. Poutine and two burgers and a Diet Coke."

Matt grinned at the woman inputting their order. "That sounds perfect. Except I'll just have one burger."

Once he'd paid, she handed them their soft drinks and they picked a table for four by one of the windows and sat down. The windows were framed with multicolored Christmas lights and there were small poinsettias on all the tables. Holiday music blasted from the speakers, and the smell of fried food filled the warm air. "So, Avonlea not as bad as you'd thought?"

Adam smiled and leaned back in his chair. "Standing in the mud in the freezing cold, watching you help that horse was way better, but I think the food will make up for it. Thanks for letting me get all that."

He let out a laugh. "I'm glad you came along. And no problem about the food. I remember my mom saying I was going to bankrupt them because of how much I ate when I was a teenager."

Adam toyed with the ketchup packet in front of him, staring at it as he spoke. "You have a nice family, Uncle Matt. I had kind of forgotten what they were all like, it had been so long since I'd seen them."

Matt nodded and took a sip of his drink. "Consider them your family too. In no time they'll feel like it."

Adam nodded, looking out the window. "I guess. Thanks. I kind of wish we had a bigger family. Like my dad's family is all gone. My mom's is basically all gone too. My grandparents were really nice, and I miss them. All we have is my weird Aunt Val, who basically stalks Mom and only pretends to be interested in us.

Matt swallowed hard. There was a lot packed into that statement, and he had to choose his response carefully. These weren't the years for sugar-coating things, and he wanted Adam to feel like he could open up to him about anything. Cam and Annie were counting on him for this. He drew a breath, pushing against the heaviness in his chest. "I know it's hard when you see all these other people with these huge families, cousins and aunts and uncles and grandparents. It can really hurt and make you feel like you got pretty unlucky.

"But as I got older, I realized that no one's life is perfect. Some of those people were only happy on the outside but were really hurting inside. Some of those families did end up broken apart. And some? They were really lucky and they were the real deal. But then I had friends who came from really messed-up families and it made me realize that I was beyond blessed with the family I did have. Yeah, my dad took off, but I had a mom that would do anything for me. A sister who, even though we drove each other crazy, I love very much. Now that we're grown up, we're even closer and we're good friends.

"I know you must know this already, but moms like yours don't come along every day. I mean, she'd do anything for you, Adam. The only reason you're here is because she wants to give you what she feels she hasn't been able to. Yeah, you may not think we're real family, but we can be. Family isn't just family because of blood. Sometimes people use that as an excuse for horrible behavior—they think that just because they're related, they're allowed to treat their family like garbage and get away with it. That's not real family in my books."

Adam nodded. "Yeah, like Aunt Val. You should see some of the stunts she's pulled on Mom and Dad. I think part of the reason Mom wanted to come here was to get away from her. She's always trying to control my mom and tell her what to do, and she's never around for us. I actually think she's even jealous of us, that we take Mom away from her. She always had some drama going on, and when my grandparents were alive, she treated them like crap and didn't do anything to ever help them. Then there was the whole trying to get me to move back to Toronto behind my mom's back. I still feel guilty about that. I was just so mad and nervous about moving here."

Matt filed away that piece of information. That was something else he'd have to watch out for. Valerie always gave him the creeps, and Cam couldn't stand her. She was someone who needed boundaries. Hopefully the distance would slowly push her away. "Don't feel guilty. Valerie should feel guilty for going behind your mom's back. I know a little about her but didn't realize things were so hard on your mom. My sister is really supportive, not at all like Valerie. Me and Kate are kind of like you and Maddy."

Adam shrugged. "Maddy's just a kid."

"Well, now she is. Four years may seem huge at this point in your lives, but as you get older, four years is nothing. When you were little, four years was nothing. You used to play with her nonstop. Don't lose that connection with her. You know, all those things you didn't have, the family you didn't have, that can all change with you and Maddy. You can both grow up to have your own families—big families. And then your kids can all play together."

Adam took a sip of his Coke, his expression a little brighter. "That's crazy to think about."

"Life goes by faster than you can imagine. Don't let these years slip by and tell yourself they don't matter. Keep your sister close, keep that relationship going. Don't push your family away."

Adam stared at his cup for a long moment and Matt sensed there was more there. Just when he thought Adam wasn't going to say anything, he started speaking, his head still downturned. "There's something else . . . I don't know. I just don't know how this can ever feel like home. Toronto is where I grew up. It's where I remember my dad. My grandparents. I could still walk to their house if I wanted to. It's where they're buried. If we stay here, we're going to have to sell our house and then the last place he ever lived will just . . . be gone. Like him. How will I go back there? How will I remember everything? It's like it'll all just be erased and I don't know who I am without my dad."

Matt's chest ached and he swallowed against the lump in his throat. He didn't pause, didn't search for the right words, because this wasn't about that. It was about giving this kid as much of his heart as he could, more than he'd given anyone, and he would. He reached across the table and gripped his forearm. "Your dad is right there," he said, pointing to Adam's heart. "He's always there. He's always been there and he always will be. No matter where you go in the world, your dad is there. He's a part of you. You can't ever lose him. As for visiting him at the cemetery, I visit your dad.

"I haven't told anyone this, but I talk to him, Adam. I know it's not the same, but he was family to me. He was a brother to me. I talk to him in my head all the time, as though he was still here. Sometimes I still laugh at some of the things we used to do. I don't need to visit him at the cemetery to feel close to him. But that is something I'm sure your mom would help you with. You could go back every summer or whatever. Don't shut her out."

They paused when their order came and it was a good time for a break. "Thanks . . . I didn't know that you still talk to my dad."

Matt shrugged and picked at his fries. "He was unforgettable. He'll never not be my best friend. There are some people in the world you have a connection with, and that doesn't go away. I can't make you love it here. But I can help you give it a chance."

Adam nodded and took a deep breath before reaching for the poutine. He watched as the kid basically shoved his face into the poutine, and frankly, that might be the best therapy at the moment. The gravy and cheese curds were inhaled at a speed that Matt had never seen before. Adam didn't even look as though he was struggling to finish all his food. He dug into his own food and they ate in silence until Annie and Maddy showed up.

"Wow, that looks delicious," Annie said, staring at the remnants.

Matt wiped his mouth and laughed. "Oh, it was. Why don't you two sit down and I'll get your order?"

She waved a hand. "Oh, that's okay, I don't mind."

He stood, happy to see her sit down and let someone else serve her for once. He wondered when the last time was that happened. "Seriously. Sit. I don't mind. Tell me what you want."

She glanced at the board with the menu. "I'll be daring and have whatever you had."

He smiled. "Perfect. You can't go wrong." He turned to Maddy. "What about you, Maddy?"

Her face lit up. "I want to come with you."

He nodded. "All right, let's go."

He led the way and ordered. Once their order was placed, he waited with Maddy for her drink. "You having a good day, Maddy?"

She smiled up at him and his heart squeezed. She had a smile that made him want to promise her that everything would be okay because they all deserved that. This kid deserved so much credit. She took everything in stride, looked at everything as an adventure. There was a warmth to her that reminded him of Annie. He had never felt so needed until today, with these kids. It was as though, somehow, he'd found a new purpose to his life. He didn't take it for granted that Adam had opened up to him, and it gave him an entirely new perspective. He wasn't just a kid too stubborn to make a change. He was a kid grappling with memories and holding on to a past that he didn't want to lose.

"This place is so cool. I can't believe we live here now and I can come anytime. It's so cute and the shops look like the olden days."

He smiled down at Maddy, shifting his attention to her and away from his conversation with Adam. "Yeah, and this is just the beginning. There's so much more to see. Wait until all the beaches are open this summer. I know the best ones on the island that the tourists don't know about."

Her eyes lit up. "I can't wait!"

"How was your first week of school?"

Her smile dipped slightly. "It was okay. The kids are nice and stuff and so's my teacher."

"Yeah? That's good. Something not so good?" he asked, detecting more.

She glanced over her shoulder at her mom and then back to him. "It's not the same. Even though the kids are nice, it's not the same. I don't know any of them really. I don't want to tell Mom because I know she's super stressed, and I don't want her to be worried about me."

His heart squeezed at the vulnerability in her voice. He placed a hand on her shoulder. "You can tell your mom anything. You don't have to hide from her. And you know, she's kind of in the same boat. She had all her friends at work and now she's starting over. Getting to really know the kids will take time. It can't be the same yet because you have to make new memories and new friendships with these kids. In time you'll start to build the same bonds. Can you keep in touch with your old friends?"

She nodded. "Yeah, a couple of them FaceTime. But it's not the same."

The server brought their tray of food over and Matt picked it up. They walked back to the table. "I know, hang in there. It's only been a week. You'll make amazing friends here, and you'll still have your old friends, so basically you've doubled your friends. Just be patient. And you can talk to me anytime you want, okay?"

She smiled up at him, her eyes twinkling. "You're right. But you need to help me with something."

He gave her a nod, the lump in his throat becoming a familiar thing today. She was trusting him and opening up to him. His best friend's daughter. Annie's little girl. He'd give her the world if she asked. "Anything."

"Help me convince mom to get a real Christmas tree this year."

"Consider it done. Of course, you have to get a real tree."

She let out a little squeal, confirming her faith in him, and it made him feel ten feet tall. He shot Annie a glance and hoped like hell this wouldn't be too difficult. "Okay, let's go eat. I'll ask about the tree after she's had a few bites of poutine. Everyone's happier after they eat this."

Maddy practically ran back to the table, almost knocking Annie over on her chair as she sat down. "We've got poutine, Mom. You should eat before it gets cold."

Annie put her arm around Maddy, smiling. "It looks amazing. Thanks, Matt."

He gave them a wink and sat down beside Adam. "You're welcome. Okay, so eat up but save room for ice cream. Can't leave Avonlea without going to the ice cream shop."

"Omigosh, this gravy is so thick and filling. How are we going to eat ice cream after this?" Annie said, panic in her eyes, as she moved her fork around the fries and fresh cheese curds and gravy.

"Trust me, there's no way you'll be able to walk by those homemade waffle cones. The smell just wafts out of there," Matt said, finishing off his drink.

"I've got tons of room saved," Adam said.

Maddy nodded, stabbing a forkful of fries dripping in gravy and cheese curds. "Me too! What flavor are you getting, Adam?"

Matt held his breath, watching as Adam's face went from sullen to almost polite as he answered his little sister. "Chocolate."

Maddy's face lit up as though he'd just told her he'd buy her the entire ice cream shop. "I'm getting vanilla."

"That's so boring," Adam said, almost smiling.

Matt cleared his throat. "So, any thoughts on where you'll get your Christmas tree this year?"

Annie took a sip of her drink. "I thought I'd just order an artificial one online. I sold our old one instead of dragging it out here."

He avoided eye contact with Maddy, who he already knew was hanging off the edge of her chair. "What about a real one? We've got some amazing tree farms on the island."

Maddy let out a theatrical gasp. "What a great idea, Uncle Matt!"

Much to his surprise, even Adam piped up. "Yeah, we've never had a real tree before."

Annie hesitated. "I don't know, guys; I've always heard real trees are a lot of work. You have to water them and . . ."

"It's actually not that hard at all. They smell amazing. I could go with you; we could put the tree in my truck, and I'll set it up. You will have to do nothing but decorate it."

"I'll even water the tree! Pleaaaaaase!" Maddy said, clutching Annie's arm, jostling her so much that Annie almost dropped the drink she was holding.

Annie was laughing. "Maddy . . ." She looked at all three of them and he knew they had her. "Okay! Let's get a real tree!"

He held Annie's gaze from across the table, that sparkle in her eye making everything worth it. That's what he wanted. More than anything, he knew that if Annie got her sparkle back, her kids would be okay. They would be okay. The way she was looking at him . . . like he'd just brought her the world. It was a feeling he could get addicted to.

CHAPTER EIGHT

Four weeks until Christmas

"I need to talk to you."

Annie gasped as Matt's sister pulled her into the powder room and shut the door. It was their second Sunday night dinner and Annie loved the idea of coming here every week. And she loved it for her kids. Routine and structure and family. They had only just arrived and she had no idea what Kate had to tell her. Judging by the fact that they were standing in the tiny powder room, it wasn't good. "What's up?"

"Jessica is coming."

Annie's stomach dropped, and then she realized that was a ridiculous reaction. Why should it bother her if Jessica was there? No, maybe it wasn't that Jessica was coming, but more like it seemed odd that she was coming. Clearly, from Kate's reaction it wasn't a typical thing. And then there was the fact that Jessica hadn't warmed up to Annie at all in the last two weeks.

In the past, Annie would have bent over backwards to make Jessica like her. But she was determined to be more assertive, to care less about people liking her or approving of her. She smoothed her hair and tried to look serene. "Oh, that's nice. What's the problem?"

Kate flipped her hair over her shoulder with a huff. "Please don't tell me you are oblivious to what is happening."

Annie looked around. "Happening?"

Kate rolled her eyes. "Listen, I'm not one for gossip, really. But she's bad news. For some reason, though, my mother adores her. She is actively encouraging Matt to date her."

Annie ignored the flash of insecurity that swept through her. Maybe that was what she was detecting from Matt's mom. She had been perfectly polite and kind to Annie, but not warm. Not the way his grandmother was. That first night they'd arrived, she had been so welcoming and sweet, and then something had happened. Maybe she thought Annie had too much baggage or she was taking up too much of Matt's time. "Oh, well, maybe . . . they should."

Kate crossed her arms. "While I commend your attempts at neutrality, you can't honestly think this would be good for Matt. Or that she would be good for Matt. I see the way he looks at you."

Annie stared at her, panic bubbling inside. "What? He doesn't look at me any way other than as a friend. A brother. We're friends. He's actually my best friend."

Kate shut her eyes and shook her head for a moment. "Oh, Annie, how can you be so oblivious? I know my brother. You bring out this side in him we rarely see around here; a more civilized, mature side. Besides, Jessica is a train wreck."

"Your mother obviously doesn't think so," she said, trying to steer the conversation back to Jessica and away from whatever it was Kate thought Matt felt for her.

"My mother is interested in one thing—keeping Matt on this island for the rest of his life."

A bubble of laughter escaped Annie. "This isn't *Gilligan's Island*; he can find his way off if needed."

Kate pursed her lips. "This isn't funny, and that's not what I meant. I need to fill you in on what actually happened to Matt—"

The slow knock on the door interrupted Kate's tell-all while simultaneously giving them a clue as to who was on the other side. "Uh, Kate, Mom wants you to help her with something in the kitchen."

Kate made an irritated sound. "In a minute. I have indigestion."

Annie slapped her hand over her mouth, trying not to laugh, feeling like a teenager again. She adored Matt's sister. They had become easy friends as she helped her with the house. She was funny and genuine and easy to talk to. In the last two weeks of Sunday night dinners, Annie already felt comfortable with her and was looking forward to getting to know her even better.

"Really? Is Annie helping you with the indigestion?"

This time Annie burst out laughing. "I'm sorry, Kate."

"Ugh," Kate said, unlocking the door and glaring at Matt, who was standing there not even bothering to contain his gloat of victory. She poked his shoulder as she walked by him. She gave Annie a pointed stare. "We'll finish this conversation after dinner."

"Sure," Annie called out after her. Now her curiosity was really piqued. She had no idea what she was going to say.

"Everything okay?" he asked, his eyes sparkling.

They were standing quite close, and she had to tilt her head up to maintain eye contact with him. Had this been another room other than the powder room, it might have been a moment. As it was, she was very happy it was the powder room. She wanted to ignore all her feelings for Matt and think of him as family and nothing more. She didn't want to complicate any of their lives. She also didn't want to notice how handsome he looked tonight. He'd shaved and dressed up in dark jeans and a navy sweater. Standing this close, she could smell that cologne of his and tried to take a step back, but that would mean going back into the powder room. "Of course. Kate's just, um, filling me in on some of the upcoming holiday events."

A corner of his mouth tilted up. "Ah, the holiday events. It's a shame she felt she needed to do this in the powder room."

She found herself staring at his mouth and was mortified. She bit her lower lip and looked away from his gaze. Instead, she focused on the cranberry-scented hand soap with the little illustration of a sled on the front of the bottle. "Well . . . because of the indigestion."

"I see, so you don't mind being cooped up in a closet-sized room with someone having major digestive issues?"

She burst out laughing and gave him a light shove so she could get out of the powder room. But there was something about that barely-there touch that made her pulse race, that imprinted itself beneath her fingertips. "Fine, Matt. You're so clever and you know your sister very well. But she knows you just as well, I think."

They were standing in the corner of the hallway now, the dim glow of the lamp on the console table highlighting his handsome features. It felt very intimate to be speaking in low tones and quiet laughter, like they were sharing a moment away from everyone. Maybe he felt it too, because the sparkle had left his eyes, replaced with something deeper. Or maybe it was just the shadows in the hallway. She preferred to think the latter. "Maybe so. But then again, I'd wager you know me pretty well too."

Her mouth went dry. What did that mean? And it wasn't just what that meant, it was the way he said it. Or maybe she was just on high alert now because of what Kate had said. She waved a hand. "Well, it was nothing big. And as much as I know you, we haven't lived in the same province in years, so I'm sure there's a lot I missed."

He shoved his hands in the front pockets of his jeans. "I'm an open book. Ask anything you'd like."

But she had no business asking because asking meant she was interested in his personal life and she wasn't. Or she didn't want to be at least. And she certainly didn't want him knowing any of this. "Your personal life is your personal life. It's not up to me to judge. And I really don't need to know any more after that whole contract conversation. But your sister did say something about Jessica joining us tonight?"

He ran a hand over his jaw. "Yeah, that threw me for a loop. I had no idea until my mother mentioned it a few minutes before you guys came."

She tilted her head. "Does she usually invite your exes over without letting you know?"

"I think it's that she sees her as more of a family friend. Remember, she wasn't actually an ex. And she talks to her a lot on the phone when she calls the clinic for me."

Annie tapped her finger on her chin. "Oh, right. That makes sense. She's a family friend then. She's been here before and your mom was just extending a friendly Sunday night dinner invitation."

Matt rubbed the back of his neck. "She's never actually been here for Sunday night dinner and, honestly, this is a little weird."

Oh. *Oh.* So maybe Kate was onto something. Maybe this was personal. What Kate had said about the island, though, was interesting. Was his mom worried that Annie was going to go back to Toronto and Matt would go with her? That was absurd, of course. It's not like they were in love. Or even dating. Or maybe she thought he would go back with them out of duty, like Annie couldn't cope. Maybe she didn't like that Annie had kids and she didn't want Matt overly involved in their lives. "Did you, um, mention anything about the six-week plan to convince Adam he loves the island?"

He shook his head. "Of course not. I hinted that we needed to make this the best holiday season since . . . well, in a long time. That was it."

"Hmm. Okay. So maybe we're just reading too much into this," she said with a shrug. Not that she believed it. She didn't want to read too much into this because if she did, it made her feel insecure and a bit hurt.

The doorbell rang and they watched, silently from the sidelines, as his mom burst out of the kitchen to run to the front door. "Matt! Matt! Jessica is here! Come and say hello!" she yelled before opening the door. Claire definitely looked like a woman with an agenda. Annie's heart sank. She wanted Matt's mom to like her.

"Matt has a bad case of indigestion!" Kate yelled from the kitchen as Jessica walked into the house.

Matt laughed as his mother hissed at Kate to keep quiet. "I guess the payback is warranted. Do you want a drink?"

Annie looked up at Matt, forcing a smile. She was not going to burden him with her insecurities. She was not going to listen to Valerie's voice in her head, telling her all the things that were wrong with her. *Too bad you didn't get the tall gene like me. Being short just doesn't do you any favors, Annie. Curves are so out and, after you had your kids, well, not good. I can show you some exercises at the gym to make you look thinner.* She hated that voice. She'd hated it as a child and she hated it as an adult. Whenever Annie was insecure about something, it would sneak in, like a bad dream.

She smoothed her hair, bringing it to rest over one shoulder, and crossed her arms over her chest, a wave of self-consciousness washing over her. Her dark green sweater was modest and flattering, as were her dark jeans. She usually wore really boring things. Nothing to draw attention. She had felt fine getting dressed that day. In fact, she'd felt good, especially knowing Valerie wouldn't be around, looking at her and judging her.

"I have a feeling I'm going to need one. I don't think I'm Jessica's favorite person. But I'm sure if your mother likes her, I will too."

* * *

Matt needed a minute alone with his mother. What should have been an enjoyable evening was turning into one of the most painful, awkward situations he'd ever been in.

"I have no idea what your mother was thinking, bringing that Jessica over tonight. Tonight should have just been about Annie and the children. No one needs to deal with Jessica's tactics."

Matt turned the coffee pot on and took down the mugs his grandmother had asked for. "I couldn't agree more. Do you have any idea what this is all about?"

She looked up from the pumpkin pie she was placing on a serving platter. Her lips were in a straight line, her eyes serious. He knew that look. He'd been on the receiving end of it a few times during his teen years. "I'll tell you exactly what this is about—your mother is worried that you're going to fall for Annie and her kids and Annie is going to move back to Toronto and take you with her."

Hell. He had guessed as much. How was it the women in this house were aware of his feelings before he even made them known. That was the most disconcerting thing. Then, of course, there was the fact that his mother thought she could try and interfere in his life to suit her own needs. He knew the thought was harsh and that she was coming from a good place, but it was still selfish. And very premature to be thinking any of this.

And what? He was just going to fall head over heels in love with Jessica because she complimented his mom on her Sunday night roast five thousand times and wore a dress that looked like she was going to prom? This was a huge mess. And seriously, none of them had time for petty games like this. They were adults, for crying out loud.

"Are you sure about this plan, Grandma? Are you sure Jessica didn't invite herself over?"

Her eyes narrowed on him. "Have I ever been wrong about these types of things?"

He crossed his arms over his chest and leaned against the island, preferring to watch the coffee drip into the carafe than stare at his grandmother's expression. "You're right. I'm going to have to talk to Mom after everyone leaves."

Of course, his grandmother didn't stop there. She walked over to him, placed her hand on his arm and looked up at him. Her green eyes held all the answers, always. They held a mix of the past they shared as well as a past she shared with no one. But her eyes always held the truth. "I think you should. You can't let other people tell you what's best for you. You are in charge of your own life. No one else, no matter who they are . . . and for the record, I think you're a wonderful man. And I think Annie is a wonderful woman. She brings out a side of you that I'm so proud to see. It's a noble thing to be there for people, Matt. To not run from our responsibilities when the going gets tough. I have watched you since Cam died, I have watched you change, deepen in your love for your family. That takes courage, to love that deeply after loss. But it takes even more courage to go after what you really want. You can't ignore feelings forever; you don't want to live with regrets."

The coffee percolated loudly and the conversation from the dining room dimmed as he absorbed his grandmother's words. What he really wanted. Or who he really wanted. "What about wanting too much? Ruining something that's already great? What about the feeling that that I'm betraying my best friend?"

"You deserve all good things, my dear boy. And Annie and her kids are those things. As for betraying your best friend, that's not what this is. Don't you think it would bring him comfort to know that Annie and his kids are with a man like you? Do you really think he would want them to be alone or with someone who doesn't treat them well? And who could possibly be a better husband and father than you? No one, that's who."

He let out a chuckle and drew her in for a hug. "Grandma, the amount of confidence you have in me is humbling. Thank you for always believing in me."

She held onto him tighter before letting go and leaning back to look up at him. Her eyes glistened with love. "Always. You have a piece of my heart, Matthew. Live your life, don't get hung up on all these other doubts. If what you have is really special with Annie, and I think it is, then it can't be ruined. Sometimes, we don't know what we want, sometimes we need someone to come forward. Annie must have a lot of faith in you to uproot their lives and move here."

His grandmother patted him on the arm before walking by him into the dining room. He stood still, letting her words sink in, battling it out with his conscience. The sound of Annie's laughter floated through the kitchen and he found himself smiling. He didn't want to be just another person in her life that added pressure, that wanted something from her. Especially if it wasn't something she wanted to give. But he didn't know how he'd live with the regret of never trying, either.

"Hey, what's the hold up? Did you go out to buy new mugs? The situation in there is dire, hurry up," Kate said, charging over to him.

"Yeah, yeah, I'm coming," he said.

She grabbed the tray of mugs and shot him a look. "Fix this Jessica situation. Tonight, Matt."

"Thanks. I know. Coffee is ready. I'll bring out the pot," he said, grabbing it from the base.

"Can I help with anything, Matt?" Annie asked as he walked back into the dining room. His mother had a wintery greens floral arrangement in the center of the table with candles flickering in hurricanes. She and Jessica were talking about the florist, and of course it wasn't anyone Annie would know.

He held up his hand. "Not a chance. I've got this." He poured his grandmother's cup first and then for Annie and his mother and Jessica. He pretended to forget Kate.

"Hey!" She laughed.

He finished pouring their cups and sat back down beside Annie, trying to avoid Jessica's attempt at eye contact. His leg brushed against Annie's as he settled into his seat, and it was as though he was branded with heat. Even being this close to her made him long for things he wished he didn't. It would have been so much simpler if he were interested in Jessica. But he couldn't deny how Annie affected him on so many levels.

"I'm so glad you're adjusting to the island so well, kids," his grandmother said, giving them each a warm smile. They were both eating the pumpkin pie and ice cream.

Both kids nodded and smiled back, their mouths full of pie. He was happy to see them sitting beside each other, and he even caught them whispering together a few times. He wasn't so naïve as to think he'd solved their problems with one chat, but maybe it had made a bit of a difference.

"They've done great. New school, house, friends. Next week should be even better," Annie said, giving the kids an encouraging smile.

"It'll start to feel like home soon. Especially with all the Christmas events coming up," Kate said.

Annie put down her coffee mug. "Oh, that sounds fun. I haven't even had a chance to look at everything."

"I'll be sure to text you dates for all the good stuff," Kate answered, taking a sip of her coffee.

"Always good to plan and sort out the week ahead of time. Sometimes I even like to do it a month in advance when it's busy season," his grandmother said.

Annie leaned forward, her gaze fixed on his grandmother. "Oh, would you suggest meal planning by the month?"

His grandmother nodded. "Sometimes. But be flexible too."

Annie was nodding slowly. He had no idea they discussed these types of things. "Great advice."

"Wow, mom life sounds so hectic. I'm glad I can just pick up whatever I want depending on what mood I'm in!" Jessica said, scrunching up her nose before smiling. He knew that scrunch. It wasn't good.

"Well, the chaos is worth it. I've got great kids," Annie said, shooting Maddy and Adam a smile.

"So, did you guys get a lot of homework this week?" Matt asked, trying to include the kids in the conversation again.

They both nodded. "Especially since I missed that day because I was sick," Maddy said.

"At least those stomach bugs seem to be gone quickly," Matt said. Everyone at the table nodded, echoing his sentiment.

"Well, this was such a lovely evening. We should probably get going, especially now that you reminded me about homework. Adam was telling me on the way over that he has a lot to finish still before Monday morning," Annie said, standing and picking up her empty plate and mug.

"I hear you saw all the Anne stuff, Maddy. And you even got both guys to come along?"

Maddy smiled as she picked up her plate. "Yup. We also had the best poutine and ice cream."

"I had a great time too," Matt said, joining them and gathering up some dishes.

Jessica raised her eyebrows, looking back and forth between him and Annie. "Oh . . . did you all go sightseeing together?"

"We did. Uncle Matt took us *everywhere*. I was so wiped when we got home, I went straight to bed. Then next weekend he's taking us to get a real Christmas tree and we're going to the Charlottetown festival, whenever that is," Maddy said, following him into the kitchen.

Jessica gave a smile tighter than the perfectly wrapped bows on his grandmother's Christmas presents. "How cozy."

He let out a sigh when he was out of earshot. Annie quickly stacked their dishes in the sink while the kids headed to the door. "Hey, no worries. I'm on dish duty with Kate tonight."

She wiped her hands on the front of her dark jeans, not making eye contact with him. Her smile wasn't the usual, and she was in a hurry as she left the kitchen. "Okay, thanks. Uh, we'll get going. I'll see you at work tomorrow."

"Hey, hey, I can at least walk you to the door," he said, picking up his pace to keep up with her.

"You have company, and I don't want to be a bother," she said, searching for her coat in the front closet.

"Uh, you're company as well, and you've never been a bother to me a day in your life. Quite the opposite, Annie."

She stilled for a moment, or maybe he imagined it because then his grandmother and mother came barreling into the entranceway. For a half second he contemplated checking on his sister and Jessica but decided against it. He didn't want Annie to leave like this. He didn't want her to think that she was an outsider and that Jessica was more important to him than she was. Hell, he hadn't wanted to make her aware of how he felt, but he also didn't want her to think she was . . . just his best friend's wife. "Uh, thanks for dinner again, see you!" Annie said, shuffling the kids out the door.

With everyone hanging around, he couldn't possibly continue what he was saying, but he hated the look on Annie's face when she left.

As soon as he shut the door behind them, he turned around to find Jessica standing there. This needed to end. "Hey, can we talk?"

She nodded, grabbing his hand and pulling him into the dining room. "We can have some privacy here."

He took a step back from her and ran his hands through his hair, blowing out a breath. "Jess, I don't know what's going on here. If I led you to think there was more between us than friendship, I'm sorry. I thought I was quite clear last year."

Her mouth dropped open. "What? Well, I just assumed that you hired me because you were interested in me."

He clenched his teeth. "You needed a job, so I gave you one."

She raised a brow. "Like Annie needed a job?"

Clearly, he needed to stop hiring people he knew. "Annie is different."

She crossed her arms over her chest. "How so?"

"Okay, I'm not going to get into all this, but you and I are friends. We've been friends a long time, and I don't want to ruin that. But there's nothing else there for me. I'm sorry. I just want things to go back to the way they were before Annie got here."

"Your mother thinks Annie's going to break your heart. You know, your mom asked me to come here tonight because she likes me and she knows that I'll never take you away from here," she said, her voice softening at the end.

Anger swept over him, hearing, rather than just suspecting, his mother's involvement in this. "I'm an adult, I make decisions for myself. But I'm sorry that you were caught up in this plan my mother has. I really am, Jess."

She waved a hand. "It's okay. I'll get over it. I'm, um, going to head out. Please thank your mom for dinner for me."

He gave her a nod. "Come on, I'll walk you to the door."

After saying goodbye to the second woman who appeared to be disappointed in him that night, he walked to the kitchen. Everyone stopped what they were doing when he walked in. But his mother kept her back turned as she wiped down the counters. His sister was gesturing to him that she needed to know what was going on, and his grandmother was drying a serving platter, watching carefully.

He searched for the right words. "Mom, what the heck were you thinking?"

She paused and then slowly turned around, guilt gleaming in her eyes. "I just really like Jessica. And she's from the island. Her family is here. She's a lovely girl."

He braced his hand on the island, telling himself that his mother was just acting out of love and to hold onto his temper. "Your interference is out of line. You are entitled to have those feelings—I can't control who you like—but you can't act on them. You can't manipulate people in my life or me. And frankly, I think you made Annie feel lousy. Instead of giving her a chance and being a source of support to a single mother—something I would think you'd know a lot about—you alienated her and made it very clear that you thought she wasn't good enough for me. Well, you'd be blessed to have her as a daughter-in-law and have those kids as grandkids. And for the record, you're the odd one out here. Kate loves her and Grandma thinks so highly of her that she gave her the recipe book."

There was a collective gasp in the room, and he cursed himself for letting that slip. What the hell had he been thinking?

How he had grown up in a house full of women and survived was beyond him. They never missed a beat, never missed an opportunity to analyze a sentence. His grandmother was smiling, picking up another platter. His sister was smiling in victory. And his mother's face was as white as the cloth napkins she was holding.

He turned toward the door, suddenly needing his own space. "Good night."

It was only when he was on the porch that he realized he'd referred to Annie as a potential daughter-in-law. Hell.

CHAPTER NINE

Three weeks until Christmas

"Hey, Jessica, if you could let me know when Matt's grand-mother is here, I'd appreciate it. I've got some files to update and I'll be in the lunchroom," Annie said. She couldn't remember the last time she'd looked forward to a Friday so much. She was so excited to have lunch with Matt's grandmother and get to know her better and to thank her for the recipe collection.

Then Matt was going to meet her back here and they were going Christmas tree shopping with the kids. Since the Sunday night dinner debacle, things had been awkward. Well, awkward between her and Jessica and Annie and Matt. It was a dynamic she really wanted no part in. The week had been hectic, both with the kids and with Matt having a lot of after-hours calls, so they hadn't picked up their conversation from Sunday night.

Jessica turned from her computer screen to look at Annie. "Oh. Is everything okay?"

Annie nodded, not wanting to get into a discussion. "Of course. We're just going out for a late lunch."

Jessica rolled her eyes. "Oh, that'll be fun."

Annie stilled. "Why wouldn't it be?"

"All I'm saying is that she's a little old. No need to go sucking up to Matt's entire family in order to impress him."

Annie clutched her stack of files to her chest, offended on so many levels. "I'm not trying to impress Matt, and as for Lila's age, that is so rude. I'm not even going to continue this conversation."

The door opened and with it a gust of cold wind. Lila stepped into the office with a presence as big as Santa Claus. She was wearing a red knit poncho with a matching beret, black leather pants, black leather gloves and boots. Her white hair was in a smooth and sleek bob and her lipstick was the exact shade of her poncho and beret. Annie really needed to take some fashion lessons from her. "Hello, ladies!"

Jessica jumped out of her chair and made a beeline for Lila, hugging her as though she were her long-lost sister, and not the woman she'd just been smack-talking. "*Hiieeeeee*, Mrs. Harrison!"

Annie clutched the stack of files even tighter as she walked forward. She reached out to give Lila a hug, once Jessica had untangled herself like a set of Christmas lights. "So excited for lunch. I just need five minutes to change and get my things."

"You take your time, dear."

Annie gave her a quick nod and left the waiting room. She didn't even spare Jessica a glance. But as she walked down the hallway, she could still hear the conversation.

"Wow, it's almost my lunch break too," Jessica said.

"That's nice, dear. I'm sure Matt appreciates that you wouldn't leave the office while no one else is here," Lila said.

Annie smiled as she grabbed her bag and headed into the bathroom to change. Lila's response to Jessica's subtle attempt at an invite almost rid her of her own irritation at how two-faced Jessica was. Five minutes later, hair brushed, with a touch of makeup, and in fresh jeans and a navy cowlneck sweater, she headed toward the waiting room feeling like a new woman.

"My dear, you look stunning! Now let's go and have a fabulous afternoon—you deserve it!"

Annie fumbled over a reply. Lila's unabashed compliments sounded so sincere and felt like a hot cup of cocoa on a stormy winter's night. She hadn't had anyone tell her she deserved an afternoon off in . . . years. "I can't wait, Lila. And you look gorgeous. I can't wait to see what you have planned for us."

"I'll be sure to call if something comes up!" Jessica yelled after them as they opened the door.

"You can call my grandson first, Jessica. Have a nice weekend," Lila said, with a crisp bite of authority as they stepped outside.

Annie let out the breath she'd been holding. Jessica was . . . a lot. And after that Sunday night dinner fiasco, things had been awkward to say the least. But she didn't want to think about Jessica or Sunday night dinner right now. Lila's shiny black Porsche was sitting there, looking like the biggest adventure she'd had in years. "Lila, you are like a Porsche-driving guardian angel."

Lila gave her a wink that wasn't reminiscent of anything angelic and hopped into the car. Soon they were whizzing down the island's country roads, holiday jazz filling the car with cheer. Snow hugged the hills and trees in a comforting blanket of hope. The roads were so quiet that there was time to think and breathe. Annie was so used to city driving, where there was no room for daydreaming. Everything out here was liberating.

Lila shot her a glance. "I hope you have an appetite."

"I'm starving, actually. So where are we off to? I'm dying to know what you have planned?"

Lila laughed, her eyes on the road as she drove along. "It won't take long at all. I'm going to take you to a famous little place here on the island, beloved by locals and tourists. It's the PEI Preserve Company. They have an adorable little restaurant overlooking the river, but my favorite part is the shop attached to the restaurant. All locally made preserves. Jams and jellies, organic candies—which I thought might make wonderful stocking stuffers—and then housewares."

"This sounds perfect! And I'm in desperate need of stocking stuffers."

"Bonus is that it's all organic, no food coloring or chemicals in that candy either. I'll let you in on a secret—I still buy Matt and Kate candy from here every Christmas," Lila said, her eyes on the road as she took a turn that led them down a narrow road.

Annie smiled. "Good to know."

A few minutes later they pulled into a spot not too far from the bright yellow, siding-wrapped building and made their way inside. The warmth of the shop welcomed them. It smelled like apple pie and cranberries. The sight of bustling shoppers holding baskets filled with items, and rustic shelves lined with jars and housewares was straight out of a Hallmark movie. Garlands with big red bows hung from each of the wooden shelves and doorways. Christmas music and chatter filled the air. "I have lunch reservations for us if you're good with shopping after we eat?" Lila said.

Annie nodded and followed Lila through the store and into the restaurant. "That sounds perfect."

Once they were seated, Annie took a moment to let her surroundings sink in. The restaurant had high ceilings and enormous windows that overlooked a river and were framed with twinkling white lights and garland. All the tables by the windows were filled and just a few tables in the middle were empty. Delicate white roses and branches of berries sat in small vases on each of the tables.

"This feels like an escape. I don't know what it is, but I feel so relaxed," Annie said as she studied the menu.

"This place has that effect on people. I think it carries the ambience of simpler times with it. There is something comforting about a restaurant that feels like grandma's kitchen," Lila said.

Annie blinked rapidly as she stared at the menu, not processing the items, but rather Lila's words. Instead of ignoring her emotions as she might normally have done, she looked up at Lila. "That's exactly it. How do you manage to know all this? I feel like you can evoke all this . . . feeling or emotion in almost anything. I've been reading your recipe book and I'm addicted to it. It gives me so much comfort."

Lila smiled gently, her eyes warm, so similar to Matt's. "I've been around a long time, and I like to think I've learned a lot of lessons. The biggest of which is the importance of the comforts of home."

"I get that, more now than ever before. And that's because of you and that recipe collection you gave me. That is a treasure box. The best life advice I've ever been given. I had stopped thinking of my home as a sanctuary, even for the kids. It was like, after Cam died, the house held all these disappointments. It didn't feel safe and happy anymore. The kids were sad, there were fights, then my sister . . . it just became a place to go to, not to make memories in anymore."

The server came and they paused their conversation as she poured them both water and took their orders. Once she left, Lila leaned forward, her brows knitted together. "I've been there, Annie. Those are my notes from the trenches. That is all the wisdom I've gained by going through some really hard times. I'm glad to share them with you. So many of them may seem small, but sometimes the only things we are capable of doing are small things. But when you stack the small things, that little hill can become a mountain. Doing little things every day, you'll make big changes.

"You'll get your confidence back, your joy back. Of course, laundry is boring and it's the last thing you want to do when you have a thousand things going on, but it can also be mind-numbing. It can allow you to shut your mind off for a bit. And then, the next day you won't be so overwhelmed by the idea that you have five loads of laundry waiting for you. Little by little."

"You make it sound so easy. I started a few things. The basics, as you call them, and it almost seems silly to think they can have an impact, but they do. When life is so insane, they do give me a sense of control. Like, I'm regaining control over my house, so I can regain control over my family."

Lila's green eyes gleamed. "I knew you were a kindred spirit. I knew you wouldn't give up. So, how are things with your sister? I don't know much, just that Matt said your relationship was strained and now you also brought her up. Also, if you don't want to talk about it, that's fine."

They paused as bowls of seafood chowder and freshly baked bread were brought over. It was straight comfort. The gently falling snow on the river, the fresh chowder and warm bread, were enough to make Annie open up. Lila was someone she wished she'd had growing up. She took a spoonful of soup and closed her eyes as the creamy broth burst with flavor in her mouth. "This is unbelievable."

Lila chuckled, plucking a piece of bread and dipping it into her own bowl. "I'm glad you think so. It's my favorite."

"As for my sister, it's not that I don't want to talk about it, but it's hard to explain. Or I should say, there is so much to explain about my sister. It's not just her. She impacted our entire family. Valerie is ten years older than me. I have a lot of memories of my childhood that involve her . . . um, intimidating me and physically hurting me. There was a lot of ridicule. Open hostility. Putting me down about my weight or the way I looked, or everything wrong with the way I looked I should say. Nose too big. Hips too wide. Too fat. Memories of running away from her and locking myself in the bathroom. Then it evolved into bickering as I grew older and realized that she wasn't a very nice person.

"I didn't understand until I hit thirty that she was abusive. It was presented to me as sibling rivalry. Our mother would always dismiss it as the two of us just never getting along. I bought that line until I was thirty. When it dawned on me that she was ten years older than me. It's like, when we were growing up, we were treated as though we were the same age. What could a fifteen-year-old possibly have against a five-year-old? Or a twenty-year-old woman against a ten-year-old girl? But the abuse didn't stop with me. She interfered in our parents' marriage. She pitted my mother against my father. She would go through their bills and tell my father that my mother was overspending, and they would argue. She would make up health crises all the time.

"After I had Maddy, I developed a few issues with my thyroid and a lot of tests were done, and for a while it was pretty scary because there was a possibility it was cancerous. Thankfully it was fine. Well, Valerie couldn't handle the attention, I guess, because a few months later she developed thyroid issues. But no doctors could find anything wrong with her thyroid, so she dropped it. But then she said Penelope had thyroid issues."

Lila put down her spoon. "Who is Penelope, dear?"

Annie blotted her mouth with a napkin. "Her dog."

Lila's eyes widened.

Annie nodded. "It gets worse. She once even told my parents that she had cancer and then told my mother not to contact her again and then didn't speak to them for months. When she finally came back home, she forgot she had told them she had cancer and everything went on as though none of that had ever happened. That's what she would do. When my father had cancer, I took six weeks off work to drive him to his treatments. The kids were small at the time and they'd pile into the car and we'd go, five days a week, an hour each direction, then time at the hospital. My sister was MIA. She left Penelope there with them while she went away on vacation for a week."

"My dear, why didn't you ever say anything?"

"I know. I sound like an idiot. A sucker for punishment. A total doormat. Except because my parents never put an end to her behavior, the only chance I had for peace was to just suck it up and go along with it. Because every single argument I ever had growing up wound up with me trying to explain myself to our mother. So we all just played this game of trying to keep Valerie happy. But it never worked, because she is a deeply unhappy person.

"When I got married, she was so angry. As soon as the wedding was over, she came home with this guy and announced their engagement. They moved in together right away, and all of a sudden, I was expected to host events so that extended family and friends could meet him. We had to host him all the time.

And then she ditched him, ended the engagement over email, and blamed me for it. She said that if I had done more to make him feel welcome, they never would have broken up."

Lila was shaking her head. "My dear, she is out of control."

Annie didn't want to stop talking now. It was like she finally felt brave enough to get it all out, knowing Lila wasn't going to judge her. "I know. I could sit here until it's dark and regale you with the things she's done. She gets angry and then doesn't speak to anyone, then comes back months later as though nothing has happened. Once, our mother was in the ICU for a life-threatening infection and then Valerie disappeared and blamed our mother for her losing her job and wouldn't speak to any of us for months.

"The worst was when Adam was born—that was when she bought Penelope. She presented her as Adam's little sister and would leave her with my parents to take care of. Then she made up a whole new set of lies. I tried to stand up to her, but I was a new mom and struggling with everything and I just couldn't deal. My mother fell for all her lies, just like she did when I was growing up. I felt like, over the years, I lost my parents. I never really got over my mother not being there for me when I needed her. Their inability to realize how destructive Valerie was until it was too late. She broke up our family. And now it's just the two of us left."

"Oh, my dear, this Valerie is . . . well, I hate to use buzzwords that all the young people are using, but please forgive me: Valerie is toxic. You need to set boundaries."

"I know. I'm trying. I have this guilt that looms over me because of my parents. And also, the kids, she's the only family they have left."

"Are they close with her?"

Annie shook her head. "Not really. She makes and breaks a thousand promises. They've learned not to trust her. She doesn't show up for their birthdays but expects everyone to celebrate her birthday like it's New Year's Eve. That and the fact that whenever she has a minute alone with them, she badmouths me behind my back. They always tell me, of course, but it still hurts. I don't even trust the kids with her, really. I mean, they're older now, but sometimes I feel like she hates me so much that she would do anything to get back at me."

"Get back at you for what?"

Annie shrugged, trying not to feel the emotion behind her words because it was too painful. "Being born. There is this underlying anger she has that my parents refused to acknowledge. Same with all the physical stuff—it was always chalked up to sibling rivalry and fights."

Lila let out a long sigh and then reached for Annie's hand. "You need to get your life back. You owe her nothing. But you owe your children the best of you. What you have been through has been traumatic. You don't need to shoulder the burden of your sister's hatred. You can have a fresh start here. Maybe the physical distance is what you need."

"Yes, I thought of that too. She's very upset we moved away."

"I gather she doesn't have many friends?"

"None. She has no long-term friendships. And even with us, it was always one-sided. She wasn't even consistent with holidays. She would say she was coming and then just not show up, and then the next time we saw her, she would pretend nothing happened. She wasn't there for us when Cam was in the hospital because it meant there was no attention on her. I know this is going to sound really dark, Lila, but I think, on a subconscious level, a part of her was relieved when Cam died. Then we were both unmarried. And I think she was hoping I'd move back into my parents' house with the kids and then she could move back in and control me again. She never really grew up. It's like she still thinks I'm ten and she's twenty and I have to do what she says."

Lila was staring at her, her lips thinned. "My goodness."

"I feel like a bit of an idiot, now that I've gotten that all out. I mean, there is so much more, like I said. But I feel foolish. Like, hearing it all, what kind of a person would allow themselves and their kids to be treated like this?"

"A person who was trying to keep everyone happy. A person who was raised to think that peace was more important than their own self-respect. That being family meant that it was okay to be treated horribly. A person who felt loyalty for her parents. But this is your life now, Annie. You are an adult. You get to decide when you've had enough. You get to decide your own boundaries. If she can't handle them, that's her problem. You have to ask yourself, are you willing to let more years go by where you can't enjoy your kids because you're upset by the latest antics of your sister? Are you willing to let her continue to push you?"

"Well, when you put it like that, no. It's always been drilled into me to forgive. I just don't know how many more times I can forgive. Especially because she never actually asks for forgiveness. She will never admit she's done something wrong or hurt people. She can't even admit she didn't show up for a holiday—she will just ghost everyone for a month."

Lila glanced around the room and leaned forward, the expression in her eyes fierce. "Forgiving someone doesn't mean you keep taking abuse. It does not mean you can be a punching bag. Trust me. There is more than one way to hurt someone. There is more than one way to wind up in a hospital. More than one way to break. Don't wait until you're pushed to that point. Know where your line is."

"Line?"

"The line that cannot be crossed. Everyone has one. I hope it never comes to that for you, but you'll know it when it happens. I don't want to be pushy. Please accept that it comes from a good place. From a person who is sitting here at seventy-five wondering how life passed by so quickly. You don't get to my age without having regrets.

"If I could go back, I would have asserted myself much sooner. I would have protected the life I was building with my family. Because I learned that, in the end, family that can't act the way family should isn't worth saving. You and your children are your family. If your sister wants to be a part of that, then she needs to act the way a sister should act and not like an enemy. Now, I'm not telling you what to do. Only you can decide how to handle this."

Annie broke Lila's stare, the intensity of it forcing her to realize that she wasn't capable of what needed to be done. But Annie also sensed something in Lila's past that she was referring to, and she didn't want to pry. Maybe one day. They sat in silence for a few moments, finishing their soup.

"The Christmas Song" played in the background and the nostalgia hit her hard in the chest. She'd had good parents who were flawed, who couldn't ever muster the backbone to keep her sister in line when she was growing up, and then she'd turned into an adult who unleashed so much harm on all of them. But their parents were gone. Annie wouldn't have to face their disappointment if she finally told Valerie to either act like a normal person or hit the road.

It was strange, being here, surrounded by Matt's family, and feeling like she was home. Valerie always tried to make home feel like a place on a map, but maybe that wasn't always the case. Maybe home could be people, could be love, acceptance, trust.

The server came and cleared their plates and they both ordered coffees. "I think your advice is great."

Lila put a hand over her heart. "I'm glad. I was really worried there for a moment. You were deep in thought and I was berating myself for going off like that."

The server came back with their coffees and Annie added cream to hers after Lila. "Not at all. You just prompted me to really think about all of this. It's funny, because as a kid you want to please your parents and you think that just goes away as an adult or when you have your own family, but it's always there. Or for me it was. I felt like I wanted their approval and I never really got it, and that hurt, Lila."

"I'm sure they were so proud of you. How couldn't they be?"

Emotion clogged Annie's throat, and she quickly took a sip of coffee. "I could never have anything that was truly my own to celebrate because of Valerie. No one was allowed to outshine her. We tiptoed around things. It got so bad I stopped sharing my successes with them because I knew the responses would be muted out of fear that Valerie would be jealous."

Lila made a tsking noise under her breath. "Oh, my dear, that is all so wrong."

Annie nodded quickly. "I know. I know that especially now as a parent. But I'm okay, Lila. This conversation has helped more than you know. I will reflect on it tonight. Maybe . . . I'll even journal about it. Where do I get those traveler's notebooks?"

Lila sat up straight, her eyes shiny. "Well . . . how about we go and look for some after the holidays? I know just the place."

Annie smiled at her, feeling a sense of hope trickle through her. Maybe it was all part of the magic of the season, but she hadn't felt this hopeful in years. "That sounds perfect."

They finished their coffees and made their way through the busy restaurant and out into the even busier store. Soon Annie had a basket filled with homemade preserves and was making her way over to the candy section. "I don't think one basket is going to be enough," Annie said to Lila, who had already filled up her own basket.

"I know what you mean. Why don't I go drop these off at the counter and get you a new basket?"

"That would be great, Lila. Look at all these candies," she said, handing Lila her basket. They were all in clear jars with old-fashioned labels that reminded her of the kind she might have seen at Oleson's Mercantile on *Little House on the Prairie*. As soon as Lila came back, she picked out jars with an assortment of gummy worms, sour bears, and chocolate-covered raisins.

"Make sure you get a few for yourself," Lila said, grabbing two jars of the gummy worms.

Annie laughed and added another jar of the colorful gummies. "Good idea. They'll be a nice treat when I'm doing my meal planning."

Lila gave her a wink. "I also have it on good authority that my grandson is obsessed with the worms."

Annie's jaw dropped open. "You're kidding me."

Lila shook her head. "I always pick up a few jars for him at Christmas . . . but if you were looking for a little gift for him . . ."

Annie's cheeks grew warm as Lila's voice trailed off. "That sounds like a perfect idea, if you don't mind. I'll also enjoy teasing him about it."

Lila laughed. "Please do."

They finished their shopping with time to spare. As soon as they got in the car, Lila turned to her with a mischievous smile that reminded Annie of Matt's. "I have a few more things to show you. How would you like in on all those top-secret places I mentioned in my recipe book?"

Annie's jaw dropped. "You mean like . . . the shepherd's pie and cinnamon rolls and . . ."

Lila winked and held a finger to her lips. "Exactly! You don't need to make those things from scratch! They're still homemade if someone else made them and you reheat them!"

Annie felt as though she were in Santa's sleigh as Lila drove them around the island to remote bakeries and little restaurants. They were all off the beaten track, places Annie would never have known about. She felt as though she'd just hit the jackpot on a homemaker's treasure chest. By the time they pulled into the clinic parking lot, the trunk was packed with enough supplies to fill her freezer entirely.

Wind and snow swirled around them as Annie transferred her bags from Lila's car to her trunk, careful to hide the bags under a blanket in case nosy kids were peeking back there after school. "Do you still have enough time to pick up the kids from school?"

"Right on schedule! Matt should be here any minute," she said, closing the trunk.

Lila reached out to give Annie a big hug. "Perfect. Now you all have a wonderful time together, and I will see you for Sunday night dinner."

Annie hugged Lila tightly. "Thank you for a wonderful afternoon and for listening. And for all your advice . . . the food, the recipe book, the life advice I didn't even know I was missing. I will never be able to thank you enough for how welcome you've made me feel, Lila. I hope we can spend even more time together. You've made me feel like family."

Lila pulled back but grasped Annie's hands. "You are family, Annie. And you're a good person, a good veterinarian, and an amazing mother. Don't ever forget that. It's never too late to start living the life you were meant to live, to start being the person you always wanted to be. And for the record, I think you're pretty great too."

And with that, Lila blew her a kiss, got into her Porsche, and sped off down the rural highway. Annie stood there, emotion clogging her throat until her chest hurt. No one had ever told her that other than Cam. But there was a maternal warmth to Lila that seeped through the layers of self-defense Annie had built up over the years, layers made up of all the negative things she'd heard about herself, layers that had never been penetrated because her own mother had simply validated all those thoughts. Annie closed her eyes and let the cold breeze and whisper-soft flurries of snow hit her face as she let Lila's words replay in her mind.

CHAPTER TEN

"I'm so excited we're getting a real tree at a real farm!" Maddy yelled from the back seat as though they weren't all sitting within a foot of each other. Matt chuckled as he sped along the winding roads to his favorite tree farm on the island. Annie was sitting beside him in the front and the kids were both in the back. Adam had been thrilled when Matt had picked him up from school and he didn't have to take the bus home.

"I think everyone heard you all the way back in Toronto," Adam said, a smile in his voice.

"Well, they can smell you back in Toronto," Maddy said, giggling as she spoke.

"All right, let's keep the spirit of Christmas in this car ride, please," Annie chided. "It looks like more snow is on the way."

Maddy clapped. "Perfect Christmas tree weather!"

Everything Maddy said came out at a volume level of ten, and Matt couldn't help the smile on his face at the sound. A few minutes later he pulled the truck onto the gravel-lined driveway and then parked in front of the barn. Cedar garland was draped around the barn doors, and twinkling lights made the old place look festive. Maddy hopped out of the car, barely waiting for him to park.

"Kids these days, amiright?" Adam said, before following her out.

Matt and Annie laughed as they joined them. The wind and snow had picked up, and even though it wasn't dusk yet, the sun had disappeared, giving an extra chill to the air. "Okay, so let's walk up to where they have all the trees and pick our favorite. Then we'll bring it down here and I'll talk to Herb."

Maddy ran off in the direction he pointed and Adam followed. Matt glanced over at Annie and tried not to notice how beautiful she looked. Her cheeks were pink and her eyes were shining as she watched her kids already disagreeing about what tree to get. They could hear them from here, even though they were walking slowly. "I don't even mind how cold it is. This is one of the nicest days I've had in a long time. I think I even like the sound of their arguing because I know it's all in good fun."

"The Christmas spirit must really have a hold on you," he said, shooting her a smile.

"I think you're right, because I think I might be just as excited as Maddy at the prospect of having a real tree this year. We've never had one, and this seems like the perfect time to start a new tradition."

"Agreed. And how was lunch with my grandmother?"

"I feel like a new woman. Honestly, she's like a grandma, a wise sage, and a therapist all rolled into one. I adore her, Matt. You are so lucky to have her in your life."

"I know. She's one in a million, and she loves you and the kids." He resisted the impulse to reach out and take her hand. It would come way out of left field and he'd never do that in front of the kids because of what it implied. The longer he spent with Annie the harder it got to ignore his feelings for her. He had also been fooling himself. But after his ridiculous slip at his mother's house on Sunday, it was clear that ignoring his feelings was going to become more and more of a challenge. But he would never jeopardize their friendship by making things awkward, and the last thing he wanted was to add more stress to her life. She was here for a fresh start and he was going to stand by her, even if that meant standing on the sidelines. "Perfect. Let's see if there's a tree you can all agree on."

One hour and one seven-foot Fraser fir later, he was parking in front of Annie's house. "Okay, how about Adam and I haul this thing in and you tell us where you want it?"

"Done. I've got the tree stand you dropped off ready to go," Annie said, as they all got out of the truck.

Maddy was already racing up to the door. "Jingle is waiting for us!"

Sure enough, he spotted the cat's orange head peeking out from the sidelights. Soon the four of them were inside. Maddy had turned on the local radio station, and Christmas music filled the air. Annie hauled out bags of new Christmas tree ornaments from the hall closet. Jingle was front and center, poking his head into the bags.

"Jingle, you can't go in here, there are some glass ornaments," Annie said.

Maddy picked him up and held him like a baby.

"That cat is bigger than you, Maddy," Adam joked but made no move to hold the cat.

"He's so sweet," Maddy said, showering his orange fur with kisses. Jingle scrambled to jump free. Even he had his limits.

Annie took out some boxes of ornaments and placed them on the coffee table. "Here we go. Maddy and I picked these up last weekend. Brand new decorations for a brand new house. But I do have something special to add. I'll be right back!"

She ran out of the room, a sparkle in her eyes.

Matt picked up a box filled with glass ornaments in the shape of red trucks with Christmas trees hanging out the back. "Why don't I open these and you two can start hanging the ornaments. Adam, you can take the top of the tree and, Maddy, you can get the bottom."

"Sure," they both said, in a rare show of unity.

Annie came walking back into the room a few minutes later, holding a box to her chest. "I've got the decorations that are just too valuable to ever buy in a store."

"What are they?" Maddy asked.

Annie opened the lid and smiled. "All the ornaments you two made at school and at home. These are all my favorite," she said, her voice cracking.

They all laughed and joked at the decorations they pulled out. They were the most hideously special decorations he'd ever seen. "I didn't think you brought these," Adam said, his voice thick.

"It's not our Christmas tree until it holds our memories," Annie said, reaching out to hug him.

Adam's face went red, but Matt witnessed a softening in him, a few defenses coming down. "I like Maddy's three-eyed snowman the best," he said, his voice dripping with sarcasm.

Maddy snatched the snowman, which did indeed have three eyes, and placed him in the center of the tree. "Me too."

He and Annie laughed. "I think I'll make us some food," Annie said.

"How about I help?" Matt added, following her to the kitchen.

"Sounds good. Okay, you two, keep decorating and no arguing," Annie said with a smile as she began pulling some things out of the freezer.

"I don't mind picking up some takeout," he said, joining her at the kitchen island.

She glanced from him to the windows. "It's so cold and snowy out there, I honestly don't mind making something easy. Are you okay with shepherd's pie for dinner? I have a homemade frozen one," she said, turning on the oven while she spoke.

"Love it. Actually, I have a lot of good memories of eating that at my grandmother's house."

Annie fumbled with the plastic wrap on the pie. "Really? Well, it's definitely comfort food. We haven't had one yet this season and it's perfect on a night like tonight. Do you mind turning the fireplace on? I feel like I can't shake the chill from the wind this afternoon."

"No problem."

She placed the pie in the oven. "I was thinking of warming up some apple cider for the kids. Do you want some?"

"Sounds good. I haven't had any since last Christmas." He turned the fireplace on, while Annie lit one of the apple-scented candles on the island and the one on the kitchen table.

He helped set the table while Annie let the cider simmer. Soon, the place felt as though he was in one of those ridiculous Christmas movies his mother, sister, and grandmother watched every year. It was ridiculously perfect. Annie was. These kids were.

Except he wasn't. He was an imposter. He didn't know how he would ever get over the guilt of being here when Cam wasn't.

If he couldn't get over that, there was no way in hell he'd ever get over the guilt of his feelings for Annie. He wanted to, but he couldn't help but think that this wasn't his family. It was his best friend's family.

An hour later, they were seated enjoying lively conversation about the kids' school. He tried a bite of the shepherd's pie and was instantly brought back to his childhood. "Annie, this is incredible. I know it's been a while since I had my grandmother's, but it reminds me of hers so much."

Her eyes widened. "I'm glad. I hear your grandmother is a great cook so I'll take that as a compliment."

"I hope so. I meant it as one. Actually, she's an incredible cook but notoriously tight-lipped about her recipes. My sister still can't believe she handed you that recipe book."

Annie's mouth was full, so he was assuming that was why she didn't say anything.

"Yeah, Mom, this is delicious. Is there more?" Adam asked, even though he hadn't finished his yet.

Annie laughed. "Yup. Lots more. There are also apple turnovers in the oven for dessert. And I made extra for tomorrow morning. Nothing like a lazy, snowy Saturday morning with apple turnovers."

"This is the best day ever," Maddy said.

"Pretty good," Adam said, shoving the remaining contents of his plate in his mouth and then standing and heading over to the island to grab another helping.

"So has everyone made their Christmas list?" he asked.

Maddy nodded. "Mine's been finished for weeks. But I have another list for everything I need to buy for everyone else. I'm planning on getting a bunch of gifts for people at the Christmas Festival next weekend."

Annie smiled. "Me too. I can't wait. I guess yours is a long list?"

Maddy blushed. "Maybe. But it also depends on what ships out here. I did check with American Girl and they do ship here, so that's a relief."

"What a rip-off," Adam said as he polished off his second plate of food.

"And I'm hoping I get a moose stuffy, since we didn't get one in New Brunswick."

Matt had already planned to pick one up. "That shouldn't be too hard to find."

"And then the next weekend is the Christmas Bazaar, and Mom's volunteered to make ten dozen sugar cookies."

Matt almost dropped the dishes. He made eye contact with Annie. "Wow. That's a lot of cookies."

Annie offered him a wan smile. "Well, you know how these small schools are. The bazaars are great fundraisers, and it's also a good way to meet the other families."

He had a feeling there was more to it than that.

"I'm going to head up to my room, I've got some friends I'm talking to tonight," Adam said, taking his plate to the counter.

"Sure, buddy, thanks for helping with the tree," Matt said, giving him a slight nudge on the shoulder.

Adam shot him a grin and ran up the stairs. He seemed to be doing a lot better. Maddy was racing up the stairs too. "I'm going to call my best friend back in Toronto!"

Matt turned to Annie once he heard the bedroom doors click shut. "So, what's the deal with the cookies? You couldn't volunteer for just one dozen?"

She laughed, and he was relieved that she knew he was teasing. "No one else volunteered for sugar cookies. I also have to package them into dozens to make them look pretty to sell. But it'll be fine."

"You're worried about Maddy."

She sighed before loading the dishwasher. "Sort of. Maybe it's premature, but she always used to have friends over after school or would go to friends' houses. So far, she hasn't invited anyone or been invited. She seems happy enough, but she also hasn't really talked about any new friends."

"It's only been a few weeks, Annie."

"I'm worrying for nothing, right?"

He shrugged. "I'm not saying that either. You're her mom, your instincts are telling you something. Or maybe you just need to give it time. It's the holiday season, everyone is busy doing something."

She closed the dishwasher and leaned against the island. "You're right. So that's the reason I volunteered to make all those cookies. I thought it would be a great way to meet some of the other parents and then maybe invite a mom from Maddy's class over for coffee."

"Pretty good plan. Too bad you need to make a hundred and twenty cookies in order to have someone over for coffee."

She crossed her arms and lifted her chin. "No cookies for you."

He laughed. "Well, just so you know, I'm an excellent baker so if you need help, I'm available."

She lifted a brow, a smirk at the corner of her mouth. "I did not know this."

"I'm a man of many hidden talents." Dammit, where had that come from? Why would he have said that? All of a sudden, the mood shifted, like one of the winds off the ocean. She quickly grabbed a spray bottle and started spritzing the counter, probably wishing she could blast the cheese factor out of his line.

He cleared his throat. He needed to bring things back to neutral subjects. "So, was this week better at work?"

She paused for a moment. "It's been great. I was hoping to make some inroads with Jessica, but I don't think it's happening."

"Still?"

She finished the counters and moved on to the table with that spritz bottle that smelled like pine. "Yeah. Not exactly the warm welcome I got from everyone else. I'm sensing she's threatened by our relationship . . . I mean, friendship."

Her face went red, and he knew it didn't mean anything because the feelings here only went one way between them. She was still wearing her ring. The one he remembered Cam showing him before he proposed. This was all so hard and so impossible to make right. He couldn't be in love with a woman he could never have. "Jessica's fine. I, uh, did talk to her and made it clear that we're just friends. I don't want her getting hurt. She just doesn't make friends easily."

Annie shot him a look before putting away the spray bottle and tossing the paper towel in the garbage. "Fine. Well, everything else is going really well. Actually, it's been an even smoother transition than I'd hoped."

"How are you adjusting to working fewer hours?"

"I thought I'd have a hard time at first, but it feels right. I'm needed here. That's the season of life we're in, so I'm trying to embrace it. It does help that it's a new house and I've been busy making it feel like home, and then there's Christmas, so lots of time being spent preparing for the holidays."

"The kids are looking great."

She gave him a soft smile and it echoed in her eyes as she looked up at him. It affected him, somewhere deep inside. "That's because of you. You're making them feel like this is their home.

Never in a million years would I have expected Adam to adapt so easily. He smiles more than he frowns now. I mean, I don't want to jinx myself or anything here, but it's like a miracle."

"Well, it is the season. Speaking of, how do you feel about coming with me on Wednesday for some farm calls. I know you wanted to get some experience. The farms I'm going to are close to Confederation Bridge, so after I thought we could head over to New Brunswick to pick up a moose?"

Her brows knit together. "A moose?"

He grinned. "You know, the one Maddy mentioned."

She smiled up at him. "You're a total sucker. You don't need to drive to another province to order one from New Brunswick. Just get one online."

He crossed his arms. "I'm insulted. That would be low. Besides, it's not like it's a five-hour journey."

"Okay, fine, but only if we can stop at the Gateway Village shops before the bridge. I have a feeling there will be some good gifts to buy, and since the kids won't be with us, it'll be perfect."

He gave her a salute. "Deal."

They started walking to the mudroom. "I need to find something for Adam. But I'm just so hopeful that this is all going to work out. We've had four Christmases without Cam and none of them have gotten easier. In fact, the holidays have always been the worst time. But this year he's being social, engaging in conversation. He seems lighter, his shoulders aren't slouched over like every day is the end of the world."

"Good. I see it in him too. All we can do is continue to be there for him."

"I think he knows we are. I think he instinctively feels like you and your family will have his back and that he has a real place here. Your entire family has been so welcoming. Sunday night dinners are the perfect routine. They're a tradition that had been missing in our lives."

He didn't want to bring up last Sunday's disaster of a dinner because what was there to say without revealing how he felt? Sometimes when he thought about what Annie had been through, everything she'd had to handle on her own, he wanted to protect her, even though she didn't need it. She was so put together, so stoic, but he knew she had her moments. Hell, he still had his moments when he thought of his best friend being gone. "It feels right, having all of you back here. Maybe the timing is right, finally. I think if you had done this right away, it wouldn't have been good. I want you to know we think of all of you as family as well."

"Thank you. We think of you the same way."

He held her gaze and, for once in his life, was at a loss for words. "Okay, so I'll get going and, uh, see all of you Sunday night for dinner."

She nodded, her hand on the doorknob. It was like she was suddenly awkward as well. He hoped it wasn't him, like she was detecting his feelings for her. "Thanks again for everything, today, Matt."

They were standing in the small mudroom, the porch light glowing through the window. The space felt intimate and filled with unspoken truths. Things he'd never reveal. Because the woman standing in front of him was the love of his life, he knew that, deep in his soul. "My pleasure. Good night, Annie."

CHAPTER ELEVEN

"I still cannot believe you are traveling to another province to buy a moose stuffy."

Matt shot Annie a lopsided grin before turning his attention back to the road. She tried to ignore the little skip her heart did at the sight of his smile. It was something she was getting used to, now that they'd been in Prince Edward Island for three weeks. Even though she'd known they would see each other a lot because of work, she had never expected she see him almost every day.

It was starting to feel like home. Their house, the island, Matt's family . . . Matt. He was becoming the person she relied on, to talk to, laugh with, confide in. He had stepped into their family effortlessly and now that he was here, she couldn't imagine not doing life with him. But that also made her wary. He was stirring up feelings and emotions she didn't know what to do with. She didn't want to be noticing how handsome he was, she didn't want to get a little jolt of electricity when he smiled at her, or feel all giddy when they shared a laugh. They were friends.

Good friends. And she needed to remind herself of that because what they had was too special to risk. There was no way she wanted him to detect anything other than friend vibes from her because she didn't want him to feel awkward.

She turned her attention to the view outside, remembering how it already seemed like ages ago that she'd driven across this bridge with an angry teenager who'd been hell-bent on leaving.

"Maddy is pretty convincing, not that she asked for this or anything. But that tragic story about trying to collect an animal stuffy from every province, but missing out on a moose from New Brunswick was pretty sad."

Annie rolled her eyes but couldn't help but smile. "You are easy prey, Matt. A total sap. We just didn't find a roadside stop that had any moose stuffies left, but I promised her that we'd get one. I had no idea you'd actually be driving to New Brunswick to get one."

"It's only an hour from here and since our last farm call was so close to the bridge, I thought it was perfect. All the other stuffies were picked up in the provinces you drove through, I'm not going to cop out and just order one from Amazon. That's not authentic. You even got Christmas shopping done at the village. Besides, we'll be back in time to pick the kids up from school."

Annie ignored the stab of whatever it was that hit her. It was an innocuous statement. It was factual. They had to pick up the kids from school. But he made it sound like they were their kids. That it was a given. That they were their responsibility. She liked that, very much in some ways. Her kids had been just her responsibility for so long now that she'd forgotten the comfort that came from having someone else care about them. She could never rely on her sister to help with them. But coming from Matt it was so different. Matt was so different. Their relationship was changing and she wasn't sure what to do with that.

She stared out the windshield, noticing now how the snow and wind had picked up. "I checked the weather this morning and I don't think they were calling for much accumulation."

He gave a shrug. "They're usually wrong. But I'm sure this will pass. We're not that far from home anyway. A little bit of snow is no big deal, we're used to it. We'll get the moose and then turn right around."

She nodded, her eyes on the swirling snow as it seemed to blanket over the harsh waves of the Atlantic. "Does this bridge ever close?"

"Not that often. Not once last year, I think. Don't worry. It's not going to close. This is a nothing storm. I mean, maybe for you Torontonians this is a big deal, but we're made of tougher stuff out here."

She laughed. "Yeah, well, Adam was questioning why we'd move somewhere that has an even worse winter than ours."

"Different, not worse. Ours is way more scenic. If you'd like, I can go into all the reasons the Atlantic has a better winter season."

She kept her eyes peeled on the endless snow that seemed to pour out of the sky and tried to relax and keep up with his banter. "Ugh. No thanks. As much as I appreciate the offer, I'll be the judge of the kind of winters you have out here. But the fact that this went from flurries to blizzard in a matter of minutes, I'm thinking I'm right."

"Blizzard? Where's the blizzard? We haven't fishtailed once."

Annie turned to him slowly. "You judge whether or not you're in a blizzard by whether or not your truck fishtails?"

He grinned, looking perfectly at ease driving over the Atlantic on a two-lane bridge during what most certainly was beginning to look like a blizzard. "No, that's just the fun part. But I'm telling you this isn't a blizzard. We'll be turning around and crossing back to the island within the hour. Trust me."

She let out a sigh, trying to relax the knot forming in her stomach. "I do, Matt."

* * *

Half an hour later, in the parking lot of a souvenir store, moose purchased, Matt cursed under his breath and tossed his phone on the seat. "So, uh, it appears the bridge is closed."

Panic erupted inside Annie's chest as she slowly turned to look at him. "You have got to be kidding me."

He shifted in the driver's seat to look at her. "It, uh, is closed for the night, but listen, no need to panic. We can find a place to stay and head home as soon as it's open in the morning."

"My kids! Are buses running? Are they able to get home from school?"

His eyes were serious and he spoke in a really slow manner. "I'm going to call Kate and she can pick them up and stay with them. It's *fine*. This will all be okay."

She frowned at the slow-motion speak. "Uh, last time you told me that, you also said that the bridge doesn't close."

"Trust me. It's all going to be okay."

"I did trust you and that's why we're still on this side of the bridge!"

"Okay, well, maybe if you didn't have to go into each and every shop at the village, we would have been finished sooner."

She sucked in a breath. "What! I'm not the one who had to eat samples of every type of local cheese. You *live* here! You've eaten those cheeses a thousand times!"

"Cleary, it won't serve anyone if we sit here and blame each other. I'm sorry for making this sound like it's your fault. But also, I shoved those pieces of cheese in my mouth and kept walking. You're the one who got sucked into talking to the sample lady."

"That's not really an apology, is it? Also, at least I have manners and made an effort to speak to her and listen about the variety of cheeses, instead of grabbing cheese like a child and running away."

"I'm going to refrain from this petty arguing and call Kate about the kids." Once he started speaking with his sister, she shot him one last exasperated look and then checked her email and was relieved that the schools were still open and that the students were getting bused home early.

As soon as he finished speaking, she turned to him to let him know what she'd found out.

"Okay, buses are running but kids are being sent home early. They are fine on their own technically, but I'd feel so much better if your sister was there. Especially if there's a power outage or something tonight."

He put his phone down. "She's already on her way and more than happy to stay with them."

Annie let out a sigh. "Wow. Okay, that's amazing. Way less stressful than I thought it would be. I'm going to text her as soon as we find a place to stay and thank her. Oh, I'll also text the kids and contact the school to let them know. I put your entire family on the emergency contact list so this should be fine. I can't even express what a relief that is."

"I told you when you moved here, you've got family. We won't let you down. We all love those kids. And you. As in the collective. Love. Anyway, let's find a place to stay before we're really in trouble."

She picked up her phone, desperate to move on from the awkward tension at the mention of love. "I don't suppose there are any really great recommendations in the area?"

He let out a gruff laugh as he searched his phone, and she did the same. "Well, no five-star places . . . wait a minute. Apparently, there is a five-star B&B about five minutes from here. It has ocean views, a historic home, award-winning food . . . want to try it out?"

She forced a smile. "I don't think we really have a choice."

Matt pulled the truck out of the parking lot, and the accumulation of snow in such a short time was visible as they traveled along the empty road. The yellow lane dividers weren't visible anymore and it was impossible to see more than a few feet in front of them. "This place should be just up ahead. Not more than a minute or two."

They drove in silence until a white fence with twinkling lights and cedar roping became visible. The long circular drive welcomed them with lit lampposts. "Omigosh, this looks just like this amazing B&B we once stayed at a few hours outside Toronto! It was called the Christmas House and there was the sweetest lady who ran it. This has to be a good sign, Matt."

He pulled up in front of the house. "See? Didn't I tell you this would be fine? I'll park here until they confirm they have some availability," Matt said, before opening his door.

She joined him outside, shielding her eyes against the onslaught of snow.

Maybe things would be okay. Her kids were old enough to not panic without her being home. She trusted Matt's sister. Maybe this was all happening so that she could see she really did have people here she could lean on.

Maybe Matt was right and everything was going to be just fine.

CHAPTER TWELVE

Matt held open the front door open while Annie walked in. He hoped to hell she was right and that there was a vacancy. They stepped into the warm entryway and were greeted by an elderly man with a white moustache and sparkling eyes. Annie was commenting on how gorgeous everything was, but he was more interested in securing accommodations for the night. He hadn't wanted to let his worry show, but according to the latest weather updates, the storm that was blowing through was going to be a big one. But if this place came through, at least it would be luxurious and might make up for the having to spend the night away from her kids.

"Good evening, folks. How can I help you?"

Matt cleared his throat. "We're looking for two rooms for the night."

The man shook his head. "I'm sorry, but we're all booked. I've got nothing."

Matt didn't have to turn to Annie to already know the *I told you so* he'd be facing. "Is there another place nearby that you'd recommend?"

The man tapped the tip of his pen against the large, leather-bound appointment book. "Well, I'm afraid the only place that might have a vacancy would be Buck's Cottages. It's only about a five-minute drive from here. Keep going east on this same road."

"Um, okay, thanks. We'll get going right away," Annie said, her voice tinged with panic.

"Thanks," Matt echoed before turning to Annie, who was already marching out the door.

He joined her outside, the snow slapping him in the face promptly. He had a feeling she might be wanting to do the same for getting them into this predicament. "Hop in. We'll get a place, not to worry."

"Worried isn't exactly the word I'd use," Annie said when they were both buckled in.

He turned the wipers to the highest setting as they drove out of the circular driveway and back onto the road. "I'm not sure I want to know the right word. But I'll preempt however you might want to tell me off—this is totally my fault. I should have paid attention to the weather before we left the island. So, I'm sorry. But I do know that the kids will be fine because my sister is completely trustworthy."

She let out a long sigh. "I can't be mad at you. How can I? We're here because you're buying a moose for my daughter. Of course I trust Kate and I know . . . on a rational level that the kids will be fine. I think I've been operating on an irrational level a little too long now. That's my problem," she said with a rueful laugh.

He slowed down a little as the truck fishtailed slightly. He braced himself for what was next.

She let out a smug little noise that might have irritated him if it had been anyone else, but since it was Annie, he found himself enjoying it. "So, this is officially a blizzard?"

"My previous statement doesn't count because we're in a different province," he said, his eyes on the road and his speed slow so there would be no more fishtailing.

"Uh huh," she said, sounding almost happy.

"Maybe you should text the kids," he said, trying to distract her.

"Already did, and they seem thrilled by the idea of me not coming home tonight. I've learned not to take things personally from kids," she said, sounding less stressed and more like her usual self. In fact, she'd been sounding more and more like the woman he remembered, and that filled him with gratitude. He'd only ever wanted her happiness and the kids'. His own personal feelings and attraction for her could be kept under wraps.

A wooden sign, mostly covered with snow, dangling off a leaning post, told him they'd reached Buck's Cottages. There was a small one-story cabin with a blinking vacancy light in the front window. Matt followed the winding drive. Snow from the towering balsams blew occasionally across the windshield. Judging by Annie's silence, dread had trickled in from their prospective accommodation rental. "I'm sure this place will be great," he said, parking the truck and turning to look at her.

She gave him a wobbly smile. "I'm sure."

Five minutes later, he wasn't so sure. They were standing in the "lobby" of a one-bedroom log cabin. The owner, Buck, was sitting on a lawn chair behind a folding table. There was a string of blinking, multicolored lights strung on the front of the table. A far cry from the last establishment. "The cabin *does* have heat, right?"

Buck puffed his already broad chest and snapped his suspenders. Buck looked exactly how Matt had pictured him to look. He was friendly, though. "Well, of course it does, son. There is also a wood-burning fireplace, so youse folks can warm up nice and toasty. And you won't find a cleaner cabin in the province. We pride ourselves on that."

"Okay, great, we'll take it," Matt said, needing to move this conversation along before Annie changed her mind about staying here.

"All right. So, just sign here. I've got a nice cabin by the water for you and the missus."

Matt was about to say something, but Annie beat him to it. "Great. We appreciate that."

Matt handed Buck his credit card, silent. Annie still wore her wedding rings. That's why Buck had assumed. She hadn't corrected him, but maybe she just didn't feel like answering a bunch of questions. Matt didn't know why it felt odd. Of course she was wearing her wedding rings still. She still loved Cam. She had never talked about remarrying. He'd never once heard about her going on a date or being interested in anyone. This should not come as a surprise to him or bother him. But it did. Kind of.

"Okay, folks, so you'll want to keep driving toward the ocean and then make a left where you see the road split off in two. You keep driving toward the water. You'll go past a little shack. Don't worry, that's not your cabin. Keep going, up a hill, down a hill, and then hang a right. Your cabin will be right there. Mind the road, you don't want to end up in the water!" he said with a booming laugh.

Matt glanced over at Annie, who clearly didn't find any humor in what Buck was saying. It was time for them to leave. "Thanks for the tip, Buck. Have a good night."

Buck waved them off. Matt held the door open for Annie and she shot him daggers as she passed through. The minute the door closed outside she stopped. "What is this place and did you even understand those directions?"

He squinted against the snow that was coming down on a diagonal thanks to the wind. "His directions were very clear. We should be there in five minutes."

"Five minutes? It sounds like we're going on a *Lord of the Rings* type of journey."

He barked out a laugh. "Let's go before the road completely disappears."

"Right. Don't want to end up in the freezing ocean," she said, hopping into the passenger side of the truck.

A few minutes later, Matt spotted the "shack," which looked as though it was only good for kindling at this point, and then turned right. "See, there's our cabin, yonder."

Annie rolled her eyes at his humor but he didn't miss the curl of her lips as she fought her smile. "Fine, this is impressive that you managed to find the cabin with those directions."

"Honey, you haven't seen impressive."

Hell. He hopped out of the truck, his ears burning listening to his own stupidity. That was a line he'd use on anyone but Annie. He needed to get his head in the game and remember that though she was a beautiful woman and he loved everything about her . . . including her, he was not allowed to let his thoughts go there. And he was not allowed to be charming, even though it seemed ingrained in him.

He felt a tap on his shoulder. Annie was standing there, squinting against the snow as she stared up at him. "What was that line? I'm not Jessica."

He let out a resigned sigh. "No, you're not. Clearly. Sometimes old habits die hard. These charming lines fall out of my mouth and it's beyond my control."

She burst out laughing. He hid his grin and opened the back door of the truck. "I'm grabbing my backpack; do you want yours?"

"Sure. Thanks."

They made their way up to the small cabin and he unlocked the door and held it open so Annie could go through. They stood in the doorway and he flicked on the light switch. "Well, not bad," he said, his gaze roaming the studio-style cabin. There was a giant fieldstone type of fireplace with a large couch in front of it and a coffee table and two end tables. A kitchenette with a small fridge and warming plate and coffee maker and sink. One door, which he assumed led to a bathroom. And then one giant bed tucked in the corner of the room. "I'll take the couch," he said, dumping their bags on the ground.

"No, no, that's not fair. I'll take the couch, I'm smaller. Your legs will probably dangle off the sides," she said, her gaze darting around the room.

"I'm taking the couch, Annie. No arguing."

She took off her jacket and then put it right back on with a shiver. "We'll see. It's freezing in here."

"Yeah, it is. Why don't I get a fire going? There's a nice stack of logs by the fireplace and there's more on the porch. That'll warm the place up."

"Sure. Are you hungry?"

"Starved."

"I guess there's no Uber Eats out here?"

He grinned. "I think we both know the answer to that."

She let out a dramatic sigh. "I guess that means we're digging into the stash of Christmas gifts we bought. Good thing I bought all that cheese!"

CHAPTER THIRTEEN

Half an hour later, Annie was arranging their food assortment on paper plates while Matt was dealing with the fire. She was glad they both had their work backpacks with them, filled with a change of clothes and toiletries.

There was a change in the vibe somehow, and she was desperate to get things back to normal. "Is this water safe to drink?" she asked, looking at sink.

"Eh, I'm sure one night won't kill us."

"Great. I'll be drinking the raspberry cordial I bought."

He joined her in the kitchenette and suddenly the open space didn't feel so open. She was very aware of him. His flannel shirt brushed against her as he reached for a bottle of the Anne-branded bright red beverages. He'd rolled up his sleeves when he was starting the fire and she found herself noticing his forearms, the way they were roped with muscle, the smattering of dark hair. "This is such a tourist gimmick; I can't believe you fell for it."

She quickly drew her gaze from his arms to his eyes, which wasn't much better because up close his eyes were very green, filled with a sparkle because he was baiting her. Things were much less awkward when they were just best friends on the phone. "I think you'll be asking me for some in no time. And actually, these were for Maddy, for Christmas. We'll have to stop and get more on our way back."

"Sure. And too bad these aren't spiked with whatever Diana Barry drank."

She held up her finger, pleased she could correct him. "Actually, Diana got drunk on Marilla's currant wine by mistake. So that's not happening . . . although . . . I did happen to pick up a bottle of local potato vodka . . ."

"I regret everything I said about your shopping trip and about Anne. I have a feeling vodka and raspberry cordial are going to be a hit. I'll head out to the truck to get the vodka and meet you on the couch," he said.

She let out a laugh. "I'll try not to take it personally that the mention of vodka is the happiest I've seen you tonight."

He turned to her, and it was as though everything stopped. Her whirlwind thoughts and worries, the wind howling outside, the sound of the fire crackling. The world stopped. He was standing close to her and it was as though the intimacy of sharing a cabin with him suddenly hit her. It was just the two of them with these feelings she didn't know what to do with. And she felt something from him. Something that told her she wasn't alone in this hazy place of emotion.

For a pulsing moment, she imagined what it would feel like if she took that last step into him and he reached out and held her and then kissed her. She had no idea. What they could be like. He held her gaze and she stared into his eyes, taking in the lighter flecks of green in them, the emotion in them, and she almost thought he wasn't going to reply, because the only words she had seemed stuck in her heart, not ready to be voiced yet. She held her breath. "You have no idea. And for the record, I'd sit in this place with you without a drink or food or electricity. Anytime, Annie."

And then he walked out. When the door closed behind him, she clutched the counter. Her heart was racing and she just replayed that moment again in her mind, when the sound of his deliciously deep voice was still clear. She shut her eyes and told herself to get a grip on reality. And the reality was that Matt was a dear friend. A best friend. Family.

A minute later the door opened again, a flurry of snow and wind coming in with it. "It's a disaster out there. I could barely see the truck," Matt said, stomping his feet on the front rug.

"I guess it's a good thing we have food and drinks," she said, determined to sound normal as she met him by the couch. This was normal. How many times when she was in Toronto and he was in PEI did they have a drink and food over the phone? But it wasn't normal because now they were in the same room. She hadn't let herself think of him in any other way than her best friend. Pushing aside those thoughts, she placed the plate of food on the table.

A few minutes later they were sitting side by side in front of their food sampler while he mixed the Anne drinks in plastic cups. He handed her a glass and held his in the other hand, raising it. "Here's to a warm cabin, raspberry cordial, and vodka."

She clinked her cup against his before taking a sip. "I'll drink to that."

A burst of flavor hit her mouth and they both slowly turned to look at each other. "This is not bad," he said, taking another sip.

"Uh, it might be the best discovery in this entire shopping trip," she said before taking another sip, almost giddy with their discovery. Surely, vodka would help with these sudden jitters she had sitting next to him. It probably didn't help that he seemed to take up the entire couch and every now and then his arm or leg would brush against hers.

She leaned forward and grabbed the cheese plate, placing it on the couch between them, pleased to be erecting a physical barrier between them. "Okay, I think I need food before I drink any more of that. Eat up. This is all of it. Oh, and of course, I have the PEI potato chips and popcorn on the counter. I maybe have also purchased a bunch of caramel Anne chocolates."

His eyes widened and then narrowed in on the food left on the counter. "I'm actually thrilled for all this tourist food. But I didn't know you bought chocolate," he said, standing and marching over to the kitchen.

"Help yourself, but while you're up, bring the chips over here."

"Got it. This is shaping out to be a pretty good spread," he said a moment later as he joined her back on the couch with the treats.

"Now, I could tell you what all these are, but you might be more qualified since you've sampled them all."

He gave her a grin that warmed her insides faster than the fireplace and vodka combined. He pointed to one corner on the plate. "I recommend the Avonlea cheddar. But I didn't sample any of these crackers, so that'll put an entirely different spin on them. You can go ahead and start with the cheese; I'll be cracking open this box of chocolates." He lifted the lid, unceremoniously tossing the smiling Anne-branded box on the table. Before he picked a chocolate, he held the box in her direction.

She shook her head. "No thanks. I'll be an adult and eat the cheese first."

He shrugged and put two chocolates in his mouth. "Your loss. And that's the whole point of being an adult—you don't have to eat dinner first. You've been adulting all wrong. Also, I bet these go really well with Anne's vodka drink."

She choked on her drink and looked at the image of Anne with braids, smiling on the front of the glass bottle. "I don't think that's what they intended when they made this adorable bottle." She helped herself to some of the cheese and crackers.

"Maybe not, but a delicious new drink for sure," he said before trying some cheese.

"Agreed."

"Did you text the kids?"

She nodded. "And your sister. They are having a great time and Maddy told me not to hurry home. Oh, and Jingle likes pizza."

He laughed and the sound made her warm and flustered . . . or was it the vodka? Or both. She didn't care because right now she was feeling . . . free and happy and safe. She was feeling like maybe everything could be okay. Maybe the worst was over. She took another sip of the Anne cocktail. "That's great. I guess they figured there'd be no way we'd let Jingle eat pizza. When the vets are away . . ."

He took another drink. "Yeah. Have you heard from your sister lately?"

She reached for her drink and finished it off. "I think I'll need a refill before I answer."

"You and me both." He proceeded to fix their second round before shoving the box of chocolates in her direction. "Sorry for bringing her up."

She grabbed a chocolate and then chased it down with Anne's drink, belatedly realizing this might not have been her most attractive look. But then again, as she glanced at her short nails, she didn't have too many different looks going for her at the moment that weren't practical mom looks. "No, it's fine. I actually haven't heard from her since . . . our little argument over Adam."

He frowned. "This potato vodka is hitting me really hard because I thought you said she hasn't spoken or texted you in over twenty-four hours? How is that possible?"

She let out a laugh, before taking a sip of her drink. "We haven't spoken since then."

"What the hell?"

The anger in his voice reminded her why she loved telling him things. She didn't have to explain, she didn't have to justify her point of view; he saw Valerie for what she was. "Yeah."

He added vodka and more raspberry cordial to both their glasses. "Maybe I should have left out the cordial."

She took a long drink. "The cordial makes it civilized."

"What a selfish, manipulative thing for her to do and not take ownership of. Talk about taking advantage of a kid's insecurities," he said, the harshness in his voice actually comforting her.

"Agreed. He felt awful. Embarrassed. And we really didn't need another thing between us. When I confronted her on it, she tried to turn it all around. Anyway, long story short, she did what she always does when she's called on her bad behavior—she lies low. So she's gone from serial dialing and texting me to being completely MIA. But that's fine. Really, the times she decides not to talk to me for weeks on end are the best times in our relationship."

He put his arm on the back of the couch, turning to her. It was a casual movement, very natural, but one that made his physical presence almost unbearable to ignore. If she had one more refill of vodka, she might even imagine what it would feel like to lean into him. "I can see why. Maybe now that you're living here, you'll get a break from her."

She stared into her cup so she wouldn't get sucked into the warmth emanating from his eyes. This close up, it was becoming impossible for her to convince herself she didn't think of him as more than just a good friend. A best friend. It was this drink. It was blurring lines. "I hope so. It was one of the perks of coming out here, for sure. My hope is to maintain a relationship, and I'm hoping distance will help."

"Me too. For your sake."

She finished off the rest of her drink and they sat in silence, the wind howling and the fire crackling away. Normally, their silence would have been pleasant and relaxed. Maybe it was for Matt. But for her, everything felt alive. The silence was alive with so many unspoken feelings.

So many unprocessed emotions for him. Things she tried to deny for so long. They all flashed in front of her as she stared at the fire, like a PowerPoint of her relationship with him. How had she been in denial for so long? He was the first one she called when she needed a true friend to talk to. His was the only voice that made her heart pound, his laugh the only one that made her heart squeeze. He was the only person in the world she trusted with her heart and with her kids. And all it had taken for her to realize this was a bottle of raspberry cordial and three shots of vodka. And now that she was actually aware of all this, what did she do with all these feelings?

She stood up abruptly, needing to distract herself. "I'm going to put this cheese in the fridge before it melts. Unless you want more?"

His brows shot up. "Uh, nope. I'm good. We can keep the chocolate out, though. Maybe while you're doing that, I'll throw another log on the fire."

"Sure, sure," she said, cringing at the high-pitched tone to her voice as she collected the plate of cheese. She needed distance from him. Maybe it was time for bed. Glancing at the clock, she saw it was only eight. But it had been a long day.

"Wanna watch a movie?"

She slammed the little fridge door shut. "A movie?"

He nodded, poking the fire. "Yeah, while we still have Wi-Fi. I have my laptop."

She couldn't say no without looking like something was up. But a movie meant two more hours of sitting side by side, and if she kept drinking vodka and cordial she'd pass out or say something she might regret. Maybe she could dissuade him with movie suggestions she knew he wouldn't like. "*Anne of Green Gables?*"

He made a choking sound. "Uh, sure."

She frowned, walking back over to the couch. "Really?"

He shoved his hands in the front pockets of his jeans. His features were illuminated by the glow of the fire, which seemed to accentuate the hard lines of his jaw, the stubble that lined it. The fit of his flannel shirt hugged his broad shoulders and strong biceps—all things she had always known existed, but for some reason she could not stop looking at now. Or the jeans. Why did he have to own jeans that were all worn in and fitting like he was some kind of model for a Ford truck driving on back roads? "Yeah. I'll get *Anne of Green Gables* set up."

She felt guilty. She hadn't expected him to say yes. He was actually going to watch that movie just because she'd asked? He was . . . he was one of the good ones. She tucked a strand of hair behind her eat. "No, no, let's watch something we both want to watch."

The look of relief that flashed across his face only endeared him to her more. "*Die Hard?*"

Well, that solved that. "Not so much. *It's a Wonderful Life?*"

He tilted his head. "Deal."

"Crisis averted. I thought our friendship was going to end over movie differences," she said with a laugh.

He turned away, grabbing his laptop from his bag and then joining her. "Yeah," he said, his voice sounding strained.

A few minutes later they were sitting side by side, their feet propped on the coffee table, chocolate and popcorn between them, George Banks in front of them.

He lifted the bottle of vodka. "Do you want some more spiked cordial?"

She was about to shake her head and then stopped herself. This was the most fun she'd had in years. Maybe the first night without kids around in years. She was in a cabin in the middle of nowhere with her best friend. It was time. She lifted her glass. "Fill 'er up."

He let out a noise of approval and filled up both their glasses, but didn't add the cordial to his. "If I remember correctly, you could pound these back at the school pub like a pro."

"Great. That's a flattering memory from university. Me getting drunk at the bar?"

He let out a soft laugh, one that was filled with memories and affection. It was a laugh that made her smile and want to bask in the warmth he offered. He was leaning forward, his forearms on his thighs, and tilted his head to look at her. His eyes were filled with something that made it impossible to breathe, caught somewhere between the present and the past and everything that could be. "I have so many memories of you. So many. Including the one when we first met, at the pub, before you knew Cam. But I don't want to go back there, because it takes me to a place where I was immature and insecure. But I remember every smile and every laugh and every study session where the three of us were drinking coffee and pulling all-nighters."

She blinked back tears at the clear image of those days. "Sometimes it feels like yesterday and sometimes it feels like I don't even know all of us from back then."

He clenched his jaw and then took a drink, keeping his head down. "It should be Cam here. I'm sorry, Annie."

Tears clogged her throat and she took a long drink as well, knowing she'd regret that tomorrow. But she wouldn't regret this, she wouldn't regret this closeness. She wouldn't regret reaching out to touch his arm, as best friends did to comfort one another. "He loved you like a brother. And I'll never be able to express how much it's meant to me to know that you're here for me. For all of us."

He stood abruptly and she dropped her hand. He rubbed the back of his neck as he crossed the room to the kitchen. She felt awkward suddenly, like maybe she shouldn't have reached out to touch him. "I'll always be here for you. I value our friendship very much. And don't underestimate what you've done for me. We grieved him together. You let me into your family, close to Cam's kids. You've trusted me with them, right from day one and, uh, I'll never forget that."

She held his gaze, and it was as though something had shifted. Something had changed between them. "I've always trusted you."

He took another sip of his drink. "Did you ever . . . start seeing anyone back in Toronto? Did you ever consider moving on?"

She looked into her cup for a moment. This was one area of their lives they hadn't discussed as friends. He'd always had someone in university, there had always been a gorgeous girl with him on the weekends, and she assumed that was just the way he still was. And how did she answer that question when she didn't know the answer to moving on? She ran a sweaty palm down the front of her jeans. "I don't think there was anyone I was ever really interested in. The last couple of years have been about keeping my head above water, I guess."

"So, you mean to tell me no minivan-driving soccer dad divorcé has been interested in you?"

Her mouth dropped open. She was slightly relieved that he'd broken the tension with his trademark teasing. "Oh, I see, the gorgeous blonde is your choice, but me, it's the minivan-driving soccer dad?"

"What gorgeous blonde?"

She rolled her eyes. "Jessica."

"If I had known how this was all going to turn out then, Jessica would never have happened. No one would have happened."

The wind rattled against the windows, the fireplace crackled and popped, and all she could hear was the pounding of her heart as his words sunk in. As all the teasing vanished from his eyes and he stood there, alone and strong and so handsome that she wished he was hers. He'd always been alone, emotionally. He'd had women around him all the time, but no one ever got close to Matt. But he had let Annie in, from time to time. He let her into this side of him. He let her into those feelings and thoughts that simmered below the surface, behind the gorgeous face.

She shot him a smile and glanced at the laptop open on the coffee table. She needed to do something to break up this tension or wherever it was this conversation was headed, because she didn't trust herself. She didn't trust herself with the amount of vodka in her system that she wasn't just imagining something changing between them. What if he'd had too much vodka and he was saying things he'd regret tomorrow morning? She couldn't do anything that would jeopardize their friendship. The kids counted on him too much. So did she.

He cleared his throat and walked over to the couch, sitting with a bit of space between them. "You're right. It's getting late."

He started up the movie in silence and she put her empty drink on the coffee table. "I think I'm done with Anne's drink."

He leaned back into the cushions and stretched his legs out, propping his feet on the coffee table. "Yeah. I think we might regret this in the morning."

She smiled, feeling relieved that they were going back to their usual friendly conversation. Relieved and the tiniest bit disappointed. But it was safer this way.

After a few minutes of movie watching in silence, she found herself huddling further into the cushions, her eyelids feeling heavy.

"You warm enough?"

Matt's voice was low and husky and more comforting than the fire during the blizzard. She nodded, slowly succumbing to the exhaustion of the day. She was vaguely aware, as she drifted off, of leaning her head on Matt's shoulder, and her last thoughts as she fell into a deep sleep, as he put his arm around her, was that she couldn't remember the last time she'd felt this safe, this happy.

CHAPTER FOURTEEN

Matt stared at the ceiling of Buck's cottage and wondered when his life had become this torturous. He was currently lying on his back, on a couch that was way too small for a grown man, with Annie sandwiched by his side and one of her legs locking him into place. Normally, this might be some kind of heaven, but considering she'd made it very clear to him last night that they were in the friend zone, this was torture.

It was exceptionally cruel torture because she was perfect. Everything about her. Her laugh, her smile. The curves pressed against him. Almost as perfect as the gold and diamond wedding rings on her finger, which were being showcased on the hand she had on his chest. If he believed in the universe nonsense, he'd be seeing this as a sign that it meant hands off.

He didn't need signs. He just needed Annie referring to their friendship. As for the fact that at some point during the night, her snuggling into him had become the two of them reclined and her holding onto him for dear life, he attributed to her trust in him. As a friend.

She stiffened against him and he knew she must be waking up. "Matt?"

"Morning."

She scrambled to sit up, kicking him in the process. "What time is it? Sorry, was I crushing you?"

"I'll live, and it's seven."

She sat cross-legged on the other end of the couch, smoothing out her hair, her eyes kind of wild before she snatched up her phone off the coffee table. "No calls. I'm going to text the kids and see how their night was."

"They are probably sleeping," he said, sitting up.

She put her phone down with a frown. "You're right. Do you think it's safe to go back?"

"I can check if the bridge is open," he said, picking up his phone.

She quickly stood, grabbing things and tidying up as though they were being evacuated imminently. "Okay, that's good. Ugh. I just realized we don't have coffee."

"Okay, bridge should be open by eight."

She let out a huge sigh. "Great. Perfect. I'll just use the bathroom and, um, pack up this stuff and then it'll for sure be almost eight."

"Uh, sure," he said, watching her move like her hair was on fire before she ran to the bathroom and shut the door.

What the hell was even happening? They were awkward and distant. He ran his hands through his hair and decided he needed fresh air. Maybe he'd go in search of coffee. He was pretty sure if he remembered correctly there was a Tim Hortons a few minutes from Buck's. He left Annie a note that he was running an errand, then got his jacket and boots on.

He opened the door and was greeted by a winter wonderland. He took a deep breath, hoping it would fill him with some much-needed clarity; instead, the dull, nagging start of a headache brought on by that damned cordial-vodka drink which had seemed so clever only eight hours ago was now mocking him. He trudged through the snow and pulled out the scraper and began the tedious process of cleaning off his truck. A few minutes later he was headed down the snow-covered road that led to the main roads.

He didn't even want to acknowledge that the real reason he was out here was because he knew Annie loved her morning coffee and he wanted to surprise her and make her happy. Because whatever it was, something had her rattled this morning and he didn't want that. Last night had been the strangest thing. And it had been nothing like any other night he'd spent with a woman. They had talked. They had laughed. They drank. And they slept. Fully clothed.

Twenty minutes later, he opened the cabin door, holding a cardboard tray of coffee and a bag filled with bagels and muffins.

Annie looked as though she'd slept a full night. Her skin was glowing, hair brushed and glossy, falling gently over her shoulders. Her plaid shirt was ticked in the front of her dark skinny jeans and she looked like the best thing he'd ever woken up to. "Hey! Omigosh, I can't believe you got us coffee."

He stomped his feet on the rug and held out the tray. "No worries. I scoped out the roads, the main ones are clear, so as soon as we have our coffee we can head out."

She took her coffee and snapped the lid open. She closed her eyes as she took the first sip. "That is so good. Omigosh. I will forever be indebted to you."

He forced a smile and put the tray and bag down on the coffee table. "As if," he said, as he pulled his own coffee.

She sat down on the couch, crossing one leg over the other. "Seriously. I don't think coffee has ever tasted so good."

"I got some bagels and muffins too if you're hungry," he said, pulling out a bagel for himself.

"No thanks. Maybe on the ride back, though."

His gaze scanned the room. "Wow, you already packed everything up?"

She nodded. "And spoke to the kids and Kate. Apparently, they all had a great night and are now making French toast."

He grinned. "I'm glad. It's probably good for them to have a night without you too and get used to my family . . . not that I know anything about kids."

She paused, her coffee cup halfway to her mouth. "That's not true at all. You know my kids very well. And you're absolutely right, I think last night did them good. I know it did for me. For so long I've been panicked about leaving them. Well, the worst didn't happen. The world is still here. We're all still here."

His stomach tightened at the emotion in her voice, and he was again reminded of how strong she was. So strong that on a daily basis he forgot about what she'd been through, but every now and then he saw it when she accidentally let her fears slip through. The image of her holding onto him last night hit him. She trusted him. She may not be in love with him, but she trusted him. He was just going to have to decide if that was good enough, or if it was time to tell Annie how he really felt about her.

Her phone vibrated on the table, the sound jarring against the silence. Valerie's picture lit her screen, but Matt was watching Annie's expression. It was like watching the sky go from clear blue to stormy in a matter of seconds. Annie just stared at the phone, her posture going from relaxed, with her feet on the coffee table, to upright, at attention. "I'm not going to answer it," she said out loud, even though it sounded like that statement was meant for herself.

"Then don't answer it," he said, trying to sound nonchalant. Because he didn't want her to answer it. He thought her sister was actually a very destructive, selfish person, especially after what Annie had revealed last night.

She nodded and sat back, taking a sip of coffee. When the vibrating stopped, she took a deep breath. Except it started again.

"Wow, she's, uh, pretty pushy."

Annie drummed her fingers against her leg, holding her coffee with the other hand. "I might answer it. She might not stop calling. Omigosh, I have to answer it because if I don't, then she'll call Adam and who knows what she'll say."

Matt watched her silently as she snatched up the phone like a person being held at gunpoint.

"Hey, Val, what's up?"

He tried not to cringe at the sound of her voice. It was painful to listen to and watch. Her face was devoid of all joy, and that tension was back. "Oh, that's great. Yeah, no, remember I said Penelope can't be the vet mascot."

He choked on his bagel and she put a finger to her lips. This was just insane. He placed his own feet up on the coffee table and continued to eat while listening to the conversation.

". . . No, the bridge was closed. Matt and I had to spend the night in New Brunswick . . . What? No, I know that. Listen, Val,

I need to get going, the bridge opens soon . . . right, well, yes, Penelope is very charming . . . hmmm . . . yes, I do remember the time I had mono, yeah, no, I didn't change. I'm still the same person. Okay, well, gotta run. See you later."

By the time she ended the call, Matt was ready to revisit the Anne drink with vodka. For both of them. Annie's face was bright red, her usually gorgeous, full lips now in a thin line and she was staring out the window without blinking.

"For the record, if you'd asked me about Penelope, I would have said yes to a vet mascot."

She slowly turned to him and he grinned.

A small bubble of laughter escaped her mouth. "It's ridiculous, right?"

He nodded. "It's what I would call batshit crazy."

This time, the bubble turned into laughter and the trust she'd had in him felt as though it was back. And as they sat there and laughed, he tried to hide the worry that had risen. Her sister was not okay. The way she spoke to Annie was not okay. It angered him that she had to deal with this. He didn't even know if she was aware of the physical reaction she had to speaking with her sister. But it couldn't continue.

Annie deserved so much better. She deserved people who could make her happy, who would be there for her. He wondered if she even knew that she deserved that.

CHAPTER FIFTEEN

Annie ran down the stairs like her hair was on fire. Today was her day off but she'd gone in to work to cover for another veterinarian who was sick. She had gotten home by four and was ever so thankful for Lila's crockpot recipe for Irish stew because she had come in from the cold to the rich aroma of beef with vegetables. She popped a loaf of frozen bread into the oven and they had eaten dinner together. She hadn't dumped her stress onto the kids. But now, she *was* stressed. She was also sweaty. And feeling . . . clammy. Brushing off the idea that she was getting sick, she forced herself to focus on the task at hand.

It was almost seven and she'd showered and put on her jogging pants and a Christmas T-shirt and had to start making ten dozen sugar cookies for tomorrow morning.

She had planned to make them last night, but had to help both kids with their homework. Grade nine math was way harder than she remembered and had taken way longer than expected.

Racing into the kitchen, she turned on some Christmas music and started pulling bowls out of the cupboard. She was so glad she'd packed up the Christmas mixing bowls her mom had given her one year. It didn't feel like Christmas without using them. They were a deep green, with embossed holly leaves around them. She swallowed past the lump in her throat as she remembered so many holidays baking together. Her mother would have been here to help her bake all these cookies. Now she was stuck doing them all alone. She could ask the kids to help, but they were both upstairs working on school projects due on Monday, and Maddy looked run down.

Annie pulled up the recipe she'd saved on her phone. Of course, Lila's recipe for sugar cookies had been something along the lines of *"Go to the bakery and order them. The holidays are too busy to be rolling out dough."* She had laughed at that but knew she couldn't because they'd look way too professional and the bazaar list had stipulated that these were supposed to be homemade.

Once she laid all her ingredients out on the counter, she made the mistake of glancing at the time. Dread pooled in her stomach and she decided she was going to have to make coffee. There was no way she'd stay awake without it. She pulled out the coffee canister just as there was a knock at the door.

She didn't even have the time or headspace to worry that it was Matt. Of course it was Matt, who else would come here unannounced at this time of night? Except she and Matt had kind of been awkward around each other since their night at the cabin. She felt awkward for her own reasons, but she had no idea why *he* was awkward.

She ran to the back door to find Matt standing there. Opening it quickly, he stepped into the house, bringing a blast of cold air with him. "Hey, sorry for just dropping in."

"You always just drop in, and you're always welcome."

"Are you baking?"

She frowned. "I was just about to start; how did you know?"

"I have a great sense of smell."

"You can *smell* sugar?"

He nodded.

"I'm not sure if that's concerning or impressive," she said as he hung his coat up and they walked toward the kitchen.

"Are you feeling okay?" he asked as they entered the kitchen.

"What do you mean?"

"You look flushed. Your eyes look glassy."

She stood a little straighter and tucked a strand of hair behind her ear, trying not to look mortified. Did she look that awful? "Just tired. Maybe a little under the weather, but I'm sure it's nothing. One of those days where I feel pulled in a hundred different directions, I guess."

"You shouldn't have worked today."

She waved a hand. "It's not a big deal. Believe me. I've just got these cookies and then Adam had a ton of homework."

Maddy appeared on the landing of the stairs, her face as white as the sugar on the counter. "Mom . . . I don't . . . feel so well."

Before she could reach her, because she knew instinctively what was going to happen, Matt was already up there, catching Maddy before she fainted and hit her head on the railing, or worse, fell down the stairs. He gently laid her down.

"Maddy, honey, wake up," Annie said, trying to stay calm.

Maddy opened her eyes and she turned to her side quickly, "I'm going to puke."

Sure enough, before they could help her up, she threw up on the landing floor.

"Ugh, you poor thing. It's okay, you're going to be okay," Annie said, stroking her hair.

"I'll get paper towels," Matt said, already in the kitchen.

"I feel so bad, my throat," Maddy rasped out.

She tried to take the paper towels and spray from Matt. "I'll clean this up," he said. "You help Maddy clean up."

"Matt . . ."

He shot her a look. "Please, I'm a vet. I've seen rat vomit, this is nothing."

"Omigod, so gross," Adam yelled from the top of the stairs.

"Adam, be quiet. Your poor sister is sick," Annie said, leaning against the railing. She was feeling worse by the minute herself.

"Are you sure you're not sick too?" Adam said.

That's when Annie knew she was really in trouble. Adam never noticed anything. "I'll be fine. I think I'm just a little tired. And have a bit of a sore throat."

"There's one after-hours clinic less than fifteen minutes from here. We can get there before they close at eight if we hurry," Matt said at the bottom of the stairs. The bag of vomit was in one hand. Annie stared at him, desperate to hold onto her dwindling health even though she felt worse by the minute.

"I really want to argue with you, but I think you're right," Annie said.

"Adam, grab a couple of water bottles from the fridge while I help your sister to the car," Matt said, as he helped Maddy down the stairs. "All right, kiddo, let's get a jacket on you and head outside."

"Sure, I'll get a couple of puke bags for the car," Adam said, rushing by them.

Maddy nodded weakly and they made their way to the mud-room. Matt tossed the bag onto the back porch while they got their coats on. Poor Maddy couldn't even stand and just sat on the bench. "Why don't we take your SUV? I'll drive," Matt said.

Annie nodded, her sore throat making it hard to talk. Adam handed her the bottles of water and two plastic bags. "Here, Mom. Hope you feel better, Maddy."

Maddy gave him a weak smile.

Matt frowned, looking at both of them. He crouched down in front of Maddy. "Okay, Maddy, how about I just pick you up and get you into the back seat. You look too tired to walk. Is that okay?"

Tears filled Maddy's eyes and she nodded, lifting up her arms.

Annie's throat ached even more as she watched Matt pick her daughter up effortlessly. Maddy's legs dangled down, and her head rested on his shoulder. He turned to her before heading out the door. "Let's go. You going to make it?"

She nodded, grabbed her purse, and followed them out. "Lock up behind us, Adam. I'll text you if we're going to be a long time."

"Okay, Mom. Love you."

"Love you too," she said before heading out.

As she walked toward her SUV, the cold night air felt welcome against her flushed skin. The sound of the howling wind almost drowned out the sounds of the ocean crashing against the shoreline. It was a night that could have been intimidating. A night where she would have yearned for the reassuring city lights, instead of the foreboding darkness of a winter's night in the country. Exhaustion was seeping into her bones faster than the damp air. But instead of panic or sadness, the long-forgotten sense of security trickled through as she watched Matt buckle Maddy into the back seat and get in on the driver's side.

Adam had said he loved her, without being prompted by Annie saying it first.

Annie was out here, as the passenger, for the first time in forever.

And she saw the stars shower the sky with lights, with hope, for the first time in years.

The whole world wasn't resting on her weary shoulders tonight.

* * *

"I've got it all under control. Just go to sleep, Annie."

Matt tried to hold back his grin, because he didn't want her to think he was laughing at her. He wasn't. Well, not in a mean way. He leaned against the doorjamb of her bedroom and pulled out his phone when it buzzed: Annie was texting him because she couldn't speak.

I have to bake cookies.

He smiled and spoke. "I already told you; I'll take care of the cookies. Adam will help."

She made a panicked noise and then furiously texted.

He's a disaster in the kitchen. He won't measure things correctly and he'll eat the batter.

This time he couldn't hold back his laugh. "Annie, trust me. Just go to sleep and let the antibiotics work. You'll feel better in forty-eight hours. I'll sleep on the couch and I'll help Maddy if she wakes up. But by the looks of things, she's out for the night. You've got water on your nightstand and Advil if you need it."

She frowned and furiously texted him again. *I can't believe I have strep throat. I haven't had that since I was a kid.*

"Well, now you got it *from* your kid. Rest up. Lie down. If Maddy really wants you, I'll come and get you, okay? I can't stay and chat, I've got a lot of stuff to deal with here."

She rolled her eyes.

"What time do the cookies need to be delivered to the school?"

Nine!!!!

He tried hard not to laugh out loud again. "No need for exclamation points, I've got it under control. No problem. Anything else?"

Thanks, Matt.

"You don't have to thank me."

He turned around and shut the door to her bedroom and headed down the stairs after peeking in on Maddy. Sure enough, the kid was fast asleep. Adam was downstairs in the kitchen his head in the fridge.

"Hungry?"

"Starving. It's been hours since dinner."

Matt pulled out his phone. "I hear ya. I've got a plan that will solve all our problems."

"You're not going to tell me to go to bed, are you?"

Matt scrolled through his contacts, leaning against the island. "It's nine. On a Friday. You're fourteen. I'm an adult, not a monster. Besides, you've got to help me with my plan."

"Sure, what do you want me to do? Wait. Do we have to bake hundreds of cookies?"

Matt shook his head. "Of course not. I have a few favors to cash in at all times. One of them happens to be with the woman who owns a bakery not that far from here. She sells dozens of these cookies a day. I'm sure she has a fresh stash ready to go for tomorrow. So here's the plan: I call her. While we wait for her to get them ready for us, we clean up this kitchen so it's spotless for your mom tomorrow morning. On my way back from picking up the cookies, I'll get us some burgers and fries. Because it's the Christmas season, when I come back, we'll put on a classic Christmas movie—"

"Uncle Matt, this was sounding like the best night ever, but I can't watch black and white movies."

Matt grinned. *"Die Hard."*

Adam's eyes widened. "I've never seen it but just the name sounds amazing."

Matt's chest squeezed. "It is. Classic eighties. Classic Christmas. So we watch while we eat and package up the cookies. We should be done and in bed by midnight, I'd say. Tomorrow morning, we swing by the school and drop these off before nine and then on the way back pick up some breakfast. Sound good?"

Adam's eyes were wide and he was looking at him as though he were Santa. "This sounds like the best night I've had in years. I mean, I feel bad that mom and Maddy are sick."

"Right. Of course. But you and I get to hang out."

"Do you think Mom will be mad you didn't bake the cookies? Or are you going to lie?"

"I'm not going to lie; I'm just not going to tell her until she's feeling better."

Adam nodded wisely. "I personally think this is a brilliant plan."

Matt gave him a fist bump. "Good. Me too. Okay, I'm going to head out and make my calls on the road."

"I'll start cleaning up."

* * *

An hour and a half later, Matt and Adam were finishing up their burgers and fries. The Christmas tree and fireplace were on, guns were being fired on the TV, and there were a hundred forty-four decorated sugar cookies on the kitchen island. Annie and

Maddy were both sleeping soundly. Adam was looking happier than Matt had seen him in years. Life was good.

"Uncle Matt, do we have to wrap those cookies up or something?"

Matt crumpled up the wrapper from his burger and tossed it into the open paper bag, landing a perfect shot. "Nope. Sally did all of that. Twelve dozen cookies, ready to be sold for charity."

Adam crumpled up his own wrapper and tossed it in the bag, landing a perfect shot as well. "I think we only needed ten dozen."

"I like to plan ahead. One dozen is for you and me and the other is for your mom and Maddy tomorrow."

Adam grinned, hopping up from the couch. "Can I get them now?"

Matt threw his hands in the air, feeling like Santa. "Of course! Bring over our box."

Adam joined him, opening the box and revealing a dozen of the most colorful, detailed, festive cookies he'd ever seen. Three Santas, three Christmas trees, three snowmen, and three snowflakes, all decorated with meticulous detail. "Wow, Mom is going to know in like one second that we didn't make these."

Matt grabbed a Santa from the box. "I know, so enjoy eating them now, before we get in trouble."

Adam nodded, grabbing one of each cookie variety before settling back in and looking at the screen. "Good idea. So, are you sleeping over?"

Matt nodded, snapping off Santa's head with his mouth. "Yeah. Is that okay?"

"Yeah, of course," Adam said, his eyes glued to the screen. "I, uh, I'm glad you're here. Mom doesn't usually get sick, so it'd be kind of weird if it was just me. Not that I couldn't help or anything. It's just nice to have someone around. In Toronto, I would have been on my own."

Matt finished chewing the cookies, notes of butter and vanilla mixing with the emotion in his throat. There were so many things in Adam's statement that made him unable to answer right away. He also knew how much that must have taken for Adam to admit. Whether or not he knew it, Adam was beginning to open up to the possibility of liking it here. "I'm glad you're here too. I missed you guys. I also missed hanging out with just you."

Adam looked down in his lap and then shoved a snowflake cookie in his mouth and chewed for a moment. "Sometimes I worried that life would never be the same after Dad died. I mean, like, I knew it would never be the same, but I wanted it to. I wanted a dad again. My dad and no one else. A lot of kids whose parents were divorced at school, their parents got remarried and for a long time I didn't want my mom to get remarried. But I don't know . . . this last year, I don't know if it's because I'm getting older or what . . . but I feel guilty because I've given her a hard time and I think if I hadn't acted like such a loser, maybe she would have had time to date or whatever it is people your age do."

The catch in Adam's voice stopped Matt from laughing out loud at that last remark. Up until that line, Matt's heart was in this throat. And God, was he happy this kid was here with him right now. Not that he wanted Annie or Maddy to be sick, but it had obviously prompted Adam to reflect on his feelings. Matt's grandmother would say this was a destined night.

As he looked at his best friend's son, this young man, caught between the past and the present, caught between childhood and adolescence, Matt knew he was needed. Not as a casual friend, but as someone Adam could come to, count on. Not as a guy on the phone a thousand miles away, but as a man he saw with consistency. He didn't know what to do with the date remark, or if he had picked up on any vibes coming from Matt toward Annie, so he had to tread carefully.

He cleared his throat. "Well, I guess first, us people in our thirties would have to get approval from the nursing home staff to see if we're allowed to date."

Adam burst out laughing and Matt smiled, happy he'd relieved some of the tension in the room. "That's not what I meant. I know you guys aren't that old."

"I know, I'm just teasing. But I also know that you shouldn't feel guilty. You're a good kid, and you love your mom and she knows it. Even when you don't show it the way you want to. We've all been teenagers. No one is going to fault you for missing your dad or acting out because you miss him. But I'll also be the first to tell you that none of that stuff will take away the pain, if it's pain that you're feeling. No amount of nicotine or alcohol will do that. Because when it wears off, that pain comes right back in, hitting you harder because you're sober. So, then a vicious cycle starts. You got to push through the pain and the mud, to get out to other side. You do that with the people you love. And if you need more help, you get the help."

Adam nodded, looking down at the ground. "I know. You're right. Can I ask you something?"

Matt held his breath and nodded. "Anything."

Adam snapped Santa's head off the cookie and shoved it in his mouth. "I know it's not the same, but your dad left, right? How do you get over not being able to ever see him again?"

Matt reached for a cookie he didn't want, wishing it was vodka and raspberry cordial. He never talked about his dad.

Annie knew. Cam knew. Because when they were all drunk one night in their third year of university, they had gotten into family and had shared and bonded over the dysfunction. But he hadn't talked about it much since then. He and Kate would sometimes say a thing or two, but never to outsiders. But Adam wasn't an outsider and Adam needed someone who was open and someone who could relate. "I guess it's the same in that neither of us will ever see our fathers again, but that's where it ends. I know your dad would have done anything to be here with you. He fought. Right up until the end. And it's not fair that he's not here. As for my dad, Adam, I don't know where he is. I don't keep tabs on him. I know that he has another family, and the last I heard he was in the U.S. My dad is the opposite of yours—he didn't fight for his wife, for his kids. The going got tough and he split."

Adam stopped chewing, Santa's round body hanging limply in his hand. "I didn't know it was that bad. Mom never really got into details. I'm sorry, Uncle Matt. I don't know what's worse."

Matt took a bite of the Christmas tree cookie and shrugged. "I don't know either, I guess. But I try not to think about it too often. It has changed me, though. I mean, it's made me figure out the kind of man I want to be. Sometimes challenges like that can define who we are and who we want to be. It made me realize that family loyalty is everything to me."

Adam groaned and hunkered further into his seat. "Family loyalty. Yeah, I failed at that."

"No, you didn't. Your aunt did."

Adam shook his head. "I shouldn't have said I'd go with her. But I feel like I can't take it back now. My mom was right. Even about coming here. I didn't want to tell her, but I like the kids in my grade. I like this girl. I even like Jingle."

Matt couldn't help the grin on his face. Annie was going to be so happy. Her boy was coming back, he was coming back to her, whole. As if right on cue, Jingle came trotting down the stairs. "Why didn't you want to tell your mom?"

Adam shrugged and grabbed another cookie as Jingle appeared by his side. "Would I sound like a total jerk if I said that I think it's because I didn't want to admit she was right?"

Matt put his feet up on the coffee table. "You'd sound like a fourteen-year-old. I remember hating when my parents were right."

Adam snapped his head in Matt's direction. "Really?"

Matt nodded. "Of course. That being said, though, your mom only wants what's best for you. Not to rub it in and say I told you so. I mean, hell, kid, she drove a thousand miles for you. That's how much she loves you. That's how much she wants you to be happy. Not for her to be right, but for you to be happy. That's a pretty amazing mom you have."

Adam's eyes filled with tears and he turned his head to the Christmas tree, the credits now playing on the movie in the background. Matt tensed, hoping he hadn't pushed too hard. "I know she is. I, uh, I'm going to tell her."

"I think that would mean a lot to her. I was also thinking that maybe we could surprise your mom and Maddy tomorrow by decorating outside."

Jingle jumped up on the couch beside Adam. He looked at him and then patted him on the head awkwardly. "Like what?"

"Lights. I bet Maddy would like one of those lit-up snowmen."

Adam nodded enthusiastically, like maybe he'd like one too. He gave Jingle a piece of cookie. Jingle scooped it up and then hopped off the couch. "For sure. Mom likes those pots with the Christmas green things in them. She was saying she was going to get some this weekend. And a wreath for the door and all that."

He was totally getting into the spirit of things. "Perfect. Maybe after I drop off the cookies, we can head out to the store, buy everything, and set it up. I have a feeling they'll both be in bed all day, and hopefully by tomorrow night the antibiotics will have started making them feel better."

"Sounds good. Maybe we can pick up some lunch or something for them."

Matt nodded. "I know a great place for soup. So, uh, what about this girl?"

Adam's face turned a few shades of red. "I just like hanging out with her. We talk sometimes."

Matt tried to look cool. Annie would kill for this information. She was going to be thrilled when he told her. "That's good. Maybe you should invite her over to hang out one night?"

Adam shrugged. "I don't know. It's kind of embarrassing."

"Ah, your mom won't embarrass you."

"So, about girlfriends . . . what about you. My mom?"

Matt stilled. So Adam had picked up on something. Matt drew in a deep breath, wishing he were more prepared for this conversation, wishing he'd actually told Annie how he felt before he broached the subject with her son. He couldn't reveal too much, but he couldn't lie. But he also needed to be sure he wasn't misinterpreting what Adam was asking. "I think your mom is great. Of course."

Adam took another cookie. "But like, more than that?"

Matt swallowed hard. "What if I said yes?"

Adam looked up from the snowman in his hand to Matt. There was something there in his eyes, eyes identical to Cam's, that robbed Matt of breath for a moment, that made the hairs on the back of his neck rise, that made goose bumps flicker over his body.

"I'd be cool with that."

CHAPTER SIXTEEN

Annie looked at her reflection in the mirror, feeling like a new woman. Sure, the woman staring back at her looked a little pale, with dark circles under her eyes, but she felt like a million bucks . . . for so many reasons.

She had just gotten out of the shower and had blow-dried her hair and gotten dressed in black leggings and an oversized Christmas sweatshirt. She and Maddy had bought matching ones last weekend; they were charcoal gray with a red truck with a Christmas tree hanging out the back. Her throat was barely sore anymore, and she knew from texting Maddy and from Matt's updates that Maddy was doing better too. She and Maddy were going to meet in the kitchen.

Annie couldn't ever remember crashing so hard with anything—and not having to worry about her kids. Every time she would try and get up, Matt would insist everything was under control. And she'd trusted him. Enough to sleep as though she hadn't slept in years. The kind of deep, worry-free sleep she'd had before kids. And now, the next night, she was feeling so much better.

She could hear Matt and Adam laughing about something in the kitchen and she heard the TV, something like bombs going off. The comforting aroma of chicken soup greeted her as she opened her bedroom door and headed toward the kitchen. She stopped at the bottom of the stairs, undetected, and took in the sight in front of her. She blinked furiously, desperate not to cry in front of anyone. Matt was placing a bowl of soup in front of Maddy, who was sitting at the island. She was wearing reindeer pajamas and her hair, still damp from the shower, was in a perfect French braid. Maddy was smiling up at Matt.

Adam was sitting by the tree, playing with Jingle, who was trying to catch a Christmas mouse dangling from a stick. The house was spotless. The Christmas tree had a few wrapped presents under it. The pillows and throws were all perfectly fluffed and folded. The kitchen table had a poinsettia in the center and a flickering red candle beside it. The island also had a glowing candle, a plate of beautiful sugar cookies, and gleaming counters. Her Le Creuset pot had chicken soup simmering away, and a loaf of garlic bread sat on a cutting board beside the stove.

And the man currently smiling at her daughter was the one responsible. He had somehow managed to run this house, bake and deliver cookies, make her son look the happiest she'd ever seen him, keep her and Maddy comfortable. She would never forget how effortlessly he'd fallen into a needed role here; how natural it had been for him. She would never forget the way he'd picked up Maddy and held her and taken them both to the doctor. He'd been her rock.

He'd always been her rock. She had thought, by never needing anyone again, she would protect herself and her kids. She had thought if she could do it all alone then they wouldn't have to rely on people and risk being disappointed. She had started to believe that the world was filled with takers, that the world was filled with Valeries.

But Matt was not Valerie. Matt was not a taker.

Matt was her best friend. But so much more. Because as much as she would never forget the way he had held her daughter, she would never forget the way he had held her. It wasn't the same as when Cam died. Everything was different now. Including how she felt about him.

How it had felt that night at the cabin, to fall asleep with him, to hold onto him, to wake up with him. And she was unable to deny her feelings for him anymore. She would be a coward if she did. She wanted to believe again.

"Mom!" Adam said, rising up from the ground and giving her a hug.

She held onto him, making eye contact with Matt over his shoulder. Matt didn't look surprised, but the light in his eyes told her something special had happened here. "Hi, honey."

"I'm glad you're feeling better," Adam said, taking a step back.

"I feel almost completely back to normal," she said, entering the kitchen with him. She walked over to give Maddy a kiss on the forehead.

"Me too," Maddy said, giving her a quick hug.

"Matt took good care of us," Annie said, making eye contact with Matt. He held her gaze for a moment, just long enough to make her heart race.

"Are you hungry? I've got chicken soup and garlic bread if you've got your appetite back?" Matt asked, already ladling some soup into a bowl.

"That sounds perfect. I'll sit right beside Maddy," Annie said, taking a seat. Matt gave her the bowl of steaming soup. "Thank you so much, this smells delicious."

"Not a problem. It's an old family recipe," he said, tossing a dish towel over his shoulder.

"This is amazing," Annie said, after taking a spoonful of the aromatic soup.

"It's so good," Maddy agreed.

"There are sugar cookies for dessert," Adam said, leaning against the counter.

"Okay, I'm so impressed with you guys. I can't believe you made these. I mean, like, no offense to either of you, but these are gorgeous," Annie said, looking at the plate.

Adam looked down at the ground, and Matt's face turned slightly red. "So, here's the deal, Annie, because I can't tell a lie . . . it was really late last night and there was no way we were going to be able to bake that many cookies. Also, I don't bake. Adam can't tell the difference between sugar and flour—"

"Hey!" Adam laughed and shoved Matt.

Matt laughed and shoved him back. This continued for a few more shoves.

Annie and Maddy sat in silence, watching this exchange. Had she been asleep for a year? Her son was laughing and joking around like she hadn't seen him do in years.

"Oh! That reminds me, Maddy, when I dropped off the cookies, a girl from your class was there helping her mom. I know her mom, we went to high school together. Anyway, they heard you're new in town. She asked where you were and I told her you were home sick with strep throat. So she said she's been meaning to invite you over to her house after school. And Annie, her mom said she'll have you over for coffee."

Maddy nearly jumped off her chair. "Who was it?"

Matt pulled his phone out of his pocket. "I'll send your mom her contact info right now. The girl's name is Sarah. And she said you can FaceTime her if you're up to it."

Maddy's face lit up like the Christmas tree. "I think I will! She sits across from me in class."

"That's so nice of them," Annie said, hardly believing that all of this could be falling into place so smoothly. "And I love your French braid, honey."

"Matt did it," she said, polishing off her bowl of soup and reaching for a sugar cookie.

Annie slowly turned to Matt. "You know how to do French braids?"

He nodded, reaching for a cookie. "Yeah, I learned how to do them in grade school because Kate was obsessed with them. My mother didn't have the patience to learn. So I taught myself by reading some magazine with step-by-step instructions and then I charged Kate a dollar every time she wanted one."

They all burst out laughing. "You are a man of many surprises . . . and getting back to those cookies . . ."

He braced his hands on the edge of the island counter and looked at her. She tried not to get lost in his eyes, or admire how good he looked with his scruffy stubble and disheveled hair. His navy T-shirt was rumpled, as were his jeans. He looked delicious. "You're mad at me."

She was very aware of the kids watching their exchange with avid interest. "How can I be mad at you? You somehow managed to find over a hundred of the most gorgeous cookies I have ever seen, deliver them, take care of me and Maddy, hang out with Adam, make soup, keep our house spotless. I mean, I am so very grateful for everything you've done."

His jaw clenched and he blinked a few times before pushing off from the counter. The raw emotion was replaced by a teasing glint. "I'd be happy to share my housekeeping tips when you're up for them."

"We have another surprise too," Adam said.

It was not lost on her that her son looked so enthusiastic or that he had used the word "we." "Okay, well, I'm done with my soup."

"Me too. Let's see the surprise!" Maddy said as they stood.

"Okay, but you have to put your coats on," Matt said as he and Adam led the way to the mudroom.

They scrambled to put their coats on, and Matt held the door open for all of them. Adam headed out first. "Follow me and stand right here," Adam said, a few meters from the door.

"Shouldn't we turn the lights on; we can barely even see you," Annie said as they carefully walked down the steps.

"In a minute," Matt said. All of a sudden, hundreds of twinkling lights illuminated the yard. Matt stepped outside and stood grinning alongside Adam.

Annie and Maddy took it all in. White lights ran along the trim of the house. There was a giant Santa in a sleigh, all lit up. The door was framed with lit garland, and a fresh boxwood wreath hung on the window. Two large pots bursting with Christmas greens flanked either side of the door. It was gorgeous. It must have taken them hours.

"Oh my gosh! We have the nicest house I've ever seen!" Maddy yelled, summing it all up in that one sentence.

"Do you like it, Mom?" Adam asked.

Annie put her hands over her mouth, unable to find the words. The house wasn't just a house—the lights, the decorations, weren't just decorations, they were all symbols of the future. The four of them here, together, a sign of what could be. What the future could look like. After years of being afraid of the future, barely getting through the hours of the day, she found herself, feet firmly planted in the snow, in the present, not ever wanting to wish a second of this life away. "This is amazing. This is the best surprise. Thank you, guys."

"Glad you like it. It was Matt's idea, but we did it together. Now I've got to run. I've got a friend calling," Adam said before giving Matt an odd look and then running back to the house.

"Can I go call Sarah?" Maddy asked.

"Sure you can. Have fun!" Annie said as Maddy turned around and bolted inside.

She and Matt stood side by side. "I don't know how I can ever thank you."

"You don't have to thank me, Annie. I don't want your thanks."

There was something in his voice that made her pulse race and made her slowly turn to face him. He reached out and slowly took her hand, and she forgot how to breathe. They never really touched. Not anymore, not since she'd come to live here. Except for the night at the cabin, but that had just been exhaustion. And vodka.

This was different. This was Matt deliberately reaching for her, and the minute his large, warm hand slipped over hers, she clasped it. Never wanting to let go. When he took a step closer to her, she knew there was no going back to her safety zone.

"Annie," he said, in a tone she'd never heard before, that made her toes curl in her boots.

"Hi," was all she could say, inwardly cringing at her awkwardness. Why had she said "hi"? Obviously, they had already greeted each other. She couldn't think of anything cleverer?

His mouth tipped up at a corner, and he slowly let go of her hand, only to frame one side of her face. Her breath caught as his thumb grazed her cheekbone, sort of like he was tracing it, memorizing it. He was looking at her, even though he'd looked at her a thousand times before, but now he was looking at her like she was different. Maybe she was.

"Annie . . . I don't want to ruin what I consider the most important friendship I have. You have become my best friend in the world, and I never intended to feel anything more than friendship, but God, I can't deny what I feel for you anymore. That night at the cabin was the best night of my life. When I woke up with you in my arms, I never wanted to let you go. No one, nothing has ever felt so right before."

Her mouth dropped open, her gaze going to his mouth. He didn't stop the slow, torturous, tracing of her cheekbone and she wanted to take that last step into him and know what it was to be held by him again and to kiss him. But he was waiting, she belatedly realized. He was waiting for her to say he wasn't ruining their friendship, that she felt it too.

She looked up at him. "I feel it too," she whispered.

And then it was as though he had brought her all the stars in the sky, every wish, every dream, as he reached down and kissed her. He kissed her slowly, his mouth firm but gentle, tentative. And then his hand went to the nape of her neck, his body against hers. She slipped her hands around his waist and soon all she could taste and breathe and feel was Matt. The world was peace and fire all at once and she was alive again.

"Annie," he whispered against her mouth, his words sounding like a plea or a prayer. Her knees wobbled and she leaned further into him, knowing he wouldn't let her fall.

And she never wanted to let him go. She never wanted to stop living again. She stood there, in the snow, with the ocean at their backs, wrapped up in Matt's arms, knowing that this was where she was meant to be.

She never wanted to go back to the woman who was half alive, one foot in the safety zone. She wanted to be the woman she was with him. The one who was brave enough to start a new chapter.

CHAPTER SEVENTEEN

One week until Christmas

Matt walked down the historic Victoria Row in Charlottetown with Annie and Adam and Maddy. For the first time in his adult life, he was looking forward to Christmas like a kid. The Christmas Festival, even though he attended every year when he was on the island, felt new to him. He was seeing it through their eyes. Maddy was thrilled with literally everything, her smile, her enthusiasm infectious. Adam was filled with sarcasm, but the kind that made them laugh and was intended to be funny and not hurtful. And Annie . . . well, everything had changed since last weekend.

He had held back for as long as he could, but when they'd been standing outside her house, he knew he couldn't maintain their friendship without being honest. That openness had always been there between them and, as much as he didn't want to cross the friendship line, he also didn't want to ruin their friendship with hidden feelings. The weekend at her house had solidified what he already knew—that he loved all of them. He'd loved his time with Adam, hearing his thoughts and his laughter again. And it had felt right to be there for them, like there was a place for him in their family.

Once he kissed Annie, he knew there was no going back. The electricity between them was exactly as he thought it would be. Now they were in this new zone where he was letting her take the lead with how they approached things with the kids. But as soon she gave the green light, he wanted them to know. He didn't want to hide in front of anyone. He wanted to take her out on a real date, he wanted to hold her hand in public, he wanted what they had to be real.

"I had no idea the Christmas Festival was this big," Annie said as she sipped her coffee. The cobblestone street was bursting with decorations, vendors, and shoppers. The smell of cider and fresh evergreen filled the air.

The four of them were enjoying the afternoon, and were going to meet up with Matt's family for dinner at one of their favorite restaurants. "Can we get hot chocolate?" Maddy asked.

"Of course. It wouldn't be a Christmas market without hot chocolate," Annie said as Maddy ran to stand in line at one of the booths.

"Uh, is it okay if I meet up with you guys for dinner? I'm going to hang out with some friends from school," Adam said.

"Sure. That's great. Here, I'll give you some money," Annie said, pulling twenty dollars out of her wallet.

Adam's face lit up. "Thanks."

"I'll text you the restaurant name and how to get there," Matt said.

"Sure, see you guys later," Adam said before racing off in the opposite direction.

"That's so great. He looks so happy," Annie said.

Matt gave her a little smirk. "Remember I told you I think he has a thing for a girl? That's who I think he's meeting."

Annie sucked in a breath and squeezed his arm. "Really? Oh, I'm dying to spy. I know we can't."

"You're right, we can't," he said with a laugh.

"Mom, hurry up and pay," Maddy said as she reached the front of the line.

"Oh, I got it," Matt said, reaching her first.

Maddy gave him a smile as she grabbed her cup of hot chocolate. "Thanks, Uncle Matt."

They walked along the cobblestone street, the energy of the season everywhere—in the Victorian carolers, in the festive shop windows, on the faces of the children. Maddy stopped in front of a pottery studio that had an assortment of handmade Christmas items in the window and a big sign advertising a walk-in session all weekend. "Can we go inside?"

Annie nodded. "Of course."

They walked in and there were kids at a dozen different tables, working on projects like clay Christmas trees and mugs and bowls. Maddy looked up at them and Matt already knew where this was going. "Can I stay and make a tree?"

A young woman dressed as an elf came over to them. "Hi there, are you interested in doing one of the one-hour sessions?"

Maddy looked at Annie. "Please, Mom?

Annie smiled. "Sure you can, I know you love pottery."

They discussed the details and they waited while Maddy chose from the different assortment of unpainted pottery on the shelves. She finally decided on a Santa cookie jar. "Good choice.

Now you can pick a table you'd like to sit at, and I'll bring you some paint," the young woman said.

"I see some kids from my class," Maddy whispered to them.

Matt looked in the direction Maddy had pointed. A girl was waving and smiling. "Hey, there's someone waving at you."

Maddy's eyes grew wide. "Really?'

He and Annie nodded. "Turn around, Maddy," Annie whispered.

Maddy did and waved back to the girl. "I'll go sit at that table."

"Have fun, honey. I can't wait to see how this Santa looks. We'll be back to pick you up in an hour. Don't leave here without us, okay?"

Maddy giggled. "I'm going to go off with a stranger, Mom."

She ran off and Annie looked up at him. "I'm so happy for her that I don't even mind being made fun of."

He laughed. "Yeah, me too. She's really coming out of her shell."

"Okay, I'm just going to pay and fill out the contact info and we can go," Annie said, heading up to the counter.

"White Christmas" came on the speakers, and he looked out the large front window, happy to see flurries falling. He had an idea what they could do for their one hour together at the festival.

When Annie joined him at the window, he glanced behind him to make sure Maddy wasn't watching and then grabbed Annie's hand. "Come on," he said.

He held open the door and headed toward the square. "We've got one hour, right?"

She nodded. "What are you up to?"

He hurried down the street, his eyes on the horses and carriages lined up at the square. "How about a horse and carriage ride through Charlottetown?"

She gasped. "Yes!"

They ran up to the driver who luckily had an empty buggy. Matt paid the driver and then helped Annie into the wagon. Soon they were trotting along Main Street and sharing a red and green plaid blanket.

"This is so nice," Annie said, smiling up at him. Her eyes were alive, sparkling, and her cheeks were a vibrant pink. And her mouth . . . well, her mouth was red and full, and now that it was just the two of them, he couldn't hold back. She leaned into him and he curled his hand around the nape of her neck, her silky hair brushing against his hand. "I have been waiting to do this since the second I left your house last week," he said, an inch from her lips.

"Me too," she whispered.

That statement was all he needed to hear.

"Now, if you'll look here on the right, folks . . ." The driver's booming voice had them both jumping in the seat. "We have Province House National Historic Site. In the spring of 1864 . . ."

Matt cleared his throat. "Oh, we're not tourists, you don't need to give us an actual historical tour of the city."

The man turned around, frowned, turned back around, and continued to speak. "In the spring of 1864, the legislatures of New Brunswick, Nova Scotia, and Prince Edward Island expressed interest in meeting to discuss the possibility of a maritime union. This was before Canada was a country, you see . . ."

Annie's eyes widened, and she slapped her hand over her mouth in an attempt to cover up her laughter.

Matt was not feeling the humor as much. "Sir, we're all up to date on our Canadian history, so you can just drive along and feel free to skip that."

Annie nudged him.

He shrugged.

The driver continued speaking.

Annie laughed softly. "Well, this is still a very nice ride, even with the historical guide," she whispered.

Matt was not one to be deterred. He leaned forward and kissed Annie, getting lost in her, the driver's voice a mere inconvenience. There was nothing that would stop him from enjoying this moment. "I should have offered to pay extra for a silent tour," he said against her lips as the driver actually raised his voice.

She pulled back slightly. "Agreed. I would have pitched in."

* * *

"My dear, you look positively radiant. Glowing. There's a lightness to you that I haven't seen before," Lila whispered to Annie.

They were all seated at a long table at one of the harborfront restaurants. The two-story restaurant was packed, but they had managed a table overlooking the harbor. Multicolored Christmas lights were strung at the tops of the windows and around the restaurant. Christmas trees of various sizes were tucked into corners, and boisterous holiday music was being played by the live band. The servers were decked out with Santa hats and light-up Christmas necklaces. The atmosphere was lively and festive.

Annie leaned closer to Lila. "I feel like it too, Lila."

Lila's eyes sparkled. "And would my grandson have anything to do with it?"

Annie's cheeks grew warm. "A little something."

Lila clasped her hands together. "Wonderful! I knew it. Is this still top-secret news?"

Annie nodded. "Sort of. I'm trying to find the right time to tell the kids. I'm pretty sure they'll be thrilled. They adore Matt."

Lila picked her glass of wine and took a sip. "Of course. And what about your sister, dear? Have you heard from her?"

Annie toyed with the cloth napkin in her lap. "No, but that's not unusual when she's mad at me about something. She can go from calling me five times a day to ignoring me for months at a time. In a way it's a blessing. Especially right now. Lila, I feel like I'm getting my life back, like it's finally going in a direction that makes me hopeful again."

Lila clasped Annie's hand. "You deserve that happiness again, Annie. It's not just you who's glowing. Matt looks the happiest I've ever seen him. He's a good man. I'm very proud of the person he's become."

"So, Annie, are you all feeling better from the strep throat?"

Annie turned her attention to Matt's mom, slightly surprised that she was addressing her. That strange vibe she'd gotten over the Sunday dinners had only gotten worse it seemed. Again, there was nothing overtly hostile, but she wasn't exactly warm and friendly like Lila or Kate. Annie tried not to take it personally.

"Yes, all better. Luckily it came and went quickly."

Claire gave a slight nod. Annie was vaguely aware of Matt watching their exchange, and she suddenly felt under the spotlight. Did he sense something from his mom? Or had she said something to him? Did she not like Annie? Would Claire influence him in some way?

"That's the second time Maddy has gotten sick since she's been here, isn't it?"

Annie's gaze darted to the kids, who were thankfully engrossed in a conversation with Matt's sister at the other end of the table. Annie sat a little straighter in her chair. "Yes, but you know how kids are. This time of year, it seems there's always something going around."

"Has she seen a doctor?"

"She had strep. Of course she's been to a doctor, Mom. We didn't prescribe her horse pills from the clinic," Matt said, intervening before Annie could. She felt his hand on her knee, under the table. That gesture of solidarity made her heart squeeze. This interrogation was bringing up memories of her past, with her family, on the defensive all the time about something Valerie would bring up, causing doubt in her mother's eyes.

Claire gave a strained smile and took a sip of wine. "Of course, dear. Oh, Annie, I love your rings, dear. That is quite the diamond. I can see why you're still wearing them. I still wear mine too."

A tremor ran through Annie. The rings. She stared at Claire, wondering why she was saying this, why she was pointing that out. Clearly, she was trying to show Matt that Annie hadn't moved on. Annie wanted to tell Matt why she was still wearing them, but hadn't brought it up. But now it looked like Annie wasn't ready to move on. "I, um, thank you."

"Well, I'm glad Maddy is doing better. She must miss home very much."

Annie lifted her chin. Having a good relationship with Matt's family was very important to her, but the whole direction of this conversation was making her very uncomfortable. And now she was also creating problems for Annie, and she was going to have to address the rings to Matt. "This is her home now. She's doing fine here."

"She looks better than fine! I'd say she looks like she's loving the island," Lila chimed in, turning to give Claire a pointed look.

"I guess she must like having her mother around more at home. Careers can really take over and make a person forget their responsibilities at home to their families," Claire said.

"Mom, what is this?" Matt said, his voice thick with anger as he leaned forward.

Annie put her hand on his arm gently. She did not want to be the cause of any rift in an otherwise very supportive family. But it did hurt that Claire was insinuating that Annie wasn't a great mother, hadn't put her kids first. "It's okay, Matt."

"No, it's not okay. What is this about, Mom?"

"Yes, I'd like to know too, Claire," Lila piped up, turning to her daughter.

Claire's face went red. "It's nothing . . . nothing. I just was concerned about the children."

"They aren't your children to be concerned about. Annie is a wonderful, caring, loving mother, but again, that's not your concern and she doesn't need to prove herself to you," Matt said, his voice low but firm.

Claire's chin trembled. "Yes, of course," she said thinly.

"Food's here!" Maddy yelled above the music and the noisy crowd. As the server handed out their dinner, the tension at their end of the table was thicker than the cream-based chowder Annie had ordered. The glow from the twinkling lights seemed a little dimmer and the weight of Christmases past, when her sister had created problems, slowly descended. Annie forced a smile and a laugh when needed during the rest of the dinner, but she couldn't shake the hurt or the insecurities Claire had brought up.

Matt was quieter than usual too, and it was hard to imagine that just a couple of hours ago they had been stealing kisses in a horse-drawn buggy. Was he having doubts now? Was he thinking about her rings? This was supposed to be a new beginning for them. She was supposed to be here to show her kids real family, to be rid of Valerie's manipulations. Instead, it felt like she was trading one set of family problems for another. It was different, but the same. Being in the hot seat. The way her skin felt prickly, like she was overheating. The overwhelming feeling of things being out of control and needing to prove her innocence. Prove that she was trying her best. She was a good mom. She tried to be. She tried to be a good person. But Matt was very close to his mother . . . what if she saw something in Annie that he'd missed?

She sat there, forcing smiles, faking laughter, the happiness from a mere couple of hours ago fading like the sunset. The uncomfortable self-doubt mingled with the panic already bubbling inside her was that maybe she was wrong. Maybe Valerie was right about her. Maybe Claire was right about her. What if she was a horrible sister, daughter, mother? What if she should have done more for her sister? Would it have been so bad if she'd asked Matt to have a mural of Penelope painted in the office? Maybe she should try harder with Valerie. Maybe she shouldn't be so happy that Valerie wasn't speaking to her.

Tomorrow, she would call her and try again.

CHAPTER EIGHTEEN

One week until Christmas

"Uh, mom, just to let you know, I have a friend coming over tonight to hang out."

Annie shot Matt a look, trying to play it cool. The three of them were in the kitchen, and Annie and Matt had come home together after work. They were planning on having dinner together and going over plans for the holidays. Maddy was at her new friend Sarah's house.

Ever since dinner at the festival last night, Annie had felt unsettled and unsure of herself. She had called Valerie a few times, her parents' words about just letting things go replaying in her mind, panic building inside her chest. Then she'd wanted to talk about taking off her rings with the kids before she actually did it, but there hadn't been enough time. She hadn't wanted to saddle them with it before school in case they had questions or were sad. But now Matt was here and she was still wearing her rings. In short, she felt a bit like she was losing some of the control she'd gained here in the last five weeks. She was slipping again and spending her time trying to prove herself to everyone.

Annie watched Adam's expression for any clues as to who was coming over. "Okay, honey. Are they staying for dinner?"

Adam shrugged, putting his feet on the coffee table. "Uh, no, I don't think so. It's not a big deal or anything. Just hanging out."

"Right. Hanging out." What did hanging out even entail? And was that the girl Matt had been talking about?

"That's cool. Someone from school?" Matt asked, looking completely cool and collected as he took a sip of his coffee.

Adam nodded. "Yeah, she's in a couple of my classes."

Annie opened the fridge and kept her face in there, hoping it would calm the sudden surge of heat on her cheeks. A girlfriend? Adam really had a girlfriend? Maybe this was why he was acting so much happier and more . . . civilized. "Oh, I can whip up some dinner for you two," she said, taking the milk carton out of the fridge and adding a splash to her coffee. She needed to play it as cool as Matt was.

Adam shot her a sympathetic smile. "That's okay, Mom."

"You know what? Why don't I run out and pick up a couple of pizzas if she decides she wants to stay for dinner?" Matt said.

Adam nodded. "Yeah, that's cool. Thanks, Uncle Matt. Uh, I'm going to head upstairs and get ready."

"Sure, sure," Annie said as he ran up the stairs. She glared at Matt as he walked over to her, taking everything in stride. "You're such a show-off," she hissed.

He chuckled under his breath. "He's a guy, he doesn't want his mom making them a bowl of spaghetti like it's going to be a moment from *Lady and the Tramp*."

She choked on her coffee and then glared at him. "That's not funny. That's not what I was planning at all. I know not to embarrass him."

Matt gave her a lopsided grin, and it was very hard to stay mad at him. "I'm teasing. But still, he doesn't want us buzzing around here when he has a girl over. Pizza is casual. I'll get one for them and one for us. They can hang out here and we can go upstairs in the bonus room."

She drummed her fingers on the counter. "So, we just leave them down here?"

He nodded slowly. "Either that or they go to his room."

She choked on her coffee again. "I am so not cut out to be the mother of a teenager. Okay, you're right again, they should stay down here. I should pull out some snacks. I have chips and popcorn. Oh! I could put cookies in the oven . . ."

Her voice trailed off when he kept shaking his head. "It has to look casual. He doesn't want to look as though he told his mom that he likes this girl and she arranged a bunch of playdate snacks."

She rubbed her temples. "I can't handle being so wrong so many times in a row."

"Also? How are you going to whip up cookies that fast anyway?"

She took a sip of coffee, belatedly realizing it was only going to make her more anxious. "Thanks to your grandmother's recipe book. I now keep a stash of frozen cookie dough in my freezer. Fresh cookies in ten minutes!"

His mouth dropped open. "That's brilliant. No wonder whenever we'd show up there on short notice, she always managed to have cookies coming out of the oven. I mean, it's not like we needed all that, but there was something so comforting about entering a house to the smell of freshly baked cookies."

She gave him a smug smile. "So I guess you *don't* have all the answers."

He laughed and she smiled, for a second feeling a little lighter, hope a little brighter. The Christmas tree was already on and she was happy knowing that Maddy was having fun at a friend's house and Adam was starting to make friends. Even if she wasn't ready for girlfriends.

"I never claimed to, but I was on a roll, and you were very easy to bait."

She laughed. "Fine. But if we have to hang out upstairs, that means you have to help me wrap a bunch of Christmas presents."

"You might regret that."

"Oh, come on, if you can stitch up a hamster, I'm sure you can wrap a present."

"True, but I may surprise you. It's literally the one thing I can't do well."

She laughed. "Do they sell that kind of self-confidence?"

He grinned. "I was born with it. But if you need pointers, I can help. You're about as perfect as perfect can get, Annie."

Her mouth dropped open and heat ran up her neck. She picked up her mug of coffee again, needing something to do with her nervous energy. "Okay, listen, back to Adam's friend, though, I do get to meet her, right? Like I'm not just going to hide upstairs."

He cracked a smile. "Of course, you meet her and then you leave. It'll be more normal than them just hearing someone clomping around upstairs but not coming down."

"You are literally no help," she said.

Adam came running down the stairs. "She's here. She just messaged me. Mom, act cool," he said, whizzing by them to the door.

"I'll try not to take it personally that you were exempt from the *try to act cool* instruction," she whispered as they followed Adam to the mudroom.

Except he wasn't actually in the mudroom, he was standing in the hallway outside the mudroom. "What are you doing? Aren't you going to open the door?"

Both Matt and Adam gave her a look. "He has to wait for her to knock. He can't look over-anxious."

Adam shook his head, and before Annie could defend herself there was a knock on the door.

* * *

"Should I go downstairs and offer to make some cookies?"

Matt looked up from the Rudolph wrapping paper and wished he was stitching up a hamster rather than trying to wrap these gifts according to Annie's standards. He should have known better. "Uh, I thought we already discussed the cookie situation."

"Maybe I'll text him and let him know if he wants me to it's no big deal."

"Fine."

"I hope she liked the pizza."

"What teenager doesn't like pizza?"

"I heard lots of laughing," she whispered.

He smiled at her concern, despite the fact that he'd screwed up the corners on the box. He resisted the urge to rip off the paper and crumple it up and throw it across the room. "How many more presents do you have?"

She frowned at him and shoved another one across the games table. "Ten. And this is your grandmother's fault because that little Preserve Company place had so many things! Also, I hear you're an overgrown child who likes to eat gummy worms."

He leaned forward, smiling. "You can't try and shame me. I like candy."

Her eyes were sparkling, and he found her irresistible. More and more. Every day it was becoming harder to keep their relationship a secret. And he loved being around Adam and Maddy, it felt right. He still wanted to talk to Annie about what happened with his mother last night. He'd tried calling his mother after, but she had said she had a headache and had all but hung up on him. Then today he'd been busy with work. Something was up, and he needed to make it clear that whatever reservations she had, going after Annie like that wasn't okay.

Annie didn't need any more pressure, least of all from his mother and her bizarre questioning.

"I think this is a good thing that he's making friends. Not sure I'm ready for girlfriends, but he's looked a lot happier this week."

"I've noticed too. She probably has friends too, and that'll help him get to know other people. All in all, a positive thing—especially when it comes to your deal. This may be the exact thing that's needed to make him want to stay."

They paused when they heard a crash followed by a few "omigods" and then laughter as Jingle came charging up the stairs as though he'd just robbed a bank.

"Jingle knocked over a glass, we've got it covered," Adam called up.

Jingle jumped up onto the table and sprawled out on the gift wrap. Purrfect. Now he wouldn't have to keep wrapping the gifts. Unless Annie asked him to. "Jingle, you're a troublemaker," Matt said, scuffing up the fur on his head.

"He totally is. His obsession with knocking glasses over is funny, but not funny."

"Though I have a feeling that Ella liking the cat will go a long way in how Adam perceives Jingle."

Just as she was about to answer, her phone buzzed. She sat up as though the chair was on fire and grabbed her phone, frowned, and sat back down.

"Everything okay?"

She nodded. "Yeah. I just thought it was Maddy."

"So . . . not Maddy?"

She shook her head, her jaw clenched, and started picking up the bows like she was plucking weeds from the garden. "My sister."

"Ah. Did you want to call her? I don't mind at all."

She shook her head. "No . . . I mean, I did call her last night."

He paused, on high alert. "And?"

She sat there holding her phone, not looking at him. "I was feeling like maybe I was harsh with her . . ."

"For going behind your back and messing with your kid? How about boundaries?"

She snapped her head up to look at him. She chewed her lower lip for a moment and he regretted how harshly he had spoken.

"Hey," he said, reaching out to take her hand. "I'm sorry if that sounded harsh or like I was judging you. I know your history with her. I've heard a lot about her over the years, from Cam, then from you. We've been friends a lot longer than we've been together, so I'm just looking out for you. That's all. You make whatever decisions you want to make."

She drew a shaky breath and squeezed his hand. "Before last night, I would have agreed with you. Honestly, I still haven't gotten over her going behind my back with Adam. She could have made everything so much worse. But he's a loyal kid, and I'm glad that he understood that he was being manipulated. There's this sense of entitlement she has that I can't understand. I'm . . . I feel like I'm being pushed, and I don't know how much longer I can take this."

"Hey, you don't have to take anything longer than you have to. No one is judging you here. Your priority is your kids, right? Your own mental health. Not some conniving, manipulating, entitled forty-something sister. You had to pick yourself and your kids up after your husband died. That's the shit that life deals that we can't control. There is stuff in our lives we can control."

She shot him a look and he didn't know if he'd overstepped. But it was the truth. She nodded. "I needed to hear that. It was brought on by that dinner with your family. It made me feel like I was doing everything wrong. And I get the feeling your mother really doesn't like me. Sitting there reminded me of growing up, answering all sorts of questions and having to defend myself, because Valerie was making things up about me. I don't know . . . I wanted to make a good impression on your mom. I want her to like me. I know it sounds juvenile, but at this point in my life, I don't want conflict. I had that with my family. I grew up second-guessing myself over everything. I can't do that again, Matt."

He ran a hand over his jaw, anger toward himself running through him. He should have sorted this out with his mother that morning before work. He had thought he'd made it clear that Sunday night after dinner when Jessica was there. He didn't think it would need addressing again. Had he known Annie was now internalizing this and making it her problem, he would have. He should have known that questioning would have struck a vulnerable chord with her. "You're not in the wrong. My mother is."

She shook her head, looking down in her lap. "Your grandmother said something similar. Actually, she gave me a really great therapy session," she said with a hollow laugh, but he heard the break in it. She pulled her hand from his and stroked Jingle, who started purring loudly. "I struggle with duty and guilt and my parents, even though they're gone. Sometimes I'm really mad at them for putting me in this situation. My sister didn't just turn out like this at forty-three. She was always like this, but they could never control her or stand up to her. For a long time, they even believed her lies. I would have to defend myself over and over and sometimes I still feel like I'm being judged by others. I panic at what others think of me. I can't establish boundaries.

"I know where they should be, but I never enforce them. I can be a pushover. A people-pleaser. Growing up, I had to be in order to keep the peace. If Valerie wasn't happy, it was because of me, and I learned to just keep her happy at all costs. It wasn't until I left home for university that I realized how I'd been conditioned to please my sister at all costs. My parents had done the same, and it was almost as though they were also afraid of Valerie's temper."

He wanted to say how abusive that whole dynamic was, how her parents had wronged her, but he didn't think that's what she needed to hear right now. He also wanted to tell her that he didn't give a shit what people thought of him and that she should adopt his policy, but they were different people. He didn't want her to think that he was judging her too. He searched for the right words, the ones that would acknowledge what she'd been through but also encourage her to take control over her life. She was the strongest woman he knew, and hell if he was going to watch her go down because of her sister's deceit or his mother's interference.

"Family is family, until they're not. Until they betray that all-access pass they have and rip your heart out. As far as I'm concerned, even if you forgive, it's hard to earn back trust. No amount of blood or DNA can make up for lies or disloyalty or abuse. So you either keep looking in the past, at the way things should have been, or you start looking forward, at the way things can be. That way you don't miss out on the miracles you have coming."

She covered her face, and he couldn't just sit and watch her cry. "Come here," he said, pulling her onto his lap. She buried her face in his neck. "How are you able to do that?" she whispered, pulling back to look at him.

He wiped the tears from her face, slowly leaning up to kiss the trails of dampness. "You deserve so much more than they all gave you. I don't want to influence you, but I don't want to see you cave. You've come so far. You're almost free. You came here for a reason, don't forget that."

She stared into his eyes, and he forgot who he was without her. He forgot the years he'd spent without her here. She framed his face with her hands and kissed him. He held her to him, one hand around her waist and the other in that gorgeous hair at the nape of her neck. He kissed her with all the love he had for her, all the dreams he'd had about her. She pulled back a moment later, when they heard a crash. Jingle was watching them. Matt's glass was on the floor.

They both laughed as Jingle just sprawled out, his feather-duster tail floating back and forth, a blatantly nonchalant gesture. "Thanks, Jingle," Matt said.

Annie laughed, scrambling off his lap and picking up the glass. "Thanks, Matt."

"You never have to thank me, remember?"

She gave him a small smile.

"What was, uh, Valerie's text?"

She averted her gaze for a moment and then picked up her phone, pulled up the message, and handed it to him. A knot formed in the pit of his stomach as his gaze went from hers to the screen. *You should learn how to have peaceful relationships, they benefit everyone. Especially your children. They have already lost so much and now they are losing me because of you. One day they will ask questions and I will tell them the truth.*

He wanted to whip the phone across the room. Chuck it in the ocean. But he didn't want to look like he had anger issues, though after reading this, it would prompt even the calmest of people to vent. "Annie, you know this is bullshit, right? This is gaslighting. *She* is unable to have peaceful relationships. Does she have any friends? Any romantic relationships? Do the kids like her? Did she bring joy to your parents?"

Annie shook her head.

"Don't doubt your instincts. Don't doubt the evidence. The truth."

She took a deep breath. "You're right. She's just catching me in a vulnerable spot. But I know all this. Rationally, I know everything you said is right. It's just harder to execute. I think one thing and I do another. I cave. I'm so afraid of conflict with her."

He reached for her hand, giving it a squeeze. "What's the worst that will happen if you tell her what you're willing to accept and what you're not?"

"She would stop speaking to me."

"Is that such a bad thing?"

She smiled. "Those really are the best moments in our relationship."

He leaned forward and gave her a soft kiss. "There's your answer. Why don't you just block her?"

"Because it's a security measure. If I answer or read her texts, at least I can get a glimpse of what she's up to so I can preempt any kind of attack."

He stilled. "Annie . . . you can't keep living like this."

She shrugged and fiddled with some of the ribbon. "I know. I just need to figure it out. Also, I'm not liking you being right so often."

"You'll get used to it."

She poked him in the shoulder, laughing. He grabbed her hand and kissed it. She sucked in a breath and he wanted nothing more than to kiss her until they both forgot about Valerie. The problem was, the more he kissed her, the more he didn't want to stop. He'd loved her for so long, she'd been his best friend for so long, that all of this was happening so fast, but he didn't want to scare her off. "This is another area you really excel at," she said.

He leaned forward and kissed her on the forehead, reconciling himself to that being enough. "Good. I have something else to impress you with. What are you doing tomorrow night?"

She raised a brow. "Uh, the usual? Homework, dishes, laundry?"

"You are very easy to impress. How about I pick you up at five?"

CHAPTER NINETEEN

"I've got a little black dress, a long black dress, and a red dress," Kate said, holding up all three options.

They were currently in Annie's bedroom. Annie had called her in a panic after receiving a text from Matt, saying he had forgotten to mention to dress up. Kate had come through and shown up on her doorstep within the hour. That was a true friend. Annie's gaze went back and forth from each dress, completely torn. "They're all gorgeous, I have no idea. I'm also running out of time."

Kate held up the red one. "This is a showstopper, I'm not going to lie. Heads will turn."

Annie made a face. "I'm not really a *heads will turn* type of person. I could never pull it off, and then I'll be asking Matt for his jacket. I mean, I'm assuming he's wearing a jacket if I'm getting all dressed up, right?"

Kate rolled her eyes. "He didn't tell me where you're going. But I did yell at him for only giving you a couple of hours notice that this is a formal event. What if I wasn't here? What then, I told him."

Annie tried not to laugh at Kate's exasperation. "What did he say?"

Kate put a hand to her heart. "Are you prepared for this? I wasn't. I almost drove into a ditch. He said that you could wear a paper bag and still be the most gorgeous woman in the room."

Annie resisted the urge to fan her face. "As well as I know Matt . . . I never expected him to be this . . ."

"Romantic?" Kate asked, finishing her thought.

Annie nodded, sitting on the edge of her bed. "Yes. It's so weird because we already know each other so well. But now there's this whole other side to get to know. I mean, we never talked about past relationships. We always kept things to ourselves. Not that I've dated anyone since Cam died. But he obviously has. He's just never really said much."

"Because there's nothing much to say. All I can tell you is that when you're around, he's a different guy. Don't get me wrong—Matt is a great guy, but when he's with you, there's a depth there that he doesn't often show. You bring out a really great side of my brother."

She thought of their conversation last night about Valerie. "He does the same for me. He's got this confidence that I really admire."

"You can admire it because you didn't grow up with it!" They both laughed at that. "But you're right. He does have confidence without being a jerk about it. I like to think he uses it in the right way. And I have a feeling he's got something up his sleeve tonight. I tried to get it out of him, but he wouldn't say a thing."

Annie's heart raced. "I'm totally in the dark."

Kate glanced at her watch. "Ah! Too much talking. We're running out of time!"

Annie's gaze darted back and forth to the dresses. "Okay, I'm going to make my final decision. Okay, so let's say no to the red dress. Too much pressure. Pros and cons for long versus short dress, because they're both gorgeous?"

"Short dress is actually knee-skimming, so a very flattering length, and the long one is a bit more formal, I'd say. The neckline is gorgeous. Not too much cleavage, just enough to still be classy."

Annie laughed. "I don't think I've worn anything other than a crewneck for the last five years, so I'm sure I'll feel half-naked no matter what I wear. I guess I'll go with the long one."

Kate nodded, handing her the dress. "Good choice. It's a showstopper as well."

"Okay, so all I have to do is get dressed. Makeup is done. Hair is done. Shoes are by the mirror. Oh, and I want to talk to the kids before I leave," she said, staring down at her hand.

"Want me to get them?"

"Thanks. And thanks for everything, Kate. Even staying here with them tonight—you know you don't have to. Adam is more than old enough."

Kate smiled. "My brother isn't the only one happy to have you all here. I'm thrilled. And I genuinely love hanging out with your kids. We're going to watch another movie and eat junk food."

Annie reached out and hugged her. "Thank you."

"You're welcome," Kate said walking to the door.

Annie took a deep breath and waited for the kids to come in. A few minutes later she heard them running up the stairs and into her room.

"Oh, Mom, I love your hair and makeup! You look beautiful. Doesn't she look beautiful, Adam?" Maddy said, her eyes wide.

Adam grinned. "She looks the same. Just red lips and puffy hair."

Maddy shook her head.

"Thanks, guys. I think. So, um, I wanted to talk to you about something."

"You and Uncle Matt?"

Annie nodded.

"You've got two thumbs up from me," Maddy said.

Adam rolled his eyes. "Are you forty? Who even says that?"

"Okay, Adam, let's not argue. Maddy, thank you, honey. Adam?"

Adam lifted a shoulder and she searched for signs of sadness or anger in his eyes but found none. "He's the best."

She let out the breath she'd been holding onto. "Okay, so one last thing. You know how much I loved your dad, how much I will always love him. I think it's time I took off these rings. I just didn't want either of you thinking that I forgot about him or didn't love him."

Neither of them said anything for a moment. Both of them were staring at her hand. Adam spoke up first. "We know, Mom. It's okay."

Maddy nodded. "Go out and have fun with Uncle Matt. Besides, I think he's already here. I heard a knock at the door."

Annie jumped up from the bed. "Omigosh. Okay, just tell him I'll be down in a minute. I love you guys. You're the best kids in the world."

"We know," they both said in unison as they left the room, a rare show of agreement.

Annie couldn't even dwell on the sweetness of the moment. She quickly shut the door after they left and pulled off the rings that had been on her hand for fourteen years. But it was time. She should have done this earlier. She had grieved and she had survived. She couldn't move forward, with her whole heart, with the rings on. She took a deep breath and placed them in the jewelry box on her dresser and shut the lid. She sat there for a moment, her hand still on the lid, before slowly standing and walking toward the dress she was going to wear for another step toward her future.

Five minutes later, she stood in her heels and dress in front of the full-length mirror, taking in this version of herself she hadn't seen in so long. She looked good. She smoothed the silky fabric over her waist. The dress was held up with thin spaghetti straps, and the silky black fabric draped into a cowlneck and then hugged her body until the bottom where it flared out slightly. It felt as though it was made for her. Or for this version of her life.

This life, where she was surrounded by people who supported her and didn't judge her. All the events she'd had to go to with Valerie had felt like she was being observed under a microscope. The minute Valerie would see her dressed up, she'd start giving her pointers on how to drop a few pounds or how cutting back on carbs would give her a less puffy appearance. If Valerie was here tonight, Annie's self-confidence would be in tatters and she would probably be wearing a sweater to cover up her cleavage. Matt had never made her feel as though she was lacking in anything. She wanted to gain all her confidence back. She wanted to be an example to Maddy.

Taking a deep breath, she fiddled with one of the tendrils of hair that had been left out of the elegant, soft French twist

Kate had helped her with. She was ready. No more stalling. She opened her bedroom door and walked down the hall, hearing everyone's voices at the door. Good grief, it felt like she was going to prom. Everyone was waiting for her. The most important people were waiting for her.

She tried not to look nervous as she rounded the corner, but everyone stopped speaking the moment she did.

"Wow." Matt had spoken first and she already knew she was blushing when she met his gaze. There was a fire there that terrified and thrilled her all at the same time. "You look incredible, Annie."

Kate and Maddy did a little squeal of delight and clasped their hands together. Adam rolled his eyes.

"Thank you. So do you," she said, taking in how he'd dressed up.

His hair was actually combed and styled perfectly. He was clean-shaven, the hard lines of his jaw a contrast to his sensual mouth. His dark suit clung to his broad shoulders and athletic build. The white shirt and navy tie were a striking contrast to his tanned skin. But it was his blue eyes and all the approval there that made her breathless. He was a very handsome man. He had always been, but now even more so, somehow.

"Well, we'd better get going if we're going to make our reservations," he said, holding out her coat for her.

She smiled awkwardly and stepped into it, with everyone still watching them. "Thank you," she said formally.

"You're welcome. Goodnight, guys, we'll be home by midnight," he said, opening the door.

Annie gave them all a quick kiss on the cheek, including Kate, who gave her hand an extra squeeze, and then left. The cold night air calmed her flushed skin as they stepped outside.

She let out a sigh of relief as the door shut behind them. "Now I know how celebrities feel," Matt said, placing his hand on the small of her back as they walked toward his truck.

She let out a soft laugh, a nervous energy still buzzing through her. "I know. If it wasn't so awkward it would have been funny."

He held the door open for her. "Exactly."

She settled in her seat as he made his way to the driver's side. Soon they were on their way through the cornfield. "Okay, so now are you going tell me where we're going?"

He grinned but kept his eyes on the road. "Nope. It's about a twenty-minute drive. I wanted to get there before sunset, and we should make it."

They chatted while they drove, catching up on the day's events. She gasped when she read the sign as they pulled up to a stunning old estate. "It's the hotel from the movie. But Matt, this place is closed for the season."

"Ah, ye of little faith. You don't get to grow up on this island, become a vet, and do favors for people without having a few owed in return."

"Like the cookies."

"Exactly."

"So . . . they opened up for just you?"

He parked the truck and turned to her. "Annie, you hurt me. It's not *just* me. I'm Dr. Matt, the vet. Of course they'd open up for me. Come on."

She was laughing as he helped her out of the truck. She was grateful for it, because she was out of practice walking in three-inch heels. The wind off the ocean had a bite to it, but she didn't mind as she took in the old estate, with its wraparound porch and vast grounds. He held her hand as they walked up the steps. A man held the door open for them.

"Evening, Dr. Matt. I can take your coat, Dr. Annie," he said.

Annie shot Matt an impressed look. He gave her a little wink, which she found an adorable alternate to his smirk of triumph. "Thank you," she said, as he helped her out of it.

"We have your table all ready for you," he said, handing the coat to a woman who was waiting nearby.

He led the way and she and Matt followed. Matt's hand on the small of her back was a distraction and a comfort all at the same time. They walked through the lobby of the hotel and she soaked it all in; the massive floor-to-ceiling fireplace, lit with a roaring fire, soft lighting from the chandeliers highlighting the rich and historic décor and thick trim and moldings.

She paused for a moment, gasping as he led them into the dining room. The curved wall of windows overlooked a lake. Tables with white tablecloths lined the wall. But only one table in the center was set. White china and crystal glasses, flickering candles and white roses, filled their table. There was a woman playing the piano at the other end of the room, the soft music the ultimate touch to the most romantic place she'd ever been. Matt thanked the man and then held her chair for her before sitting across from her.

She was speechless. She leaned forward. "Matt, I don't know what to say."

He reached for her hand and paused for a second, something flickering across his eyes, before he brought it to his lips and kissed her knuckles. It was a good thing she was sitting down, because this side of him was unlike anything she'd ever experienced. "You deserve all of this. I just wanted a night for both of us to enjoy each other's company without any distraction. And I know I said it before, but it was in front of everyone else, and God, you look incredible, Annie. I mean, you always look incredible, but this. Tonight. You're beautiful."

She forgot to breathe as his gaze went from her eyes to her lips.

A server came over to their table and went over the dinner selection and wine list. Once they'd ordered, Matt leaned forward. "Would you like to dance?"

She looked around. "What? Really? Here?'

He stood, holding out his hand. "Why not? We have the place all to ourselves. We have the best pianist on the island, and we have the sunset out the window."

"Um, okay," she said, feeling breathless and swept off her feet.

He led her over to the windows at the far end of the room, where there weren't any tables, and slowly pulled her close. She hadn't danced . . . she hadn't danced in so long. And she had never danced with him. His hand was large and warm and wrapped around hers like a luxurious blanket. His body was tall and strong and she looked up at him, prepared to tell him how much this meant to her, but he beat her to it.

"I have wanted to do this for so long. I'm so glad we're here," he said, slowly bending his head and kissing her. But it couldn't be just a quick kiss, because there was too much there, too many moments, too many laughs, too much history, too many unspoken truths between them, too much lost time and dreams for the kiss to end. She didn't realize they'd stopped dancing until she felt his hand at the nape of her neck, the other pulling her close.

He'd taken her breath away, her reservations away, he'd taken away everything except her heart.

When he finally pulled back, she held onto his forearms. "I didn't know this . . . you . . . could be like this," she said, feeling ridiculous once she'd blurted that out.

A corner of his mouth rose, and his hand framed one side of her face, his thumb grazing her bottom lip. "For you, Annie. Don't think this is something I do for anyone."

She took a deep breath. "You are a man of surprises. I just . . . I just can't reconcile you right now . . . and the image of you snagging free cheese in rumpled jeans and a baseball cap and stubble."

He threw back his head and laughed. She held onto him, because she just couldn't let go. "You're a great ego check."

She placed her hands on his chest. "I'm teasing. Kind of. But, um, you've made me feel alive again, Matt. This is the very definition of being swept off my feet. And you . . . all joking aside, you, um, what am I trying to say . . ."

He bent his head and kissed the spot under her ear.

She held onto his waist and searched for the words but struggled. "You make me forget everything except wanting to be with you."

He raised his head, his eyes glittering. "The feeling is mutual. But, uh, since I do have a bit of a competitive spirit and ego as you like to mention, I think I can do better than that at describing the feeling."

Her mouth dropped open and she leaned into him as he dipped his head and whispered in her ear exactly how he felt and what he imagined them doing.

"Excuse me, Dr. Matt, but your appetizers are ready to be served."

"We'll be right there," Matt said.

Annie was staring at Matt, all her limbs feeling too weak to walk anywhere, her face on fire, her body a jumble of electricity. "Who are you?"

He grinned and took her hand in his. "Just a man falling for you, Annie."

* * *

Matt took a sip of his coffee, Annie's hand in his, and fell more in love with her by the second. It was too soon to tell her, he wasn't a complete moron, but tonight had been incredible. She was incredible. And she was gorgeous. He'd always known that, but they'd seen each other at their worst on most days, and hell, he'd still found her to be the most gorgeous woman. But tonight, there was something different and it had nothing to do with the figure-hugging dress she wore, or the way her curves were accentuated in that dress, or the makeup or the hair . . . there was an openness to her. Like she was free. And he read the desire in her eyes, he felt the trembling of her body, he felt the heat in her kiss. She trusted him. She trusted him with that desire, and that meant everything to him.

And he'd noticed very early on that her rings were gone. It had taken him a moment to wrestle with his emotions over that, to separate the guilt he felt at being relieved she'd taken them off. His best friend had bought her those rings. But he was gone, and Matt was here. He had wrestled with his feelings for years. The only thing he could come up with to make himself okay with all of this was that all he could do was treat Annie the way Cam would have wanted her to be treated. To treat her the way her kids wanted her to be treated. And after that, he had to shut off those thoughts and be in the present. Because as much as he loved Annie, and had for a very long time, he would still have given anything for Cam to still be alive.

He decided he wasn't going to ask Annie about the rings. If she wanted to bring it up to him, then she could. But tonight was supposed to be about them. They already knew they were best friends, but this other side seemed like it was a surprise to her. It wasn't to him. The attraction had always been there for him, smoldering, electric, but always present. He was glad that she was able to let herself go and feel it as well. But he'd never pressure her to move faster. Hell, he'd waited a lifetime, he could wait forever if it meant having her.

CHAPTER TWENTY

Two days until Christmas

"This meal was excellent. Another award-winning, pre-Christmas dinner I wish I could at least say I helped with," Matt said, smiling at his mother.

Claire beamed, sitting up a little straighter. "Thank you."

"You not helping is probably the reason it's so good," Kate said, with a wink.

Everyone laughed. The Christmas tree in the dining room was set in the bay window and cast a warm glow at the end of the long room. Fresh greens with gold candles were in the center of the table. China plates and platters rimmed with a gold band and images of vintage Santas made the tablescape feel as though it were from a magazine spread. Dinner conversation had been lively and the food had been delicious.

Matt's family had included them as though they'd always been part of their Christmas festivities and Annie's kids acted as though they were perfectly at home. Annie stared at them, marveling at how well they fit in, how they basked in the attention they were getting. They hadn't had a Christmas like this in . . . forever, or never maybe. Of course, when Cam had been alive, they'd had their own family traditions and had loved Christmas, but it had always been filled with drama from Annie's family. There had always been a shadow around Christmas and she'd had to work so hard to make it special for the kids. But she was so grateful that her kids were able to enjoy a drama-free Christmas for once.

Annie was actually able to breathe this Christmas—a first in her entire life. She knew it was because Valerie wasn't here. The only thing Annie wished for was a softening toward her from Claire.

"I can at least help clear the table, though," Matt said, standing.

Annie and Kate started collecting and scraping plates as well. "This is all we can trust him with, sadly."

"Well, that's not true. Remember the time he hosted Christmas dinner at his first house? That was a lovely meal," Claire said, with a proud smile at Matt.

Matt grinned and shot Kate a triumphant smile.

Kate scoffed. "Mom, he didn't cook. He called in random favors from people around the island. He basically arranged a potluck."

Annie gasped, barely containing her laughter as she watched him erupt into laughter as he kept stacking plates. "It seems to be a thing with him," Annie said to Kate.

"Don't be jealous of my popularity," he said, laughter in his voice.

"Adam and Maddy, why don't you two come with me to the family room? I have a little treat for the two of you—consider them early Christmas presents," Lila said, giving the kids a wink.

"Okay!" Maddy said as she and Adam followed Lila.

A lump formed in Annie's throat as she watched them. This was the way Christmas was supposed to be. Filled with people who loved each other, people who made kids the priority. They had taken them in as though they were long-lost relatives. She would never forget their kindness.

Matt passed by her, placing a hand on the small of her back and giving her a light kiss on the temple, before joining his mother in the kitchen.

"I'd say my brother is head over heels in love. I've never seen him like this. He even acts civil," Kate said with a laugh.

Annie let out a deep sigh of contentment, gratitude. "I never thought I could be this happy. I know that may sound cynical, but I couldn't believe it. There is just this sense that this is so right. All of you . . . you've made us feel like a part of the family from day one."

Kate out to hug her. "You are. You are always family, Annie."

They walked into the kitchen, the energy suddenly changing. Matt's mother's gaze darted to Annie before she quickly returned to loading dishes into the dishwasher.

"Everything okay in here?" Kate asked as she placed the platters she was carrying on the island.

Matt crossed his arms and stared at his mother. "I don't know. Mom said something cryptic about Annie having problems with alcohol."

A flood of heat washed through Annie, enough to make her legs and body feel like it was made of jelly. Maybe it was instinct or premonition, but she'd felt this energy before.

Matt's mom looked up with a sigh, her gaze going from Annie to Matt. "I . . . I'm sorry if I was wrong, but that's what I was told."

Annie started shaking, and she clutched the counter. She knew. Deep inside. She knew. Her stomach churned and she wanted to run. She forced the words out, because running wasn't an option. She had basically run to this island . . . only to be under fire again. "By who?"

Claire's face turned white and she stared down at the counter. "Your sister."

Matt swore under his breath. "How are *you* in touch with her sister?"

She looked up from the counter, wringing her hands together. "She started calling me shortly after Annie and the kids arrived on the island."

Annie covered her face. She knew what this meant. This had been Valerie's plan, a campaign against Annie, filling Claire's head with lies. The walls seemed to move closer, squeezing the breath out of her. Her skin felt itchy, foreign, like it didn't belong on her and she wanted out. She didn't want to be here. She didn't want to hear the rest of this. The thought of having to defend herself again, like she had growing up, here in this new life she'd created for herself, made her panicked. What things had Valerie said about her? How humiliating.

She took a step away from Matt's mother, from Matt. From this world she'd wanted to be her safe space. Valerie wasn't supposed to be here. This was her place. Her family. Not Valerie's. Would she ever have her own place? Would she forever have to defend herself, have to defend the truth? Would she spend a lifetime proving her self-worth?

Lila appeared behind her in the doorway and placed a hand on her shoulder. At least Lila knew the truth. At least Lila wouldn't believe the lies.

* * *

Matt turned to his mother, his body rigid, his anger palpable. "Mom, you can't possibly think that's appropriate."

"Grandma, I'll go hang out with the kids and keep them entertained," Kate said.

Lila was standing in the doorway; Annie didn't know how long she'd been there. But their conversation at the restaurant popped into her mind and she was relieved.

"It's not that I believed her, it just caught me by surprise. It was just chitchat for a few moments and then she thought she needed to tell me a few things about Annie . . . out of concern for me and you, Matt."

Annie wanted to cover her ears or throw up. She folded her arms across her chest in an effort to quell the trembling that had started.

"That didn't strike you as odd? That Annie's sister would be calling to protect you?"

Claire kept wringing her hands. "It was a weak moment. You are my soft spot. She said that Annie was really struggling after Cam's death, that she wasn't ready for new relationships, that she would never love anyone else. And that she'd never have more children or want more children because she was already having a hard time with Adam. She said that Annie had a drinking problem and that there was no way she'd live on the island for long, that she hadn't sold her house in Toronto and would be back by the summer."

"My God," Matt said under his breath.

Annie stepped forward, anger and determination winning out over self-pity and anxiety, before Matt could say anything else. She needed to stand up for herself. She needed to assert herself. "Claire, with all due respect . . . I . . . I'm not going to defend myself. I will not. I refuse to. I spent my entire life defending myself against my sister's crazy lies. I did not expect to have to do that here.

"If you would rather believe the things someone you have never met before says about me, then there is nothing I have to say. But I'm here, you could have asked me at any time. I guess that's why you invited Jessica over that Sunday. It makes a lot of sense now. My kids deserve better than this. Rumors, lies, talking behind my back . . . that's not anything I want anymore. That's not the environment I want my kids in. Thank you for a lovely dinner, Merry Christmas, we're leaving."

"I'll go with you," Matt said.

His mother's face had turned a grayish color, and her eyes were filled with tears. Normally, that would have been enough for Annie. She would have felt bad for making someone else feel bad and she would have caved, brushed it under the rug, maybe even helped the other person because it would have been awkward to witness someone else's pain and humiliation.

But Lila's words, about knowing where the line was, replayed over and over again in her head. The line had been crossed.

She looked up at Matt, saw the anger in his eyes, and knew she needed space from him too. "We're fine. You stay here with your mom. Maybe you can sort this out."

His eyes glittered, his jaw clenched, and he reached out to hold her hands. "Where you go, I go. I can't let you leave like this."

She forced a smiled. "I'm fine. But I can't have you leave your mom like this. Fix this between the two of you."

"This is the three of us."

"I know . . . but I'm not going to be the cause of a rift between you. I'm fine. I'll get the kids and we'll talk later," she said, pulling her hands from his, needing her own space.

"I'll call you," he said thickly.

She nodded and Lila put her arm around her, walking her out of the room. "I'm proud of you, Annie. Don't give up. On Matt. This is going to be okay. But I know how hard it was to do what you just did. I'm so proud of you."

Annie reached out to give Lila a hug, barely holding onto the sobs that had collected in her chest. She'd never heard those words from her parents. She'd never had support for standing up for herself. "Thank you, Lila."

*　*　*

Matt knew how close he was to losing everything. His mother had unknowingly played into one of Valerie's traps, and it killed him because he knew Annie was close to breaking. "What were you thinking?" he said, barely holding onto his anger after Annie and the kids left.

Saying goodbye to them and following Annie's cue of pretending everything was normal had taken Herculean effort and had given him a glimpse of how she'd been forced to live her life. Faking it in front of the kids for so many years in order to shield them from her sister's manipulations wasn't healthy. There was only so much of that a person could deal with.

"I did it for you," she whispered.

He shook his head. "No, don't use me as an excuse. You did it for you."

She crossed her arms, her chin wobbling. "Valerie said that Annie was going to leave with the kids and you'd follow. I almost lost you once to Melissa, I wasn't going to do it again."

He shoved his hands into his hair, trying to keep his cool, trying to remember that she had done this out of fear. "It doesn't matter why, it's that you did it. What you should have done was come to me, tell me how you were feeling, what your worries were. I thought I made it clear the night you invited Jessica over that I make my own life decisions. Not you. Listening to someone's whack-job sister, how did that seem like a good idea? And what kind of sibling goes calling up the mother of the person they're dating and starts trash-talking them behind their back? What, she was just so concerned out of the goodness of her heart, for you, a virtual stranger, that she would talk about her sister like that?"

She covered her face with her hands for a moment. "You're right. Matt, you're right. It was stupid and I was insecure. I should tell Annie."

He ran a hand over his jaw. "Mom, you have no idea what you've done. This goes beyond an apology. You sided with the person who has made Annie's life a living hell without ever having a real conversation with Annie. Could you even imagine me calling up my sister's boyfriend's mother and trash-talking her? How insane is that?"

She wiped her eyes and lifted her chin. "You would never do that."

"Mom, you believed that she was an alcoholic and listened to God knows how many other lies about her without ever telling any of us."

His mother braced her hands on the counter in front of the sink, staring at the pitch-black sky, her profile to them. "I wanted to believe those things. I thought if they were true, that I could keep you safe, that I could keep you here. I almost lost you when Melissa moved away, and I didn't want to lose you for good this time."

"I wouldn't have left for Melissa, but I would leave for Annie and her kids. I'd go to hell and back for them, I'd go anywhere for them. As an adult, that is my right. You may not like it, you may be sad about it, but this is my life to live. You had your decisions to make, I have mine. You can't hold me; you can't hold any of us here forever. It's selfish. That may be harsh, but it's the truth.

"Would you really have me here, miserable, but by your side? Or would you want me with the woman I love, and my own family? Wouldn't you want that? I am an adult. You can have your opinions, you can disagree with my choices, but you can't actively try and change the course of my life based on your own needs. I never thought I would have to say this to you. Again."

Tears fell from her eyes. "Of course, I want that. You're right. I was being selfish. I wanted to believe what Valerie was telling me because then I wouldn't feel guilty because Annie wouldn't have been the right person for you. It was convenient. How wrong I've been."

"How many times did you speak to Valerie?"

His mother drew a shaky breath. "She's called me at least once a week."

He cursed under his breath. What a piece of work Valerie was. "And that seemed normal to you?"

"Of course not. I'm not trying to make excuses, but she caught me at a weak moment. I was insecure and the holidays brought up so many memories. I was remembering your father and how I loved him so much and I thought he loved me just as much, and then one day he was just gone. The thought of you being gone was just too overwhelming. I saw the way you felt about Annie. It was obvious. And it wasn't just about me not wanting to lose you, it was about all these issues Annie had. I didn't want you involved with a person with so many problems."

He shoved his hands in his pockets, trying to wade through the mess of emotions coursing through him. "I'm not Dad. What he did inadvertently gave me my biggest life lesson. I know what kind of man I am. I'm not him. Me leaving here doesn't mean walking out on you and Grandma and Kate and never looking back. That's abandonment. I will never do that to you. I love all of you. I know the sacrifices you made to raise me as a single mom, to keep it together after he left. I have so much love and respect for you.

"I would always come and visit and you would come and visit me. There is always a bedroom for you in my house, a place for you at my table. All of you. I know the holidays are hard for you, but again, you should have come to me. You should have realized there was something very wrong with what Valerie was doing. And the notion of Annie having problems . . . I'm pissed for her, Mom. I was raised in a family of strong women, and she is right up there. To hear her maligned like that guts me. You have no idea what she's been through. You have no idea what it took for her to stand up to you and refuse to defend herself. But I will stand here until I'm blue in the face defending her, because she deserves nothing less. She is someone you should be proud to have as part of our family."

His mother nodded, quickly wiping the tears from her eyes with a holly printed dish towel. Christmas. This whole night was a sham. This was supposed to be the Christmas he gave to Annie and her kids. This was supposed to be him helping restore her faith in love, in the holidays. Instead, she had walked out.

"Do you know how long I have loved her? This isn't just some woman I met at a bar last weekend. I have loved her for years. She has been my best friend for years. I was so hell-bent on not allowing myself to be in love with her because I thought I was betraying Cam. The obstacles we had to overcome to get here . . . only to have my own mother conspiring against us."

Kate walked over to him and hugged him. He held onto her. They didn't often hug, but it meant a lot to know she had his back. "Do you want to know one of the things I love most about you?"

Matt pulled back, taking in her expression, shocked that she admitted to loving anything about him. They rarely did that kind of thing. There was an unspoken love and trust between them, but it had always remained in that realm and he'd been okay with that. They teased more than they cried and it had worked for them up until this point. But he'd be a liar if he didn't admit he was curious. "I'm afraid to ask."

Instead of giving him a smart-ass remark or smirk as he'd expected, she tilted her head and stared into his eyes. "Your morality. Your sense of right and wrong. For you, so much of life has been black and white. I feel like the rest of the world is living in this ambiguous gray fog where anything goes, where anything can be justified. And then there's you. You act like you're all carefree, but when it comes down to it, you have your shit together. And you're willing to stand up for the truth, even if it hurts. You're a good guy, Matt. You and Annie make a great couple, and those kids adore you."

There was silence in the room after her speech. They both looked over at their mother, who was now sitting at the table, her head in her hands. "I've made such a mess."

"What are you going to do, Matt?" his grandmother asked, walking up to him, her hand on his arm.

"I don't know. But I have to find a way to make this right."

His mother stood up again and started pacing the room. "I have to as well. I can't let Annie think that I don't like her or don't approve of her. And those poor kids, what if they think I'm rejecting them? They're such lovely children. She has done a wonderful job with them. None of this would have happened if I hadn't let myself get taken in by that woman. Why would she lie about her sister like that?"

"Because she's jealous of her. She's jealous of the life she's built for herself. She's jealous of Annie's resiliency, of her dedication to her children even when their life got derailed. She is jealous of everything that is good, and she won't stop until she gets what she wants—and that is for Annie to be her punching bag for the rest of her life. It's for Annie to never have her own life."

Everyone stilled at his grandmother's ferocious tone and vehement analysis of Valerie. She was right, though. The grim realization of what Annie already knew was that her sister wanted to keep her as a puppet. Someone to control.

He placed his hand on his grandmother's shoulder, feeling the tension there. It was amazing to him how one person could cause such a chasm in an otherwise solid family. But he was witnessing it in real time. Except his family was solid and his mother recognized that she was wrong. This was what Annie had witnessed growing up—but worse, because no one had ever stood up to her sister, stood up for her. The feeling in his gut wouldn't leave, though, the feeling that Annie was going to run. He needed to make his move, he needed to save their relationship, and Christmas.

CHAPTER TWENTY-ONE

Annie held the smile until she shut Maddy's door completely, and then it fell from her face like a boulder dropped into the ocean once she was safely in the dark hallway.

She had managed to pretend everything was fine; she had kept her smile, kept the excitement for Christmas the entire drive home and during bedtime tuck-in. Maddy had gone on and on about how this was going to be an amazing Christmas. She walked across the hall and knocked softly on Adam's door. When he didn't answer, she opened it only to find it empty.

She walked downstairs and saw him standing next to the tree. "Hey, honey, you know Santa's watching and he likes early bedtimes," she said, forcing a lightness to her voice, repeating her joke about Santa. She had vowed that as long as she was a mother, Santa would leave gifts for her kids. She joked with them that even when they were fifty and came home for Christmas, there would be stockings filled and gifts under the tree from him. But that thought was overwhelmed by the idea that Valerie would still be causing turmoil in her life years from now. She didn't know how much longer she'd be able to pretend that her world wasn't falling apart.

Adam turned to her, a wisdom in his eyes she hadn't seen before. His jaw was clenched, his hands in the front pockets of his jeans. "What happened tonight? It was Aunt Valerie again, wasn't it? I'm not a baby, you can tell me."

Her chest ached from the tears she hadn't been able to cry yet. The tears for all of them. This wasn't what she wanted. But she knew as her son—a young man now—waited for the truth, she couldn't shelter him forever. He already knew a lot, and he was asking her for the truth. She had to believe that he was strong enough to handle it. And he needed to be prepared in case Valerie began manipulating him too. "I just found out tonight that Valerie has been secretly calling Matt's mom . . . bad-mouthing me."

His jaw dropped open. "What? What was she saying?"

She blew out a breath, searching for words that were the truth, without adding her own anger. "She played on Matt's mom's insecurities about losing him, stuff about me wanting to leave the island."

"Are we?"

And wasn't that the million-dollar question? She had told Matt she'd go to Alaska to be free if she had to. She stared at Adam, remembering how he'd been when they first arrived. Remembering her promise to him that they could leave after Christmas. How far they'd come. But she'd worked for this, to be in this space with him, for him to heal. She had worked her ass off for it. "I know we had that deal . . ."

"I like it here, Mom. And you were right, Matt's family does feel like family. Matt . . . he feels like . . . he feels like home."

Tears filled her eyes until the image of her son was blurred. "I know," she whispered.

"I hate Aunt Valerie."

She shook her head rapidly and walked over to him, grabbing his hand in hers. "No, you don't. You don't hate, because hate will ruin you. What you need to do is live your life. Make good friends. Love your family. Concentrate on all your goals and all the wonderful things you can do with your life. Don't waste a minute on hate because those are minutes that you will never get back, they are minutes that take away from all the love that is meant to be yours."

"How could she trash-talk you like that? She's like a psycho stalker. Aren't you pissed off?"

"Come on, come sit beside me on the couch so we can look at the tree while we talk, okay?"

"Mom, who cares about the tree right now?"

She tried to follow her own advice and not let hatred fill her heart, but as she watched her son wrestle with his emotions, his pain, she wanted to hate her sister. She wanted to because her sister, instead of helping them, instead of reaching out to her nephew and niece as a caring aunt, had decided to try and ruin all their happiness. This was her boundary. This was her wall. Her kids.

Lila had been right.

Annie knew it in her gut. She had held her son when he was a baby and swore to love and protect him. She'd held him when his father had died, swearing the same thing. She'd held him here when he'd had his emotional breakthrough, and all those feelings had coursed through her again. She would die for them, for their happiness, to protect the love within these walls.

No one could take that away from her. Sister or not.

A line had been crossed and there was no going back.

"Because the tree is important. It's a symbol of hope and love. Do you remember when we brought this tree in with Matt?"

"I'd hope so, it was like a couple of weeks ago."

She laughed, grateful for his sarcasm at this point. "Well, I remember that night. It was so perfect. It was the first time I really felt like we were going to make it, that we were all going to be okay."

He turned to her and his face went from angry to vulnerable, as quickly as a flash of lightning across the sky. "I'm not like her."

"Who?"

"Valerie."

Annie frowned, putting her hand on his knee, wanting to ground him. "Of course you're not, I would never think you were."

"I've treated you like garbage this last year. Dad would be so ashamed of me. I'm so sorry, Mom." His voice broke and he reached for her.

She held onto her precious son as he went from young man to little boy again. She whispered that he was such a good boy, such a good son, with a good heart, and his father would be proud of him.

She held onto his broad shoulders as his head collapsed into her lap, she stroked his hair as he cried the tears he'd been holding onto for years. They were new tears of realization for what he'd lost when his father had died. Cam had died when Adam was still a child, and Adam had cried childhood tears for him. But these were the tears of someone mature enough to mourn things he hadn't yet thought of as a child. These were the tears for the graduations that would be missed, the weddings, the grandchildren. These were the tears she'd already cried dozens of times over.

She held onto him tighter as tears racked his large frame. He was still her baby. Her first child, he would always be her baby, his toothless baby smile forever imprinted on her heart. She would die to make these babies of hers happy, so these tears he was crying tonight were therapy for both of them. She had known instinctively that he had been holding back for the last couple of years, that he had been burying pain behind attitude, love behind sarcasm.

But this was her boy. The one who was crying for his father, the one who was crying out of guilt, because he had a heart and he knew right from wrong, the one who was holding onto her like a lifeline. This was the boy they'd raised. After heavy minutes passed, he finally spoke, his voice raw, the sound of it making her chest hurt. "I've missed him so much and I haven't wanted to tell you because I didn't want to make you sad and drag you down. But I missed him so much when we were coming here. I was so mad at you for making us leave our home, the one we shared with him. And then I started to like it here. I stared liking this new house, the new friends, seeing Matt and his family all the time. And I like Matt. And I liked our time together, and then I felt guilty because I thought I liked him too much. I couldn't remember talking to Dad about the stuff I talk to Matt about, because I'm older now. And it just became too much, Mom. I took it out on you. I'm so sorry."

She let her fingers stroke his hair lightly, like she used to do when he was little, hoping it would subconsciously be a comforting touch, a touch that would reassure him as he fell asleep at night. She cleared her throat, searching for words of wisdom she didn't feel qualified in voicing. "I know, honey. I actually felt a lot of those same things. I didn't know if coming here was the right thing. But I knew staying wasn't the right thing anymore either.

I know this might sound silly, but it's like trying to survive in a room that's a huge mess. You can't. Not for a long period of time, so you have to clean up the mess. You have to change the space to change your mindset. I felt like we needed that. I also knew we needed family—the kind that we could count on. And I know you had a hard time with that concept because they aren't blood family, but boy do they feel like it. Or at least the way biological family should feel."

"It's true. I had no idea I could feel so comfortable with people I'm not related to. Every time I go for Sunday night dinner, I feel like I'm a celebrity."

She laughed softly. "I know. Pretty great, right? It reminds me of your grandparents and how happy they were to see us."

"Except Aunt Val ruined that."

Her hand stilled for a moment. "Yeah, she did. But I'm trying to remember that everyone has their own decisions to make in life and we can't be sad for those decisions. Your grandparents decided they had to avoid conflict at all costs. I feel bad because, in the end, they only ended up getting hurt by Valerie. But they loved all of us and that's a pretty amazing thing."

He scrambled into a sitting position; his face still splotchy. She handed him a tissue. "Yeah, imagine loving Valerie."

She almost laughed. "Parents always love their kids."

"I'm glad she's not mine."

She needed to steer this conversation back in the right direction. "I can't say I blame you. But what you said about Dad—all those feelings are okay. You don't have to protect me. You don't drag me down. If you want to talk about Dad, I'm always around for that. If you have questions about him, anything, okay? And Matt is here too. Matt knew a whole other side of your dad that I probably didn't. I know he'd be fine with you asking him anything."

"Yeah. I've really liked spending time with him. We have a lot in common. He said we can go catch lobster this summer on a boat, and he really likes baseball and so do I. What's going to happen now with Claire? Does she really hate you?"

She took a deep breath. "No, she doesn't hate me. She just really loves Matt and fell for what Valerie told her. I'm sure Claire is feeling pretty awful, honestly. I'm kind of hurt, but I know she's a good person. I'm sure it'll all sort itself out."

"I think Uncle Matt will make sure it gets sorted out. He's probably worried we're going to go back to Toronto."

Or Alaska. "Well, you and I made a deal, and since you admitted I was right . . ."

He laughed. "Yeah, you were. Are you mad at him?"

Annie shook her head. "Of course not. It's not his fault. And he was upset too."

"But you left him there."

This was getting a little awkward. Especially since she didn't know what she felt right now. She actually almost felt as bad as when she'd had strep. Like she'd had the wind knocked out of her. She had needed space; she had needed time by herself. "I didn't want to talk about everything with his family there. I also didn't want to say things I was going to regret or speak out in anger. Some things are hard to take back. But besides all that, I wanted Matt to have time alone with his family."

Adam looked away for a moment. "I hope he knows you're not mad at him."

"Hey, don't worry about us."

He nodded, still not looking at her. "I just want you to be happy. Like you always say to me. I can feel the same for you. I want you to be happy, and I don't want Aunt Valerie to win and break you guys up. He's really fun to be around. He's a really cool guy . . . and I'm glad if you're with him. He's really funny and makes things not so serious around here. But I also think he's really good to you. I'm happy if you're happy. Good night, Mom," he said, giving her a kiss on the cheek before going upstairs.

"Love you, Adam," she said as he climbed the stairs.

"Love you too, Mom."

She closed her eyes briefly, a swell of gratitude washing over her.

Six weeks ago, she could not have imagined this conversation. Six weeks ago, the two of them were broken in so many ways. Six weeks ago, she'd lost her way, she'd lost her faith, her hope. She had lost faith in herself, in the truth. She had been desperate to prove herself again, falling into old patterns, falling into the role given to her by her family since childhood.

But she was an adult now. She was a mom. And the life she was building was being threatened by her sister, who didn't even have the courage to show her face here. No more. As soon as she heard Adam's door click shut, she picked up her phone.

She winced as she saw all the missed calls and messages on her screen.

Three missed calls and ten missed texts from Matt.

Three missed calls from Claire.

Two missed calls from Kate.

One text from Lila.

Not now. Now was the time to deal with the woman who was trying to take her down. She tiptoed to the mudroom and grabbed her coat and slipped into her boots. This was a call that was not meant to be overheard, because she had acted mature and in control in front of Adam. That was the opposite of how she was feeling now. Having her son cry in her lap had made something inside her snap. Life was hard enough with things that couldn't be controlled—like Cam's death. People causing garbage and turmoil on purpose? Not anymore.

She snuck out the front door, intending to sit in her car, but the ocean beckoned her.

It sounded as angry as she felt, the water as choppy as her breath. The waves thrashed and the faint light from the porch and moon led her along the narrow path.

She stumbled a little but made her way with a boldness she hadn't experienced in her entire adult life. There was no freshly plowed sidewalk here. No lights from neighboring houses or streetlights or car lights. There was nothing out here but nature.

She was a grown woman. This was her home, her land, her piece of ocean, and no one was going to take it from her. No one was going to steal her joy anymore.

She stared straight ahead, the moon her guide, the stars her hope, the ocean her fury.

Taking a deep breath, she called Valerie.

Her sister didn't answer.

Annie called her again.

And again.

And again.

And each time she redialed, she became almost giddy, childish, because it felt good to give her sister a taste of her own medicine—something no one in her family had ever dared do, because it would set her off. Let's see how Valerie liked being called over again.

Each time, the waves of the ocean sounded louder; each time, Annie felt stronger.

Finally, Valerie picked up. "Oh, did you remember you have a sister?"

This was it. Her big moment. Her heart was beating so hard it hurt to speak. "What were you thinking?"

"What? Something wrong?"

Her body started trembling, her legs unsteady, her hand shaking so hard she had to be careful she didn't drop her phone in the snow. "How dare you go behind my back and manipulate Matt's mother? How could you possibly do that to me?"

"What's the big deal? I was just getting to know her. She's actually a really lonely lady, Annie. You should try and spend more time with her and get to know her yourself."

Annie bit down so hard on her back teeth, she didn't know if she'd be able to unlock her jaw. Valerie would never give a straight answer. It would turn into advice for Annie, telling her what she should be doing. "Stop lying. That's not why you called her. You called her to trash-talk me. What was your game plan?"

When Valerie didn't answer, Annie kept talking, anger propelling her forward, pushing her to say everything that she'd been holding onto for years. The memory of standing in Claire's kitchen, the humiliation she'd felt when she realized what her sister had done, making her skin burn despite the subzero temperatures. Claire had sat on the phone and listened to all sorts of lies or half truths about Annie, personal things, made up things. It was such an invasion of privacy on a deep level. And then to have everyone standing there, looking at her with pity because they realized what kind of a sister she had.

"You only succeeded in making yourself look like a vindictive, disloyal sister. Do you actually think this is normal behavior? That people just call up the parents of the person their sibling is dating and start trash-talking them behind their backs?"

"Annie, you have a lot of problems in life. With people. With friends. With family. You ran away from Toronto. I'm your family. Matt is not."

Annie kicked a pile of snow, watching as the wind picked up traces of it, carrying it to the ocean. "I'm a grown woman who moved away. My children are also my family. You don't even like me, why won't you leave me alone?"

"You've never loved me, Annie. You've always treated me like garbage."

"I'm ten years younger than you. When I was one, you were eleven. How could I have never loved you? Have you ever looked at yourself? Have you ever wondered what you brought to the family? Did you once take care of Mom and Dad when they were sick? Did you ever offer anyone help? It has always been what we should be doing for you and it still wasn't good enough. We all had to jump through hoops to keep you happy. Time I could have had with my husband, my kids, was instead spent on you and your drama.

"But this, this—you have reached an all-time low and that's saying a lot considering you faked having cancer. Stay out of my life. Never contact my kids. You've been exposed. They see you for who you are. I tried to shelter them from that as much as I could. But you've hurt them, deeply. You chose your hatred of me over your love for them. You don't love them. You don't love me. You are incapable of loving anyone other than yourself.

"You made every special moment in my life about you. You made all my kids' special moments about you. I can't believe I lost so many years, so many good memories, to you and your manipulations. You hated everything I had—you hated that I was married, that I had friends, that I had a career, that I had kids, because you didn't. So then you hated that all those people took attention away from you. You can't understand why I have these people in my life because I was the loser, right? According to you I was mean and ugly and fat and stupid, so how is it possible that I have all these friends and got married? How is it possible that I have Matt in my life now? I'll tell you: because I love them. Because I know how to love people. It's give and take.

"I worked my ass off for everything I have. I couldn't give up because I had kids depending on me to be okay, to make sure they were okay, and instead of helping me during my time of need, you hijacked it and made it about you. No more. I will never come back. I'm done with your mind games, your manipulations. All of it. Unless you get some therapy, some kind of help, learn the meaning of boundaries, I can't have a relationship with you anymore. Neither can the kids."

Annie was shaking by the time she was done speaking. She waited for Valerie to say something. "Hello, what do you have to say for yourself? You seemed to have tons to say to Matt's mom and now you're silent?"

The wind howled around her, snow swirling at her feet. When Valerie still didn't say anything, Annie pulled the phone from her ear to look at the screen. Valerie had ended the call.

Annie cried tears of frustration. Annie would never be heard. Valerie would never hear her point of view. She'd kept it inside for so long, trying so hard to just tolerate it, and now this silence was all she was given. There would be no closure. This was supposed to be her cathartic moment. Finally, after years and years of living under her sister's rule, she was going to tell her what she really thought of her. But typical Valerie, she could never take it. She could only dish it out.

Annie took a deep breath, her hair furiously tangling in the wind around her face.

Well, fine. Maybe this was still cathartic.

Or maybe blocking her would be. She could not go through the rest of her life tensing up whenever her phone pinged. Every single time there was a great message coming through, from her kids, from Matt, from her friends, her initial reaction was panic or dread that it might be Valerie with a toxic message for her. How many holidays, birthdays, events had Valerie ruined? No more.

This was Annie's new life, and she would die trying to protect her right to enjoy it.

She slowly trudged through the snow, the sounds of the ocean calling her. The waves were hard and loud.

The sky was the same as she might have imagined on Christmas Eve as a child. It was a sky that was big and wide and bursting with stars. It was a sky she would have imagined Santa flying through on his sleigh. It was the sky she'd dreamed of, the one where she'd heard the bells.

She paused in the middle of the field, her little house behind her, the ocean straight ahead, and looked up.

Tears that had nothing to do with the wind filled her eyes. All those stars. All those dreams. So many had come true, but not the way she'd imagined. She had gotten married, had kids, had her career. So many blessings. But she didn't think she could ever forgive herself for the time wasted, the memories tarnished, because she'd never set boundaries with Valerie. Even when Cam was dying, her sister had inserted herself. It would never end. It would never end unless she stopped it. No one could do it for her.

She stared at the sky and wondered if Cam could see her. He would be proud of her for doing this. And she wondered if her parents could see her and she wished that they would finally understand that she was only protecting herself and her kids. And her future.

Annie walked toward the ocean, empowered by the sky of her childhood, and stood as close to the edge as it was safe to.

Her night at the inn with Matt flashed through her mind. His face, his smile, his body against hers, his words. Was she really going to lose that because of her sister? Was she really going to let another moment of joy be ruined by her?

She squeezed her eyes shut, pulled her phone out of her pocket, reached as far back as she could, and threw it into the Atlantic Ocean.

And as she walked back to the house, she listened for the bells.

CHAPTER TWENTY-TWO

The day before Christmas

Matt took the back roads as quickly as he could, but they were glistening with a thin layer of ice, which forced him to slow down. It was six in the morning, still dark out, but he couldn't wait. He couldn't risk losing everything he'd wanted his entire life.

He was on his way to Annie's house, his stomach in knots. He'd been calling her—and feeling slightly like Valerie for calling and texting so many times—but she hadn't picked up. She hadn't even texted back. And then at some point, the phone had stopped ringing and went straight to voice mail, which was even more ominous. He could have texted the kids, but he didn't want to involve them in their problems. He hadn't slept all night, and finally at five had gotten up and showered and picked up coffees at the only drive-thru Tim Hortons open this early.

After Annie had left last night, all hell had broken loose. His sister was upset on his behalf and got into it with their mom. Grandma Lila went around pouring brandy for everyone and had facilitated peace talks. It's not that they had to push, his mother had realized quickly the mistakes she'd made. She had cried and tried calling Annie. All of them had, but no answer.

He took the last turn to her house, driving through the cornfield, the ocean in the distance, blue under the sunny sky. He had to convince her to stay. Or leave. But do it with him. He had waited years for her to be ready to start over, and he wasn't about to lose her because of some possessive, out-of-control sister or his gullible mother. He should have seen this coming. And God, how he wished Valerie was a man so he could just punch him and have that satisfaction. Maybe threaten some bodily harm, not in writing, and then he'd be gone forever.

He parked his truck beside her SUV. He was relieved to see her SUV still there because he half expected her to be on her way to Alaska. Not that he could blame her. He stacked one coffee cup on the other and got out of the car as quickly as he could without spilling the coffee. He knocked on the door, hoping like hell she would answer it.

A minute later, the porch light came on, as did all the Christmas lights and Santa's sleigh, and Annie was standing on the other side of the door, wearing candy-cane printed pajamas, her hair all disheveled, looking like the woman of his dreams. She unlocked the door and he held up the coffees.

"A peace offering," he said before she could tell him to go away.

She smiled, and he took it as a good sign. "You don't need a peace offering. Hold on, I'm going to grab my jacket."

She stepped outside a moment later, huddled in her jacket. He wanted nothing more than to pull her into his arms and kiss her. But he couldn't. Thanks to Valerie. Ugh. "Do you want to sit on the steps?"

"Sure," he said. Once they were sitting side by side, he handed her one of the coffees. "I tried calling a few dozen times, feeling slightly like a stalker."

"Or Valerie?" she said with a slight laugh.

He grinned, relieved that she was able to make a joke out of it so early on. "I didn't want to say it out loud."

"Yeah . . . I'm sorry, Matt. I threw my phone into the ocean."

He almost spit out his coffee. He turned to her. She was smiling at him, and that's when he noticed the sparkle was back in her eyes. The last time he'd looked into her gorgeous eyes, it had almost gutted him. They'd been filled with defeat, persecution. He'd been able to see right into her past last night. He never wanted to see that look again. He wanted to give her everything.

"I see. How, uh, did that come about?"

She took a sip of her coffee and shut her eyes for a moment. "First off, thank you for this coffee. I don't think coffee has ever tasted so good as this morning, with you, out here in the freezing cold."

He took that as another good sign. "I'm glad. I think it's the least I could do. So, uh, about the phone?"

"I called Valerie. I told her off. All those things I'd always wanted to say but didn't because I was too afraid of making her mad. I said it all. I felt like I was in a movie. Adrenaline was coursing through me.

"I was standing on the edge of the cliff . . . well, kind of, it was a safe distance back. But words just kept pouring out of me. And then I realized she had hung up on me. Probably the minute she figured out I was calling her out on all her lies. It was the most infuriating thing to know that she never even heard me. At first, I was really mad, because I wanted her to really hear me. I wanted something to click for her.

"Then it made me feel so alone. She's the only living person from my family and she's so far gone. How can I possibly have a relationship with someone who is completely unwilling to listen to me? And then I realized that it didn't matter that she hadn't heard. What mattered was that I had spoken. I also felt determination come back. I'm not a quitter. I'm not going to be driven out of this home, this province. I'm not going to be driven away from you because my sister doesn't want me to be in a relationship if she's not.

"Anyway, long story short, I walked to the ocean and I knew I needed freedom. I knew the only way I was going to get it was a new number. I hurled it into the ocean. In retrospect, I probably should have just turned it in and, um, bought a new one or got a new number, but it wouldn't have had the same impact. Then this morning there's the guilt that I just helped pollute the ocean. But it was symbolic."

He chuckled. "I know you don't need me to say this, but I'm proud of you, Annie. I know how many things are tied to your sister. I want you to know, just in case you ever doubt it, I know that you were pushed to do this. I don't think you're wrong or cruel or cold. You are protecting yourself and your kids."

"Thank you. Your grandmother told me that there would be a line that Valerie crossed and that when it happened, I would know it. She was right. I knew it last night. Deep inside. After I got over the stuff with your mom, I realized the bigger picture. Valerie was inserting herself into my life here. She was trying to re-create the dynamic at home. She was threating my happiness. She hurt my kids. She tried to hurt us—she tried to break us up. All of that, all those things were my line in the sand. I'm sorry for running out of there on you. I was claustrophobic. It brought up so many old memories and I didn't want a scene in front of the kids."

He pulled her closer and kissed the top of her head. "I get it. You are the strongest person I know, Annie. You're incredible. And you don't owe me an apology. I owe you one. For not seeing where this was going with my mom, for not protecting you from that."

"You don't need to protect me."

"I do. Just like you were trying to protect me. I will always protect you. I will always be on your side, stand up for you. Annie, you are the love of my life, and I want you for the rest of my life. You and Adam and Maddy."

She pulled back slightly, her gorgeous mouth dropping open slightly. "You do?"

He raised his free hand to cup one side of her face. "You can't think I'd enter into a casual relationship with you, just hoping for the best. I've been in love with you forever but didn't want to jeopardize our friendship."

"Matt . . . ," she said, her voice catching.

He leaned forward to kiss her, because he hadn't in what felt like forever. "I love you," he said, against her lips.

She pulled back to look up at him. "I love you too. I've known that for a long time but was afraid to ruin everything, afraid to try again, afraid to believe that we could have a happily-ever-after. And then what your mom said about wanting more kids and that I didn't . . ."

He squeezed her knee. He hated that those private topics had been discussed behind their back, that they had been aired so flippantly. "Hey, no pressure. We don't need to talk about any of that now. I love Adam and Maddy like they're my own. It would be impossible for me to love them more than I already do. I just want the three of you."

"I can talk about kids if you want to talk about kids. And what about your mom?"

He squeezed her knee. "My mother is a disaster. She's mortified that she fell for Valerie's lies. She's angry with herself for doubting you, for letting her own insecurities cloud her judgment. She hates that she's hurt you. The one thing I can say about my family is that we make mistakes, but we talk it out, yell it out, but we listen to each other. And she listened. And cried. She wanted to come over here and apologize to you and try to make amends. I can't tell you what to do. I can tell you where it all came from, though."

She gave him a nod. "Please."

"I told you that I was engaged once. She was not the love of my life," he said with a pointed pause. Annie reached out and held his hand. "But I was in love with her. She wanted to leave the island; she had a great job offer in Vancouver. She wanted me to move there with her. I didn't want to go. I didn't want her to miss her opportunity either. I ended things. I guess that was the ultimate indicator for me—if I wasn't willing to leave here for someone, then it meant I didn't love them enough. It did hurt, though, for a long time. It brought up old feelings of my father leaving. I think my mother was so scarred by all of it that the thought of me leaving was unbearable for her."

Annie nodded slowly. "I can understand wanting to be close to your kids, even as adults. I mean, I can't imagine my life without my kids."

"Yes, but don't get me wrong, what she did wasn't right. I don't want you to misinterpret."

"I know. I know what you mean. Does your mom, though?"

He ran a hand through his hair. "She does. If you want to know more of the details of how all of this happened, I have them for you."

She toyed with the lid on her coffee. "All of it. I'm guessing this has to do with Valerie?"

"Yeah. She started calling my mother shortly after you came to the island. My mother hid all this, but it was so out of character for her. She's not a liar, she's not a gossip. But Valerie really got her with the idea that you were going to take me away to Toronto. She filled her head with all these lies about what kind of a person you are. I can't believe she fell for all of it. It's actually kind of scary that she would. And some of the stuff was pure trash, and also insulting that she would think I'd be taken in by you if you were really like that. No offense."

She covered her face. "Oh, like you mean, the fact that I abandoned my kids and my drinking and not taking my daughter to the doctor and . . . God knows what else she said about me. Straight out of a soap opera."

"Yeah, and Valerie is the villain . . . those things. I mean, just hearing it out loud, it's so absurd. You are the most responsible, loving mother. It makes me angry when I think of it. When I think of how little credit you've ever been given. Anyway, long story short, my mother is so upset with herself."

"Wait, one more thing," Annie said, frowning.

He placed his hand on her knee. "Go ahead."

"We never talked about the rings. I wanted to tell you, but then I didn't want our date to be about the past and Cam. But I wanted you to know, that night, that I was completely there with you, without shadows lurking, without mourning. That was the most romantic night of my life. You made me feel like I was a princess, and it sounds silly, but that's how I felt."

He leaned forward and kissed her softly. And then he put down his coffee and reached around to the nape of her neck and pulled her closer, deepening the kiss. She almost dropped her coffee but he grabbed it. "That's how I wanted you to feel."

She took his hands in hers. "I need to tell you; I hadn't taken the rings off before that because I hadn't gotten over Cam yet and was determined to never move on. It's hard not to cling to the past when the past is filled with more peace and love than the present. At least that's how it felt. Before we came here. Then I kept them on for the kids, because I didn't want to take something else away from them. I didn't want more change in their lives. I didn't want them to think I didn't love Cam anymore. I actually didn't give them enough credit. I think they suspected our feelings for each other before I was even ready to admit it to myself."

He squeezed her hands. "I noticed you took them off."

She nodded. "I told the kids before we went out on our date. They totally took it all in stride. They adore you. They love you. And I'm ready to believe that my present and my future can hold that same kind of love. I've found my hope again. My faith again. Those rings were a symbol of my hope and faith. But now I don't have to wear them anymore to feel that. I want Adam and Maddy to know that love is in our present and our future, not just in our past. And going back to the whole thing about kids . . ."

He put his coffee down, knowing this was the time. "How about we shelve that discussion until I get this out?"

She tilted her head. "What out?"

He pulled the envelope from his back pocket and handed it to her.

"What is this?" she whispered, staring down at the paper.

He grinned. "It's confirmation of our tickets for four to Alaska."

She looked up at him, her eyes wide. "What?'

He nodded. "You told me once that you'd go to Alaska in order to keep your family whole, in order to defend what was true and to live your life in peace. I want you to know that I'd go with you. Anywhere, Annie. These are cruise tickets for the four of us this summer, a cruise to Alaska. If you like it there, we find a way to make it work. If you want to stay here, we go on that cruise as a symbol of the lengths we are willing to go to for our family.

"The cruise wasn't planned; it was a gift inspired by Valerie. The real gift I had for you . . . the real gift requires me kneeling."

Annie tried to grab onto him. "What are you doing?"

"Trying to kneel in the snow, but you're ruining the moment," he said, with a laugh.

Her eyes filled with tears and she was shaking her head.

"Are you asking me *not* to propose to you?" he said as he pulled the ring box out of his jacket pocket.

"I don't know what I'm saying! Don't listen to me," she whispered, covering her mouth.

He smiled at her, knowing that if she said yes, he would be smiling at her for the rest of their lives, every day. "Annie, I love you. I love Adam and Maddy. I want to build a life with you, whatever that means for us. Whatever comes our way. I want to be there for you. I know you're strong, but I want you to know that I can pick up the fight for you. I can be your rock. I can build a wall so high and thick that nothing can get through.

"You've been entrusted with these kids and that means that they're your first priority. If you fall, they fall. But I will be your backup. I will always be here for you, all of you, as long as you want me, as long as you'll let me. I will love you."

She threw herself in his arms and he tumbled backwards into the snow, laughing and taking her with him. He held her there, on top of him, and she kissed him, her hands on either side of his face. "Yes. Forever yes. I love you, Matt. You gave me everything. You gave me back my hope and my faith and my courage. Yes, to everything.

"You have no idea what you've done for me. How much I love you. How all of this needed to happen in order for me to be whole again. And that's how I want to be on this next step. I thought this was just a thousand miles. A thousand miles to a new home, a new province. But it was a thousand miles to find myself. It took me finding myself to heal my family, my soul, my heart. I thought that distance would protect me from Valerie. I know it doesn't. I know throwing my phone into the ocean and getting a new number won't. It's me standing up for myself, protecting the life I've made for myself.

"But if I'd known that these thousand miles would lead to falling in love with you . . . I would travel those thousand miles over and over again if that road brought me home. You are my home."

Matt kissed her again, blinking back the moisture in his own eyes. "God, I love you. Merry Christmas, Annie."

CHAPTER TWENTY-THREE

Christmas Day

Annie opened her eyes on Christmas morning, a sense of peace, safety, and joy floating throughout her body. She blinked, staring at the ceiling, letting the feeling linger. Peace.

Valerie hasn't ruined Christmas this year.

Every Christmas for the last two decades of Annie's life had been dominated, controlled, and ruined by Valerie. No more. Today, Annie could enjoy her kids without tension, without worry. She didn't have to pull her attention away from her kids as Valerie vied for being the star of the day.

She was free. Annie had put up her boundaries. She'd created her wall. And she didn't have to do it alone anymore. Matt. She held up her hand and then clutched it to her heart. The ring was different from the ones she'd looked at for over a decade, and she was so ready. She was so ready for this new phase in her life, for this new love in her life.

She closed her eyes, her left hand on her heart, her other covering the ring Matt had given her, desperately needing to relive that moment with him, as though she were flipping back through a book to reread her favorite lines. She didn't even feel silly, smiling at the ceiling with her eyes closed as she pictured him in the snow.

I want to build a life with you, whatever that means for us. Whatever comes our way. I want to be there for you. I know you're strong but I want you to know that I can pick up the fight for you. I can be your rock. I can build a wall so high and thick that nothing can get through. You've been entrusted with these kids and that means they're your first priority. If you fall, they fall. But I will be your backup. I will always be here for you, all of you, as long as you want me, as long as you'll let me. I will love you.

She let out an audible sigh, feeling slightly like she was a Disney princess. But even better than lying here, daydreaming about Matt, was that Matt was downstairs, sleeping on the couch. Except, as she took a deep breath, she realized he wasn't sleeping because she could smell the rich scent of coffee. If she hurried up, they could have a few minutes alone together before the kids woke up. Swinging her legs over the edge of the bed, she ran across the bedroom to use the bathroom and freshen up. She brushed her hair and teeth and washed her face. She'd stay in her Christmas pajamas, of course, because Maddy was wearing the matching ones. But at least she looked civilized.

She tiptoed down the stairs, feeling like a kid on Christmas morning. Not herself as a kid, but as a kid who was free, who wasn't worried about a bully in the house. This was her house and it was only filled with people she loved and there was so much power in that, so much hope in that. Her sister had never been in this house . . . there were no awful memories of her here.

This was her fresh start. She stood at the landing, remembering how Maddy had fainted here, how Matt had taken it all in stride. She watched him as he leaned against the counter, facing the windows. The Christmas tree was lit, the fire was on, and the coffee was brewed. She studied his profile, loving every inch of him. He slowly turned to her, the love shining in his eyes making her short of breath, the grin he gave her making her weak in the knees. "Merry Christmas."

She ran down the last few steps and into his arms. "Merry Christmas," she said against his neck. He pulled back after a moment, his hands resting on her hips.

"I knew you were standing there, by the way."

"Really?"

He nodded, his lips twitching. "But it was my good angle, so I let you look."

She covered her mouth so she wouldn't burst out laughing and wake the kids. After a moment, she looked up at him, loving the sparkle in his eyes. "You have no bad angles, none."

He lowered his head to kiss her. "I'm glad you think so, but you're free to inspect at your leisure, in more detail."

She held his waist, her knees going weak. "You have the amazing ability of doing and saying these little things that make me forget everything else. You make me weak in the knees, Matt."

"That's good to know, Annie." He dipped his head and kissed the side of her neck, slowly backing her up to the island.

"Now you're just showing off," she said, breathless.

She felt his smile against her neck. He trailed light kisses up her neck to her lips as he spoke. "I'm not going to lie; I am kind of a show-off. But I make good on all my innuendos and promises."

She ran her hands up his chest, her fingertips trailing over the prickly stubble lining his jaw. "I can't wait."

He smoothed the hair off her face. "You are the most gorgeous woman to wake up to."

"You've woken up to a lot of women, have you?" she said, enjoying teasing him.

He gave her a lopsided grin. "It's a province of only one hundred and fifty thousand, so there was a limit."

She pursed her lips. "Good to know."

"But no one has ever come close to you, Annie. You are my heart, and I will love you until the day I die." This time when he leaned down to kiss her, all the teasing was gone, all the raw emotion in his voice, transferred to her kiss.

"Merry Christmas! Adam, wake up! It's Christmas!"

Matt pulled back, giving Annie a final kiss on the forehead, as they heard Maddy barrel out of her room and pound on Adam's door.

"I'll pour coffees; by the sounds of things, we'll need it," Matt said.

Annie lit her cranberry-scented candles on the kitchen island and then opened the fridge. "Sounds good. And I'll put the cinnamon rolls in the oven to heat up."

A moment later, a very awake Maddy ran down the stairs, Jingle at her side, while a very sleepy Adam followed them. "Merry Christmas!" Maddy yelled again, running toward them and throwing herself at both of them.

Adam joined them, and Annie couldn't even stop the tears that filled her eyes. She had never even dared anticipate such a moment because she hadn't had the courage to even dream it. She had lost so much hope. And now, the most precious people in the world were here, in her arms, and the only thing she could feel was the love. This was the perfect time to tell them. They had decided yesterday they wanted to wait until Christmas morning to tell the kids. Annie took a deep breath. "Guys, we have something to tell you."

Matt put his arm around her shoulder and both kids looked at them, anticipation in their eyes. "Hurry, Mom, there's a tree full of presents," Maddy said.

Annie laughed. "We're engaged!"

Maddy screamed, and Adam put his hands over his ears. Jingle ran under the couch. "Tone it down a few notches," Adam said to Maddy.

The kids hugged them. "I'm so happy," Maddy said as she wrapped an arm around each of their waists.

Matt kissed the top of her head. "I'm glad."

Maddy looked up at him, her eyes shiny with faith and love for him. "I love you."

Annie watched, holding her breath as Matt wiped the moisture from his eyes and leaned down to hug Maddy tightly. "I love you too. I will always be here for you, Maddy."

She nodded against him, squeezing her eyes shut. "I'm glad."

When she pulled back, Adam held out his hand, looking ever more like Cam, ever more like a young man. But Matt didn't take his hand, instead he pulled him in for a bear hug.

"You're going to make a great dad. Thank you for being here for us. Thank you for being so good to my mom," Adam whispered.

"Love you, buddy," Matt said, his voice thick.

Annie wiped her tears with the sleeve of her shirt.

"Can we open presents now?" Maddy asked, even though she'd already broken free from them and was running over to the tree.

"Of course," Annie said.

"Oh look, Santa came," Adam said with a grin as he joined her.

Matt handed Annie a cup of coffee and sat on the couch beside her as the kids read who each gift was for and made individual piles. Jingle sat in between them, trying to swat ribbons as they passed gifts. "I told you, as long as I'm here, Santa and I have a deal that he'll drop off gifts for you. No matter how old you are."

Adam kept his head bent for a moment, and then looked up at Annie, emotion glittering in his eyes. "I'm glad we're here. I'm glad we're staying."

Annie smiled at him, her boy, sending up a silent prayer of thanks for him, for returning his heart. "Me too."

Annie sat there in her little house on the ocean, the farthest she'd ever been from home and yet also the closest she'd ever been to home, with a heart full of gratitude. The sun hadn't even risen yet and her day was complete. Her gaze rested on the candle flickering on the island, remembering how just six weeks ago, she hadn't even been able to light a candle. And now . . . now she had the courage for life again, for love again. As Matt leaned over and kissed her temple as they watched the kids rip off poorly applied gift wrap, she heard all the bells jingling. For all Christmases past and all future Christmases. She knew she was strong enough to face them all.

She held onto Matt's hand and turned her head in the direction of the ocean she knew was there, to where the sun would rise, behind rich red sand dunes, and then let her gaze rest on the canvas she'd bought that day in Avonlea village. How much had changed since that day. But maybe that day had been the first where hope had peaked inside her soul again, waiting for whenever she was ready to answer. She read the words one more time, grateful she hadn't given up or given into the madness, grateful that she had people to hold onto and love.

*You never know what peace is until you walk on the shores
or in the fields or along the winding red roads of Prince
Edward Island
in a summer twilight when the dew is falling and the old
stars are peeping out
and the sea keeps its mighty tryst with the little land it
loves.
You find your soul then.
You realize that youth is not a vanished thing
but something that dwells forever in the heart.*

—Lucy Maud Montgomery

ACKNOWLEDGMENTS

To all the talented and dedicated people at Crooked Lane and Alcove Press: Thank you for believing in this book and me! I'm so excited to be working with you. You have all been such a dream to work with and I look forward to our next book together.

To Faith Black Ross: Thank you for believing in my stories and for being such a joy to work with! You are such a talent and I'm so blessed to work with you. Your edits and feedback are always inspiring and motivating.

To Melissa Rechter: Thank you for keeping everything running smoothly and for being such a bright spot in my inbox!

To Madeline Rathle: Thank you for your marketing attention and ideas and for being so approachable.

To Rebecca Nelson: Thank you for your attention to detail and all your hard work.

Acknowledgments

To Louise Fury: Thank you for always being so enthusiastic about my ideas and being a true champion of my books.

To my Readers and Bloggers: Thank you for joining me as we travel to new small towns together! I hope this book brings you the joy of the season and leaves you with hope and happiness. All of your emails and reviews mean so much to me.